Mouthwat

Three Fudges and a Baby

"Suspects are ultimately uncovered and problems solved in a delightful cozy larded with appetizing fudge recipes."

—*Kirkus Reviews*

"Readers will be carried along with Allie and her investigations by the swift plot that leads to a reveal sure to surprise even the most experienced puzzle-solving mystery expert."

—*Kings River Life*

Give Fudge a Chance

"An enjoyable character-driven whodunit that mixes murder with a touch of romance and the requisite sweet treats."

—*Kirkus Reviews*

A Midsummer Night's Fudge

"Charming characters and settings make for a pleasant stop before trying your hand at the fudge recipes."

—*Kirkus Reviews*

Have Yourself a Fudgy Little Christmas

"Two nasty murders, charming surviving characters, plenty of Christmas cheer, and enough fudge recipes for a major sugar rush."

—*Kirkus Reviews*

Death Bee Comes Her

"Personable characters and lots of honey lore."

—***Kirkus Reviews***

"Sprinkled with delightful notes on honey and its various uses, this debut novel in the Oregon Honeycomb Mystery series is a fun introduction to a new cozy series. Everett, the Havana Brown cat, is an animal delight, often proving to be smarter than the humans around him."

—***Criminal Element***

"The author writes a captivating story with interesting characters. Naturally, Everett [the cat] contributes to the solution. A charming read."

—**Reviewingtheevidence.com**

"This warmhearted book is fast-paced, with realistic dialogue and a captivating plot."

—***Mystery and Suspense Magazine***

Fudge Bites

"An easy romantic read complete with fudge recipes that make it even sweeter."

—***Kirkus Reviews***

Forever Fudge

"Nancy Coco paints us a pretty picture of this charming island setting where the main mode of transportation is a horse-drawn vehicle. She also gives us a delicious mystery complete with doses of her homemade fudge . . . a perfect read!"

—***Wonder Women Sixty***

Oh, Fudge!

"*Oh, Fudge!* is a charming cozy, the sixth in the Candy-Coated Mystery series. But be warned: There's a candy recipe at the end of each chapter, so don't read this one when you're hungry!"

—Suspense Magazine

Oh Say Can You Fudge

"Beautiful Mackinac Island provides the setting for a puzzling series of crimes. Now that Allie McMurphy has taken over her grandparents' hotel and fudge shop, life on Mackinac is good, although her little dog, Mal, does tend to nose out trouble . . . Allie's third offers plenty of plausible suspects and mouthwatering fudge recipes."

—Kirkus Reviews

To Fudge or Not to Fudge

"*To Fudge or Not to Fudge* is a superbly crafted, classic, culinary cozy mystery. If you enjoy them as much as I do, you are in for a real treat."

—Examiner.com (5 stars)

"A five-star delicious mystery that has great characters, a good plot, and a surprise ending. If you like a good mystery with more than one suspect and a surprise ending, then rush out to get this book and read it, but be sure you have the time, since once you start, you won't want to put it down."

—Mystery Reading Nook

"A charming and funny culinary mystery that parodies reality-show competitions and is led by a sweet heroine, eccentric but likable characters, and a skillfully crafted plot that speeds toward an unpredictable conclusion. Allie stands out as a likable and engaging character. Delectable fudge recipes are interspersed throughout the novel."

—*Kings River Life*

All Fudged Up

"A sweet treat with memorable characters, a charming locale, and satisfying mystery."

—**Barbara Allan**, author of the Trash 'n' Treasures Mystery Series

"A fun book with a lively plot, and it's set in one of America's most interesting resorts. All this plus fudge!"

—**JoAnna Carl**, author of the Chocoholic Mystery Series

"A sweet confection of a book. Charming setting, clever protagonist, and creamy fudge—a yummy recipe for a great read."

—**Joanna Campbell Slan**, author of the Scrap-N-Craft Mystery Series and the Jane Eyre Chronicles

"Nancy Coco's *All Fudged Up* is a delightful mystery delivering suspense and surprise in equal measure. Add that to the charm of the setting, Michigan's famed Mackinac Island, and you have a recipe for enjoyment. Mouthwatering fudge recipes are included. A must-read for all lovers of amateur sleuth classic mysteries."

—**Carole Bugge (Elizabeth Blake)**, author of the Jane Austen Society Mystery Series

"You won't have to 'fudge' your enthusiasm for Nancy Coco's first Mackinac Island Fudge Shop Mystery. Indulge your sweet tooth as you settle in and meet Allie McMurphy, Mal the bichon/poodle mix, and the rest of the motley crew in this entertaining series debut."

—**Miranda James,** author of the Cat in the Stacks Mystery Series

"Enjoyable . . . *All Fudged Up* is littered with delicious fudge recipes, including alcohol-infused ones. I really enjoyed this cozy mystery and look forward to reading more in this series."

—**Fresh Fiction**

"Cozy mystery lovers who enjoy quirky characters, a great setting, and fantastic recipes will love this debut."

—***The Lima News***

Books by Nancy Coco

The Oregon Honeycomb Mystery Series

Death Bee Comes Her

A Matter of Hive and Death

The Candy-Coated Mystery Series

All Fudged Up

To Fudge or Not to Fudge

Oh Say Can You Fudge

All I Want for Christmas Is Fudge

All You Need Is Fudge

Oh, Fudge!

Deck the Halls with Fudge

Forever Fudge

Fudge Bites

Have Yourself a Fudgy Little Christmas

Here Comes the Fudge

A Midsummer Night's Fudge

Give Fudge a Chance

Having a Fudgy Christmas Time

Three Fudges and a Baby

Fudge and Marriage

FUDGE and MARRIAGE

Nancy Coco

Kensington Publishing Corp.
kensingtonbooks.com

KENSINGTON BOOKS are published by

Kensington Publishing Corp.
900 Third Avenue
New York, NY 10022

First Printing: April 2025
ISBN: 978-1-4967-4372-5

ISBN: 978-1-4967-4373-2 (ebook)

10 9 8 7 6 5 4 3 2 1

Printed in the United States of America

This book is dedicated to Ann and Audrey, the wonderful librarians at the Mackinac Island library, who allowed me to wander about looking for the perfect place for the next murder for Allie to solve. Your kindness is deeply appreciated.

Chapter 1

"Allie." Alice Huff, head librarian at the Mackinac Island library, didn't sound surprised to see me.

"I'm returning these books," I said, lifting the beautiful, full-color books on wedding planning, choosing flowers by their meanings, and more. "I'm going to have a look in the library list to see if there's anything else." I placed four books and six thick bridal magazines in the return pile. Thank goodness for a library card. Without it, I may have gone broke by now.

Alice was a warm-hearted, welcoming person who lived for books and loved to help patrons. She lived in St. Ignace and enjoyed baking, ensuring there was usually a plate of cookies at the desk for everyone, but only if you were leaving with your books in a bag. Everyone knew she'd remove your cookie privileges if she ever saw you with a cookie and no protected books.

She shook her head at me, her crisp gray bob swinging from side to side and her blue eyes twinkling. "You've been checking out everything we have on weddings for the last six months. When's the ceremony?"

"Two weeks." I know I blushed five shades of red because I could feel the heat slowly rise in my cheeks. I thought the whole island knew that the wedding was in two weeks. With my involvement in the community and the fact that my fiancé was Rex Manning, the lead policeman on the island, everyone was invited. It's why we decided on an outdoor wedding. My best friend and maid of honor, Jenn Carpenter, had worked it out that everyone but the family would bring their own chair, if they wanted, and others could stand in the back. The reception was to be a giant potluck, while Rex and I paid for a caterer to barbecue steaks and handmade hamburgers, as well as brats, and even provide savory pasties as the meats for the meal. Already the senior ladies had planned a potato salad competition.

June was a lovely time on Mackinac Island, with sweet smelling flowers blooming everywhere, including our iconic lilacs. It's why I picked the Saturday before the Lilac Festival. I would have picked the Saturday of the festival, but that was a busy day at the McMurphy Hotel and Fudge shop, and the entire island, if I was to be honest.

"Two weeks," Alice said, her head tilted, her right eyebrow lifted, and it felt like she was laughing at me on the inside, but her expression only held concern. "Then why are you still devouring every wedding book and magazine available since 1959?"

"There are many details," I explained, half-embarrassed and half-desperate. "I'm not sure I'm making good decisions, and the books help me narrow down what I like. I never thought about ever getting married, let alone having five hundred people attend, and the worst part is my mom. She will scrutinize everything, down to how white my teeth are. That's a lot of pressure."

Alice held her hand to her heart. "Sweetheart, you are a bride of the island. I know we specialize in beautiful destination weddings, but no one here expects your wedding to be a royal affair. We have a lot of experts on weddings. They're helping, aren't they? Because if they aren't . . ."

"They are helping," I reassured her quickly. "And I think it's going to be beautiful."

"Then why are you still looking at books and magazines?"

"If I know my mom, and I do know her, she expects it. She's been trying to convince me we should have a private reception at the Grand Hotel, where there would be linen tablecloths on the tables, fine china and silver, and cocktails before with a trio of violins and a cello. Then a five-course meal followed by cake and champagne."

Alice laughed. "That doesn't sound like you or Rex. As for the rest of us, all we care about is that you're happy, in love, and that your marriage lasts a lifetime. The rest will take care of itself. Besides, don't you have Jenn as your wedding planner?"

Jenn was my best friend and a marvelous event planner. Ever since I'd begged her to come for my first summer and help me, she'd shared my office on the fourth floor of the McMurphy. On top of all that she also had a baby boy who would turn one soon. "Yes, and I'm afraid I've been driving her crazy. She has suggestions and decisions she wants me to make, and all I do is freeze."

"And study wedding books and magazines." Alice patted my hand. "If it makes you feel better, go on and see what's new at the lending library, and I'll see if I can get it here before you get married in two weeks."

"Thank you!" I waved and hurried to the computer. I knew in my heart that weddings aren't as important as marriage. But I also knew my mom's pride in being part of upper-middle-class society, and her expectations for her only child's wedding, which had me running in circles. And while this was Rex's third wedding, it was my first and definitely last.

I felt even more pressure because I was embraced as a local by most of Mackinac Island's society. The whole island was invited, and my parents and my entire family, some coming all the way from Florida, plus my parents' friends and business associates—thanks, Mom—and then there was Rex's family and any extended family, all of whom I hadn't met yet. Good or bad, I represented the island, and they hadn't said anything, but I knew the businesses hoped most of them would be charmed enough to come back and spend their money or plan their own family weddings here. Everyone hoped that people would talk about it for years.

No pressure there, I thought sarcastically.

Then there were my finances for what my mom still called my "little business" to think about. Even with my newly trained fudge maker, I needed to shut the fudge shop down until the Tuesday after the wedding.

And, while the McMurphy was all booked up, it was filled with relatives, my parents' friends, and everyone else my mom invited. The rooms were all comped. Otherwise, my mom would die of embarrassment. I would lose a quarter of my revenue this month.

It's no wonder I couldn't stop reading wedding books and magazines, second-guessing all my decisions.

I heard a noise and glanced over to see the side door to the library closing. Shrugging, I drew my attention back to the library computer in front of me and searched the database. As I finished the first page of scrolling, I heard two women arguing. I leaned around the computer to see if I could spot who it was on the other side of the stacks. Although the building was small, it was still a library, and the librarians tried to keep it quiet. Unfortunately, I couldn't see anything from my vantage point. They had to be a few aisles away, and if I got up, it would appear that I was far more interested in a fight than my wedding, and I wouldn't have that bad luck.

Audrey Davis, the associate librarian, who had beautiful brown skin, kind eyes, natural hair, and a welcoming personality, hurried over to where they fought. As their voices grew louder and louder, I couldn't help but listen. "Ladies," Audrey said, her voice calm yet insistent as a schoolteacher's. "Please keep it down."

"I requested the newest craft book," I heard one woman say. "It wasn't in my reserved books pile, and when I got here, she had already taken it."

"First come, first served." The second woman sounded

familiar, but then again, I had a pretty good relationship with all the seniors, and even the first lady's voice sounded slightly familiar. "Besides, this book hog has been reserving all the new craft books and then keeping them for weeks. This time, I am going to read one first."

"No, you're not. It was on the shelf, and I got it first."

There was the sound of a scuffle.

"Ladies!" Audrey used what I could only describe as a principal's voice. "If you don't stop fighting, I will give it to the four other people who have requested it before we'll lend it to you two."

The fighting stopped, but I could hear grumbling. Suddenly, there seemed to be a race to the section of books for sale, which, if I leaned back, I could see.

It was Velma French and Myrtle Bautita who had had the fight over the craft book, and now it seemed like they had elbowed each other to grab books off the top shelf, which held the newest books for sale. I knew both ladies through my interaction with the Senior Center, and I knew Myrtle was a good friend of Irma's. The rivalry between Velma and Myrtle went back decades, and no one remembers why it began. In fact, I don't think even the women remember why.

I'd never seen two women grabbing up as many books as they could hold to keep the other from finding something they wanted.

"Ha, ha!" Velma raised two books in the air and waved them under Myrtle's nose, her gray curls swinging and a vicious smile on her face. "This is the latest Karen Dionne, and it's signed!" She hugged it to her chest and waved the other book. "And, even better, this one is by Anissa Gray, and it's a first edition!"

Myrtle appeared defeated. "I've been wanting those for ages, and you know it."

"Too bad, so sad," Velma gloated, waving her books. "I got them first, and they are going into my private collection."

"Until you die," Myrtle replied. "Then they're going to have one big rummage sale. I can't wait."

"Humph," Velma sniffed and turned on her heel toward the front desk, where she could check out the books she selected and pay for her treasures.

Myrtle sighed and sat down at the computer next to me.

"That was kind of mean," I said softly.

"I know. She didn't have to wave them under my nose," Myrtle said.

"I meant telling her that when she died you were going to buy them from her estate rummage sale."

"Oh," Myrtle said, rolling her brown eyes and waving the thought away. "She knows I didn't mean it." Then she looked down at the computer in front of her. "Sheesh, it's like Velma to not return the computer to the home page." She scrolled a bit. "What on earth was she doing on the Social Security site? Everyone our age knows our retirement benefits forward and backward. Well, at least we should." She scrolled through websites for five minutes and then deftly put the screen back on the home page and stood. "She should be gone by now. Bye, Allie."

"Bye, Myrtle," I said and went back to scrolling through the list of bridal books and magazines that might get here within two weeks. I sighed. I'd read them all. I turned off the computer, grabbed my book bag, and strolled to the front of the library.

"Did you find anything?" Audrey asked.

"No," I said, trying not to sound defeated.

"That's for the best, don't you think?" she asked kindly. "Try to enjoy the experience. It only comes once in a lifetime."

"I'll try," I said with a half smile.

"Wait," Alice said. "Here, you may need this book on slowing anxiety with meditation." She held out her hand, looking for me to hand over my library card. I gave it to her. "This works wonders for me when I start to worry about details." She handed me my card back, along with the book. "I'm sure it will work for you when you get overwhelmed."

"Thanks." I put the book in my book bag and stepped out into the blue sky and the sounds of birds and lapping water from the lake.

The library itself was built to attract locals and fudgies who wanted to spend a few hours reading. A beautiful mint-green Greek Revival building with white columns and trim, it sat near the shore. There was a boardwalk that took you past the tiny, white house-shaped sign with the library's hours on it. But one of my favorite things was the brass sculpture of two young children enjoying a book. Thick bushes ran along the side, allowing for shade so that you could read on one of the benches undisturbed by the park next door.

As I walked beside the bushes, I noticed Velma's precious craft book on the ground. I bent to pick it up and brush it off. As I rounded the other side of the bushes, I noticed three things at once. Myrtle's books were also scattered on the ground. And Velma lay flat, her head turned to the side, bleeding horribly. Beside her was Myrtle on her knees, rocking back and forth keening softly.

I rushed to her side and bent down to see if I could help Velma with my first-aid skills. They weren't needed. Velma's skull was bashed in to the extent that I knew she had to be dead. Still, I did my duty and reached for a pulse along her neck. There wasn't even the slightest glimmer of a pulse. That's when I noticed a large rock beside Myrtle. It was covered with blood and gray hair.

Then a man came around the corner of the library with a fishing pole in his hand. "Velma?" he asked and dropped the pole. "Velma!" He rushed to her side and started to shake her as if to wake her.

"Don't touch her! She's gone," I said. "And the police will need to look for evidence on anyone here who touched her."

"No! Not my Velma!" he put his face in his large, calloused hands. "My sweetheart!"

I deduced he was Velma's husband. As I reached for my phone to call 911, Irma and Carol came hurrying over. The pair were always together and thick as thieves. Carol ran the Senior Center and half the senior committees. While Irma was always there to assist.

"We heard shouting," Irma said.

"Then we saw Velma on the ground and Myrtle beside her," Carol said. "Is everything okay?"

"My Velma is gone," the man sobbed. "And that

horrible woman killed her!" He pointed toward Myrtle, causing her to cry even harder.

"Now, Richard, you can't make assumptions like that. None of us know what happened, and it's not always what it looks like," Carol said. "This must be hard and shocking, but you are not alone." Carol comforted him by putting her hand on his shoulder. "We are here with you."

Irma reached out and squeezed Myrtle's hand. "Are you okay? Do you want me to go get Brian?" When Myrtle shook her head, I stood, stepped away, and called 911, but not before I saw someone watching from the bushes. They saw me and closed the bushes quickly.

"Nine-one-one. What's your emergency?"

"Hi, Charlene, it's Allie McMurphy," I said, trying to keep my voice calm and walked toward the bushes.

"Where are you?" she asked. "I'm contacting the police and ambulance for you now."

"Better contact Shane as well," I said. "We're outside the library." Shane was Jenn's new husband and the county's crime-scene investigator. I'm sure Jenn fell in love because of his nerdy good looks and his slim, but muscular build. She told me once she found the way he pushed his hair out of his face endearing.

"Done," Charlene said. "What happened?"

"I came out of the library and found Velma French on the ground with her head badly damaged. There was a large rock nearby with part of her left on it."

"Oh, dear, not Velma. She was always a sweet

woman and baked the best brownies." Charlene sighed. "Whatever you do, don't let anyone touch that rock."

As she said that, I turned to see Velma's husband angrily kick the rock, and it rolled into the lake. "Darn thing can go straight to the bottom of the lake!" he shouted.

"No!" I yelled and dropped my phone. All I could think about was that the murder weapon was in the lake, with evidence washing off. I rushed past him and waded into the water. It couldn't have rolled far. Velma was a few yards from the beach. I spotted it as pieces of hair and blood started to drift off in the current, grabbed it, and pulled it out of the water, not sure I would be able to preserve any evidence. I didn't have gloves on, and neither did Velma's husband. As I turned from the lake, I saw that the scene was charged with anger and sorrow.

"That rock should be crushed and ground up to dust, and so should you!" Richard lunged toward Myrtle. Carol ran in front of him, with her hands out, while Irma sheltered Myrtle.

"Stop!" Carol shouted, her purple tracksuit and blindingly white shoes catching his attention and causing him to pause.

Thankfully, Rex, my fiancé and the island's lead police officer, and Officer Charles Brown rolled up on their bikes. Charles dropped his bike and grabbed Richard by the arms, pulling him back and cuffing him. "You need to cool down," Charles told him sternly. "Sit here until we can assess the situation." Richard still looked angry, but he did as he was told.

More people stopped to see what had happened, trampling the crime scene. I wasn't any better than they were when it came to the crime scene. Here I was holding the rock in both my hands with my cell phone on the ground in front of me. Having touched Velma and then called 911, I would be lucky if they didn't keep the phone. Hopefully, all Shane would have to do is remove the case. With the wedding so close, I hoped I didn't have to order a new one as soon as I got home.

"Alright, everyone, step back," Rex said, with such a tone of authority that people moved. Charles pushed the crowd back and staked and rolled out crime-scene tape, while Carol and Irma helped Richard and Myrtle to the edge of the crowd. Both sobbed, with their hands covering their faces. Rex looked at me next. "Allie?"

"I think this may be the murder weapon," I said, holding out the wet rock. There were still a few spots of blood and a hair or two.

"What the heck?" Rex looked from the rock to me.

"Richard angrily kicked it, and it rolled into the water."

Rex looked up at the sky and, for a moment, closed his eyes. "You saved it from the water." It was a statement, not a question.

"Well, I couldn't let the evidence wash away," I said softly.

He looked at me with annoyance, then love, in his eyes. "I'm going to need you to hold that until we can get a big enough evidence bag or Shane arrives."

"I had Charlene call him, too," I said, as the ambulance rolled up, its lights and sirens running. The ambulance and the fire truck for emergency response were the only motor vehicles allowed on the island. Everything else moved by horse and buggy, bicycle, or walking. I personally preferred to walk.

Head EMT George Marron stepped out. George was the type of man who made women sigh with his copper skin and long black hair pulled back to enhance his high cheekbones and sensuous mouth. Of any of us on the island, his ancestors had been here the longest, making us all fudgies of a sort. Leah Harrell, his partner of the day, closed her door behind her and headed to the back. George opened the back of the ambulance and hauled out their medical bags, then rushed over to Velma. We all knew, and I suspect they did, too, that she was gone. I'm not known for calling in people they can actually help, although I wish it were true this time.

The yellow crime-scene tape left the growing crowd to watch from afar and whisper about whether or not Velma was dead, and who would do such a terrible thing to such a nice lady.

Carol sat on the ground next to Richard, far enough away to not be able to see much and to the side, where they couldn't hear the murmurs of the crowd. Irma and Myrtle sat on the opposite side of Velma, close to the crime scene. George checked Velma out and shook his head to confirm that there was nothing they could do for her. They blocked the body as best they could from the crowd and waited for Shane, who worked in his lab at St. Ignace. The Coast Guard was picking him up by boat, ensuring he got here as fast as possible.

"Allie!" Carol said, and I turned to Carol with the rock still in my hands. "Don't you have a dress fitting in fifteen minutes?"

Shoot. I blew out my breath. "Thanks for the reminder."

Rex looked up at Carol's words and said something to George, who glanced at me. He nodded and went back to the ambulance and produced the right size bag for the rock. Rex took the bag and strode over to me. "I'll take that," he said, with a flash of love on his face. When he slid the rock into the bag, his expression was all cop. "It's not an evidence bag, but it will do. We're going to need to collect samples from your hands. You should call Esmerelda and let her know you'll have to reschedule."

"That's what I was thinking." I raised my hands just enough to emphasize the possible murder weapon I was holding. "But evidence."

"Yeah," he said. "Where's your cell phone?"

"On the ground," I replied. "But it might have evidence on it."

"Has it been on the ground the entire time?" he asked.

"I touched Thelma and then dialed 911."

"Has Shane ever taken your phone for that?"

"No," I whispered.

He picked up my cell and held it up to my face to open it. "Is Esmerelda in your contacts?"

"Yes, of course," I responded. "We've been working on this dress for over six months." Esmerelda Gonzoles was the best dressmaker in the two counties. While my mom wanted a large princess ball gown with three crinolines and an eight-foot veil, I had wanted something simple. Maybe something a bit bohemian. Esmerelda thought to combine the two by making the dress out of white eyelet with enough room for one crinoline to help bring the skirt out.

Rex found her name in my contacts, hit the dial button, and put her on speaker phone.

"Esmerelda's Dress Designs. How can I help you?" She had the sweetest accent from her home country in South America, even though she had come to the United States when her parents had immigrated and she was ten years old.

"Um, hi, Esmerelda," I said.

"Allie, don't worry. Everything is ready for you. Are you excited for your final fitting? Don't forget to bring your shoes."

"That's why I was calling," I said and cleared my throat. "There's been an emergency, and it could be a few hours before I'll be free."

"Are you okay?"

"Yes, yes, I'm fine," I said. "Could we reschedule?"

"Of course," she said. "I tell you what, you call me when you're free, and we'll make a special appointment for you. I'm confident the dress is perfect, and this time I'll come to Mackinac when you have time, and we'll do a fitting at your place. Unless, of course, the groom is . . . shall we say, around too much? It's bad luck for him to see the dress before the ceremony."

Rex raised an eyebrow at me, his deep blue eyes twinkling as he tried to keep a straight face.

"Thank you, Esmerelda!" I said. "You're a doll."

She laughed. "Take care of yourself. We'll talk later."

"I will," I said, and Rex hung up, slipping my phone into my pocket. Lucky for me, Shane showed up, running from the special dock to the crime scene with his kit in hand. Shane Carpenter was a tall, gangly man with round glasses and an intensely smart brain. These days, he looked as tired as Jenn did with a toddler in the house.

"Shane, over here." Rex waved him through the crowd. He lifted the crime-scene tape and ducked under, then headed straight toward us.

"What do we have?" He pushed his glasses up and tried to catch his breath.

"Velma French was murdered," Rex said, his blank cop expression back in place. "When I got here, Allie held what may be the murder weapon." Rex lifted the bag to show the heavy rock. "It's not an evidence bag, but I didn't want to wait until you got here to collect it."

"That's fine. Allie, why'd you pick it up?" Shane asked as he put his kit down, opened it, and gloved up.

"Richard, who I assume is Velma's husband—"

"Ex-husband," Carol informed me.

As if on cue, a woman who was fifteen years younger than Velma made her way through the crowd. "Richard! My Richard!" Charles tried to stop her, but she pushed her way under the tape. "I'm Julie French, that's my husband, and he needs me." She ran to Richard, pushed Irma aside, and sat with him, hugging his head to her breast.

"Um, Velma's ex-husband," I corrected. "Was terribly upset." I pointed to where Richard sat with his around his wife, his shoulders shaking with sobs. "He kicked it hard, knocking it away from beside Myrtle. Unfortunately, he kicked it hard enough that it ended up in the lake." I sighed. "I rushed over to get it and preserve as much evidence as I could." With the initial worry about my fitting over, I realized how big and heavy the rock was. My arms hurt, and I went to rub them when he stopped me.

"Don't touch anything!" He pulled evidence-collection instruments out of his bag. "I need to collect as much as I can off your hands."

I looked down at my wet and slightly dripping hands and silently wished him the best. "At least you have my fingerprints and palm prints on file." I tried to smile, but neither Shane nor Rex seemed amused.

"Why didn't you tell me that what you think might be the murder weapon was beside Myrtle?" Rex looked like he was interrogating a witness. I'm not going to lie. He usually looked that way when questioning a witness—even me.

"I didn't mean to leave that part out."

"Is this the only part of the scene you touched?" Shane asked, as he put the last swab into a bag.

"No." I winced. They both hated that answer. "I had to check what shape Velma was in when I came upon the scene. I checked for breathing and a pulse. She was definitely gone."

Shane tilted his head down and looked at me from over the top of his glasses. "Allie, I swear, you touch more bodies than the ME."

"I couldn't call nine-one-one without any information," I replied. "If I hadn't done it before calling, you both know Charlene would have made me do it after I called."

"Right," both men said at the same time. I wasn't sure if they agreed with me or not, but at least that part of the conversation was over.

"That's all I'll need from her," Shane said, and Rex nodded. Shane picked up his kit and moved slowly to the body.

"Tell me everything from the beginning," Rex said as he pulled his interview notepad from his left breast pocket.

I told him everything—from what I saw in the library, to following the dropped books, to how I found Velma with Myrtle crying beside her, with the rock resting near her.

He flipped his notebook closed. "Sounds like an open-and-shut case."

I shook my head. "These things never are."

Chapter 2

As I walked home, my mind was on the face in the bushes and the crowd I had scanned while waiting for Shane. The people in the front had pushed their way to the tape. There were several seniors, all calling to Myrtle to ask if she was alright. One was Ralph Stanisky. He spoke to Eli Hatfield as they took in the scene. Then there were some of the book club ladies, Barbara Vissor, Judith Schmidt, and Mary O'Malley, plus two others I couldn't quite place. One was a big man about my age with a dark black T-shirt, jeans, and a blue waiter's apron around his waist. He said something to Myrtle, but I was too far away to hear. The other young guy with the same black T-shirt, jeans, and apron pulled him away. I'd have to ask Rex if he knew who they were. He knew everyone on the island.

"Allie!" It was my Uncle John. He stood about five foot nine inches and had the weathered hands and face of a farmer. He wore work jeans and cowboy boots with a flannel shirt. His round head was bald on top, with a ring of gray hair from ear to ear. An ancient suitcase was in his hand.

And it begins, I thought to myself. Only two weeks early. "Uncle John!" I gave him a huge hug outside the McMurphy Hotel and Fudge Shop. The business had been in my father's family since the mid 1800s. But my dad had refused to take it on, so it was my turn to keep the tradition going, and I loved every moment of it.

"You're early," I said, as he opened the door for me. "Is Aunt Ginny here? You beat Mom and Dad."

"Your mom's here." He politely waited for me to go through the door. "She and Ginny came ahead, while I worked out where things were going with a porter. Nice kid, that Colby Klein, don't you think?"

"Mom's here?" I asked, my voice suddenly higher-pitched. This was the part of the wedding I wasn't looking forward to, and here it was only two weeks early.

"There's the bride!" My mom rushed toward me, her designer shoes tapping on the wood floor of the lobby. I sent her a look that said I was not happy. Without acknowledging me, she engulfed me in such a tight hug that I almost squeaked. A cloud of expensive perfume surrounded us both. Before I said even a word, she grabbed my hand and dragged me to the registration desk, where my faithful hotel manager, Frances Devaney, held my pup, Mal, while she distributed keys to a group of ten. Unfortunately, nearly all were relatives.

Had Mom learned nothing from the last time she'd

dropped in unexpectedly? There was no way I had time to entertain people now.

"Allie, you remember Uncle John and Aunt Ginny," she said.

"Of course," I said. "I hugged Uncle John outside." Aunt Ginny, who looked nothing like you would imagine a farmer's wife would look, hugged me. She rivaled my mom in a designer dress, Louboutin pumps, and smartly cut blond hair. Her makeup was perfect (you couldn't tell it was contoured), and her manicure alone must have cost $200. After all, she was my mom's sister. What down-to-earth Uncle John saw in her I'd never know.

"Well, look at you," Aunt Ginny said, eyeing my cable-knit sweater pulled over my work polo, my sticky black work pants, which I'm sure had some grass stains from kneeling down to see if I could help Velma, and my sturdy tennis shoes, which I wear for safety when I handle hot sugar. I smelled like fudge from head to toe and braced myself as I waited for her to say anything negative. "You look . . ."

"Like I just finished my last fudge demonstration and ran out to do errands?" I put on my best and brightest smile.

"I was going to say that you look happy," Aunt Ginny said.

"I wanted to surprise her," Mom said as she grabbed my arm. She mouthed something to Ginny over her shoulder. I had to work hard to keep the smile plastered on my face and not roll my eyes.

"I'd like you to meet one of my closest friends, Sharon Flannery, and her husband, Cary," Mom said.

Sharon was petite, with a warm personality, brown eyes, and short dark hair that reminded me of Elizabeth Taylor. While her clothing mirrored that of the others, I felt no distress over how I looked. She held out her hand, so I took it, and she patted mine. "So nice to finally meet you, dear. I've heard nothing but pride in your mother's voice whenever she speaks of you."

I glanced at my mom. "Nice to meet you, too."

Cary shook my hand firmly, like a businessman does. He seemed so different from Sharon. Tall, with broad shoulders and thinning blond hair, he had the sun-weathered look of a consummate golfer. "Nice to meet you. I understand you have some really good golf courses here."

"We do," I said. "I've heard all three are wonderful."

"Perfect," he said.

"And you remember Uncle Wade and Aunt Felicity." Wade was my mom's brother, and Felicity was a debutante and a sister of my mom's at the most prestigious sorority at Yale. They, too, had dressed "casual," with no idea what that meant to the residents of the island.

"Uncle Edmund and Aunt Celeste will be along later. He's working on a difficult case, but he tells me that happens often when you're a partner in a law firm," Mom's tone was cheerful and bright, as if she didn't notice Aunt Felicity's up-and-down look and her efforts to make sure her clothes didn't touch mine. Which was a good thing, should she find out I had been at a murder scene. I'm sure when my mom found out, she would have both a stroke and a heart attack at the same time, if that's possible. What she would surely do is never forgive me.

These couples were the beginning of the family descending on us. My grandmother on my mom's side had eight children, and none of them would ever even think about staying at the McMurphy. The Flannerys seemed more curious than the others about the history of the hotel. Meanwhile, my family seemed resigned to their fate. I'm sure because Mom made sure they did. As they looked around and took their keys, I could hear them whisper to each other that they would only stay for the night to make my mom happy. Then they'd be off to stay at the Grand Hotel. Which was fine with me. My father's family and friends had yet to show up.

"This hotel is quite . . . quaint," Aunt Felicity said. Her expression gave away her disgust as she followed everyone up the stairs, with Frances in the lead.

"I believe it's a historical landmark," Uncle John replied and winked over his shoulder at me. I smiled and gave him a wave.

"I've booked rooms at the Grand for tomorrow," Mom said. "Thank you all for being kind and staying at my daughter's hotel. This will give you a chance to get to know her better." I could tell from her voice that she was doing her best to be bright and shiny, while secretly she was embarrassed.

Before they went up, Frances had handed Mal over to me.

"Put that dog away," Mom said to me before hurriedly climbing the stairs. "It leaves a bad impression, and things are bad enough."

With Mal in my arms, I called up the stairs after her, "We're going to talk about this!"

Mal softly grrred for the first time ever. "I agree, baby," I said and gave her extra love, letting her down so that she could sniff the floor where everyone had stood. I stayed at the reception desk, waiting for Frances to come back down. Luckily, the porters arrived with the luggage. "They may expect you to hang up their clothes," I called after them as they went up in the old-fashioned elevator.

"We were told," Colby said as they started up. "That's why my sister and her friend are here." The girls waved at me as the historic wrought-iron elevator disappeared from view. This time I rolled my eyes for real.

Soon Frances was back at her post, without a comment. At least she looked like her normal self. Her brown hair was smartly done. Her wide brown eyes and round face were enhanced by discreet makeup. She wore an orange T-shirt, and her usual mid-length, flower-patterned A-line skirt, and for that I thanked my lucky stars. I hurried upstairs with Mal.

Thirty minutes later, I had showered, washed my hair, blown it dry while trying to straighten it as best I could—I needed a haircut—and put on my best sundress and sandals. I left my pets some extra treats, closed and locked my door, and raced to my office, where Jenn was hard at work planning two weddings, the Franklins' at the end of June and mine at the beginning.

"Oh, good, you're here. The florist ordered the flowers to be shipped by next Wednesday, giving her plenty of time to have the arrangements done by your wedding day," she said, without looking up. "I need to confirm that lilacs and peonies are what you want."

"They're two weeks early," I said as I paced the room.

"What? No, the flowers won't arrive until Wednesday," she reassured me.

"I'm not talking about the flowers," I said. That made her look up.

"What am I missing?"

"Mom's here along with her brothers and sisters." I must have looked as angry as I felt.

"Why?" Jenn asked.

"That's a good question, isn't it?" I said, in an effort to let off some steam before I spoke to my mom. "I don't know, it's one of Mom's schemes. She said they came to spend time with me before all the chaos began. I had no idea. She'd better not think she can turn the wedding into some exclusive event at the Grand Hotel." I felt like I could scream.

Jenn frowned, and her blue eyes narrowed. "I won't let that happen. I have friends on the event staff there. It's my job to ensure that nothing goes wrong at your wedding."

I paced some more, feeling my anger subside a little. Jenn was right. "The worst part is that they're staying here tonight, which stinks. I have people with actual reservations that Frances and I now need to find accommodations for. Plus, you should have seen how they looked at the McMurphy, like it was beneath them. My Aunt Felicity called it quaint, and that's not a good thing."

Jenn appeared confused, even though she looked

like a million bucks with her upswept blond hair in a neat French twist and her professional attire—a pencil skirt and a blouse under a beautiful sweater; her kitten-heel pumps completed her outfit. Meanwhile, I regretted my sandals because I hadn't had time for a pedicure. My mom would be appalled. Not that I cared at this point. I simply didn't want to hear her go on about it.

"Can they do that?" Jenn asked. "Take rooms away from customers with reservations?"

"No," I said. "But you know Mom. She assumes since I own the business, she has free rein to come at any time and there'll be a room. Thank goodness for Frances. She'll figure out how to fix it."

"Please tell me she's paying for the rooms," Jenn leaned back in her chair and crossed her arms over her chest, her blue gaze flashing with anger.

"She never does, and you know it," I grumbled.

"This is ridiculous and selfish and rude," Jenn said. "I hope you're going to talk to her about this."

"I'm going to find her. I thought I should blow off some steam first before I strangle her on sight. To top things off, I found another person murdered," I said, with a weariness that always came over me following anger.

"Oh no! Who was it?"

"Velma French," I said. "I was at the library when it happened."

Chapter 3

"Allie, why don't you show the family around the island," Mom said and slicked down my hair. "Let me get some hair spray. Your hair is ridiculous. Did you even try to do anything with it when you changed?" She reached into her handbag and dug out a small bottle of hair spray and sprayed a cloud around me. "I never go anywhere without it. Look at you, dressed like a . . . a . . ."

"Mom, why are you here two weeks early? And why did you bring the family? I told you last time that I won't tolerate you popping in with no notice. It's rude and disrespectful. Then to house them at the McMurphy on top of that? I have guests who have reserved those rooms."

"Well!" Mom straightened, clearly offended by my tone. Too bad. She deserved the talking to. "I thought you would want to spend time with family before the ceremony."

"Would you pop into Aunt Felicity's work without notice? Or Aunt Ginny's home?"

"I'm not their mother," she said, sounding hurt this time. "I simply thought my daughter would want her mother around at this important moment in her life. But I see that's not true. Don't worry. I have reservations at the Grand for everyone. I suppose they won't mind if we show up early."

I hated it when she did that. "See, you have reservations for the Grand. Why not for the McMurphy?"

"I think of it as my home, since your father basically owns it," she said even though she knew full well that I was the owner. "But if it's not my home, and you don't want me here . . ."

My mom was a master manipulator. "Fine, stay."

"If you're sure," she said.

"I'm sure," I said. "But I don't have time to give the family a tour of the island."

"If you can't, you can't," she replied. "I'm sure they'll understand. Although they don't understand why you're so insistent on being a fudge maker."

"I've always wanted to live on the island, run the McMurphy, and tell Papa Liam's stories."

"The least you could do is look good doing it. I didn't send you to all those deportment classes for my health, you know." Her disappointment was thick in the air. "I know I taught you better than this. You can't look like this in front of the family, and you know it." Glancing down at my feet, she shook her head and frowned.

"You clearly need a pedicure." She took one of my hands. "And a manicure."

"Mom," I said, my tone warning her.

"If you don't mind, I'd love to have a girls' day. We can do the whole works, and then we can go shopping," she said brightly, as if she hadn't just belittled me and looked me over. "My daughter should have a trousseau. It will be fun!"

"And what will the rest of the family do?" I asked. "They don't seem the bike-riding, hiking kind of people, and they're certainly not interested in fudge or the fort."

"Uncle Wade brought his yacht. We plan on many outings on the lake," she said. "In fact, tomorrow I've put together a champagne brunch on the yacht. Bring your best swimsuit and a nice cover-up."

"Mom," I said firmly, "I've got to make fudge tomorrow. In fact, I have to do that every day this week. I must meet my budget goals so that I can take time out for the wedding and a few days off for a honeymoon. Plus, there's so much planning I still need to do, including my final dress fitting."

"I can cancel my plans and help you with the wedding," she said.

"No, no." I waved the thought away. "Jenn and I have it covered."

"Of course you do, dear. Of course you do. Most girls want their mothers to help. But I understand." She patted my hand. "I'm dying to see your handmade dress. Of course, I've been telling everyone it's couture, which is the same thing . . . nearly."

"Please tell the family I'd love to be there today, but I have wedding details to approve."

"Yes, of course," Mom said, as she turned and walked away. "Besides, you can't go out looking like that."

I rolled my eyes.

"I saw that!"

I've wondered my whole life how she's able to do that.

"I'm your mother, dear." She seemed to know what I was thinking and continued toward the door. "We have reservations at the yacht club if you need me."

I needed to gather my thoughts and make a plan, so I went upstairs. Jenn popped out of our shared office. She squeezed her eyebrows together and wrinkled her nose. "What is that smell?" She proceeded to sneeze four times in a row.

"Hair spray." I touched my hair to find it stiff as a board. "Mom was appalled at my flyaways."

Jenn gave another silent look. We'd known each other long enough for me to hear her thoughts without her even saying them. Then she said, "Girl, what is she doing? Living in the 1960s?"

I shook my head, and my hair didn't move. "I think she's too young to reflect the 1960s. It was more like the 1980s."

"Then *Pretty in Pink* or something." Jenn sneezed another two times. "Did she demand you entertain the family?"

I gave a short laugh. "That's what she wanted, but I told her no. I also told her again that she can't pop in without notice."

"Good for you," Jenn said.

"Of course, she had to give me the song and dance about her being my mother and thought this was her home as well, yadda, yadda. Oh, and she said I needed a manicure and a pedicure, and she planned an entire mother/daughter day at the salon. Right after I told her I was busy with my business."

"Does she not listen to you?"

"Let it go, Jenn," I said. "She said I couldn't do anything with the family until we had a mother/daughter day."

"What's that mean?"

"She needs me to be more . . . presentable. It seems the family would be appalled at what I'm wearing and that she didn't teach me better."

"Remember when we first met?" Jenn laughed. "You looked like something out of a fashion magazine. I was jealous. But then when you went into the culinary school building, I laughed."

"Why did you laugh?" I was confused.

"Because I knew your designer outfits wouldn't last long if you were in the kitchen every day. And guess what?"

I shook my head and smiled. "You were right."

"As far as I'm concerned, your mom and her family should love you no matter what." Jenn's tone was at once angry and disappointed. "I know I will love Benji no matter what."

"You have to understand," I argued for my mom. "The way she grew up, it was all about power and fitting into a certain group. When she fell in love with my dad, there was so much family pressure that she begged him to leave the island and the hotel and start a prestigious career instead."

"And clearly he did," Jenn said with a shake of her head. "I don't think I'll ever understand."

"Dad left the island out of love," I said. "I think she's only doing this out of love. She wants her family to accept me because they never accepted my father."

Jenn gasped. "After he left here for her? They are horrible people."

"I don't know about horrible," I said thoughtfully. "The family has a strict code of deportment. They all grew up with it and have passed it down from generation to generation. My father wasn't raised with that code, and even though he loves my mom deeply, he's never bothered with their family traditions. On one hand that's part of Dad's appeal, but on the other, it disregards everything Mom's family has endured and survived to maintain their traditional social status."

"But you're not like them," Jenn said, confused. "How come? Weren't you raised with your mom's strict rules?"

I laughed. "My poor mom. She's worked and worked with me to see that I learn them. Even put me in an exclusive private school and several deportment classes. But no matter what she did, it didn't stick. I've always broken her heart for that."

"I didn't know that." Jenn looked at me as if she had never really known me. "Did you have trouble fitting in with those classmates and their families?"

"Yes, you should have seen me in my uniform of green plaid skirts and white blouses. Even our socks and shoes had to meet standard. Once a week, Mom took me to her hairdresser, where my hair was processed to remove the wave and then straightened flat and kept that way with nearly a bottle of hair spray. It was expected that my hair would look done every day, with no flyaways and the proper amount of sheen."

Jenn shook her head. "How were you able to maintain that for a full week? I sleep half a night and have bed head."

"I had to sleep with a silk nightcap and silk pillowcases. It was also expected that I would sleep on my back. Lying on your side gives you wrinkles."

"Oh, my gosh," Jenn exclaimed. "You were never allowed to be a kid, were you?"

"Unfortunately for my mom and fortunately for me, my father ensured I had no such rules on the weekend and holiday breaks," I said. "And when I spent summers on the island with Papa Liam and Grammy Alice, I was allowed to be as free as a bird. I ran around barefoot and wore what my mom would call cheap clothes. When I wasn't watching Papa make fudge and learning the art of fudge making, I was swimming in the lake or wandering in the woods. My mom would be appalled if she knew that the designer clothes she bought for the summers and packed in my three suitcases never left them."

"Wait, where did you get the other clothes if you weren't wearing what she packed?"

I grinned. "Grammy Alice would go out and get me some 'tougher' kid's clothes for the summer. Clothes that it didn't matter if I got grass stains on the knees and fudge stains on the shirts."

"Ah, you learned subterfuge from your Grammy and Papa."

"I did," I said, sure that I had Papa's twinkle in my eyes.

"Wait, aren't those schools and designer clothes expensive? I thought your dad was an architect. Where'd your family get the money?" Jenn asked. "I guess that's a rude question."

"No, it's not rude when you're best friends for as long as we are. My mom's family has made fortunes, lost fortunes, and made fortunes. My great-grandfather was very good with his money, and my grandfather invested wisely. My mother is quite rich."

"Quite rich as in very rich? As in millionaire rich?"

"Yes," I said.

"That explains a thing or two," Jenn said. "Wait, doesn't that make you a trust-fund baby? Have you been holding out on me?"

"Nope," I said, with a shake of my head. "I lost that right when I didn't go to an Ivy League college, even though my grades were good, strings were pulled, and I was a legacy student from a well-respected family. Mom's entire family were horrified when I decided on culinary school instead of a more 'respectable' school. And I refused to be a member of a sorority. I was instead—gasp!—following in my grandfather's working-class footsteps. I haven't seen my aunts and uncles since."

"Well, I'm glad you made the choices you did because we wouldn't have met otherwise." Jenn gave me a hug.

"I also wouldn't be doing something I love, with pets I love, in a place where I feel at home. As far as I'm concerned, I would do it all over again, trust fund or not."

Chapter 4

After I finished my work for the day, I took Mal out for a nice long walk. She was excited to nose around our usual places. I liked to think of it as reading the news. I took her to the crime scene, and Mal went straight to the bushes where I'd seen someone. I studied the dirt and looked for shoe prints.

"What do you think, Mal?" I asked her.

She glanced at me and then sniffed until she sat and looked up at me expectantly.

That's when I saw them. Two footprints facing the bushes and two walking away. Using my phone, I took photos of the footprints and measured them against my own foot.

"Allie," Carol called as she and Irma power walked by. Mal rushed over to greet them, pulling me along. Both ladies bent down to give Mal the attention she sought.

"We know you're busy with wedding plans," Irma said, as she straightened. "But Myrtle's son, Brian, is worried about her, and you know she's an old friend of mine. We've known each other since kindergarten, and she would never murder someone. Especially Velma. You wouldn't know it, but as much as they fought, they loved the rivalry."

"They've been competing since high school," Carol said.

"Begging the question, what has changed now that would drive Myrtle to kill? It makes more sense that Myrtle didn't kill Velma. I'm sure if she wanted to, she would have done it long ago."

"See, I told you she didn't kill Velma. She said she found her like that, and when she checked for a pulse, Velma was already dead." Irma shook from the force of her answer.

"That's why we need you to help investigate," Carol said.

"I don't know," I said. "My family arrived early today, and they expect me to spend most of my time with them."

"The book club is meeting tomorrow night," Carol said slyly. "If you find yourself needing a distraction, you're always welcome."

"Thanks, but I doubt I'll have time," I replied.

Carol sent Irma a knowing look, waved goodbye, and speed walked away.

I glanced at my watch with a sigh. It was nearly eight, and the sun was setting. Soon any visible evidence would disappear in darkness, and I didn't have a flashlight.

I walked to the side of the library, looking for anything that might help. It was all grass, which meant the killer could have arrived and left through the side door of the library without leaving a trace. Mal sat and barked again. When I looked at her, she ran her nose over a bush, sniffing.

"What do you see, Mal? Huh, baby?" I said and carefully studied the bush. Something caught my eye. I wouldn't have seen it at all if it weren't moving in the wind. It was a torn patch of a green-and-black flannel shirt. And, if I remembered right, Richard wore a flannel shirt with the same pattern.

I used my phone to take a picture of it. Thankfully, I had several poo bags in my pocket to clean up after Mal. I turned one inside out and plucked the fabric from the sticky bush and deposited it in the poo bag, quickly tying it shut.

"The sun is really low," I told Mal. "I'm sure Mom and her family are still at the yacht club having drinks and then coffee. But we better get back before it gets too chilly; besides, Mella must be missing us."

I took Market Street and stopped at the police station. The white clapboard building was welcoming, and Mal and I left the sound of horse-drawn carriages and the smells of lilac, pine, and dew to walk inside. The smells and sounds changed dramatically to a printer, phones ringing, and people talking, along with the smell of burnt coffee and microwave pizza.

"Hey, Allie," Officer Ashbury said from behind the reception desk. Reception duty switched daily and mostly consisted of newer police officers or trainees. Officer Ashbury couldn't have been more than eighteen years old. He still had the baby face of a high schooler. His dark hair was cut with clean edges and short on top. His chocolate-brown eyes were as handsome as his deep black skin. I bet he had girls hanging all over him.

"Hi, Booker, er, I mean Officer Trainee Ashbury." Mal jumped up and stretched so she could see him.

"Ms. McMurphy and, of course, hello, Mal." He laughed, reached under the desk, pulled out a dog treat, and gave it to her. Mal took it gently and sat to chomp on it with delight. He turned his attention back to me and my last comment. "It's okay, people struggle when they see me in uniform. Are you looking for Officer Manning?"

"Yes," I replied. "I have something for him."

I held up the green bag, and Booker snorted with laughter. "Did you two have a fight?"

We both laughed at the idea that I would bring Rex a bag of poop. "No," I said when I could stop laughing. "It's evidence."

"Sorry. He left about an hour ago. He mentioned something about an appointment to have a final fitting on his suit." Booker tilted his head.

Guilt made my stomach clench. Rex took time off to prepare for the wedding, and I spent time looking for evidence.

"I found it when I took Mal for her nightly walk," I said, but it sounded lame.

"And?" He looked at me expectantly.

"Oh, right. Well, is Officer Brown still on duty?"

"He is," Booker replied. "I'll give him a call and let him know you're here."

"Thanks." Mal and I walked toward the door into the bullpen.

"He'll be right here," Booker said. Then went back to what he was doing when we came into the building—I suspected either video games or Netflix on his phone.

The door opened, and Charles greeted us. "Hi, Allie. Hi, Mal. What brings you here?" He glanced at his watch. "It's after eight p.m."

"I found some evidence that may be relevant to Velma's murder case."

"Come on back," he said. The smell of coffee intensified as we made our way to his desk.

He waved toward a seat across from his desk. I sat, and Mal jumped up on my lap. "Now," Charles said, "you mentioned evidence?"

"Yes," I handed him the poo bag, and he gave me a dubious look. "I found this—er, Mal pointed it out. It was in the bushes on the library side near the back."

He opened the bag carefully, then turned it inside out until his hand was covered with plastic and the piece of cloth fluttered to his desktop.

"I have a photo of where it was. I think it might be from the shirt Richard wore this morning when we found Velma." I leaned forward. "If I remember right, it's the same color and, I think, the same pattern."

"We'll have to see if we can get the shirt from Richard," Charles said thoughtfully. "Shane and the team decided he hadn't touched her because you and the other witnesses saw him come from the lake side with a fishing pole in his hand."

"He might have torn it on his way to fish, but I don't

see why he would go that way and not through the park," I said. "I wanted Rex to have it, in case."

"Okay," he said and examined the piece of cloth.

"There's something else."

Charles raised an eyebrow and gave me a look that said I should know better. I pulled up the two pictures of the footprints. "I said in my statement that I thought I saw someone watching through the bushes, but couldn't be sure. When I walked by the bushes with Mal just now"—I cleared my throat—"I saw footprints. And I snapped pictures of them in case it rains or someone comes to hide them."

"Why would someone hide them?" He narrowed his eyes.

"Maybe they don't want anyone to know they were there. Or they saw the whole thing but are too afraid to get involved," I posited. "Anyway, here are the pictures."

"Or maybe these prints have nothing to do with the crime." Charles took the phone from me. "There's no way to link them to it. They could have been made anytime by anyone," he said, but looked at the pictures.

"I used my foot. I wanted something to compare it to. Notice how my foot never touched the ground." I leaned forward to point it out on the screen.

"See how much smaller than mine the footprints are? I'm a women's size eight. These footprints look like a size five or six." I sat back. "They are definitely too small to belong to a man."

"I see," he said.

"Oh." I grabbed my phone. "Here's another picture

of the same footprints walking away." I swiped to the second photo and handed it to him.

"Hmm" was his only comment.

"Do you want me to email these pictures to you?" I asked. "You could add them to the case file on the off chance they become important."

Charles handed me my phone back and rubbed his chin. "Frankly, Allie, even if they were evidence, we can't prove it."

"But they can still point you in the right direction." I tapped on my phone and sent them to him.

He didn't even check to see if he got them. "Is there anything else?"

"Yes," I cleared my throat. "Mom and my aunts and uncles are in town and may want a tour since Rex works here."

"Aren't they two weeks early?"

"Yep," I answered. "That's the reason for my nice long walk with Mal."

Chapter 5

We took the front way back into the McMurphy and I saw there was a folded note in my letter box, so I grabbed it. Then Mal and I walked the steps to the fourth floor. I took off her harness and leash, then unlocked my apartment's door. My pup rushed in and jumped on Rex's lap, and he greeted her happily. Mella had been sleeping on the top of the couch, resting on Rex's upper back. When Mal leapt up on Rex's lap, Mella's tail twitched with annoyance. She leaned over Rex's shoulder and batted Mal on the nose, then leapt off the couch and climbed to the top of her cat tree.

Shaking my head at her antics, I bent down and gave Rex a nice long kiss. Then I threw my keys into the key dish near the door and took off my shoes. We'd redecorated a bit to accommodate some of Rex's things and help him feel at home here. We'd talked about moving to his cottage, but he argued that, as early as I had to get up to make fudge, it only made sense to stay here.

I was grateful that he'd thought of that, because I sure hadn't.

"What's going on?" he asked and put Mal down. "Did you have dinner?"

I stopped. "I can't remember."

"Then you didn't." He pulled some things out of the fridge. "Have a seat. You can tell me what's happening while I fix you a plate. Now do you want something hot or cold? I can whip up a steak and green salad." He held up a nice steak in his right hand. "Or a cold-cuts sandwich and potato salad?" In his left hand was one of my dishes, not a deli box.

"You made potato salad?" I felt my heart flutter with delight. I loved it, but never had time to make it. Most of my dinners were grilled cheese or a bowl of cereal or something already made from Doud's Market.

"Yes, I made potato salad," he said, without any pride, as if it was a given. "I know it's your favorite. I also know you happen to like a good steak, medium-rare."

I put the note down and rested my elbows on the kitchen bar putting my chin in my hands and blew him a kiss. It made him smile. "I'll take cold cuts and potato salad, please."

"On it," he said, put the steak away, and pulled out a stack of meats and cheese I didn't even know we had.

"Did you go shopping?"

"This is not about me," he said. "Let's start with what is that piece of paper in your hand?"

I glanced at my name handwritten on the note and sighed. Mom. "Oh, I'd nearly forgotten, although I don't know how. My mom and her siblings showed up today out of the blue."

"Two weeks early." He shook his head and got out a loaf of bakery bread.

"And two weeks early," I repeated. "And they're staying here, for free."

"I figured." He took out my bread knife and sliced a thick piece of fresh bread, and my stomach started to rumble. "And you have other guests who've reserved the rooms."

I sighed. "How'd you guess? Anyway, we're lucky they're moving to something more to their taste tomorrow. Apparently, the McMurphy is quaint."

"Which is short for not up to their standards." He spread honey mustard and mayonnaise on the bread.

"That's not what bothers me," I said with a sigh. "What bothers me is that I wasn't ready for them. Which means I haven't had a mani-pedi, my hair isn't freshly cut and styled, and I'm not wearing clothes that live up to my mom's standards."

"I thought you hated your mom's standards." He put slices of thin-cut meats and cheeses on the bread.

"Well, I can't do that around her family. I know it embarrasses her to no end that I don't play by their rules."

"Yes, you told me about your childhood." He cut the sandwich and placed it on a plate, then added a generous amount of potato salad. "They still expect you to play by those rules?" His thick black eyebrows drew in toward each other as if he couldn't comprehend why. Frankly, neither could I, even after I had just told Jenn why.

"They do." I shrugged my shoulders and let out a heavy sigh. "I was still in my work clothes, fresh from the crime scene, with wet pant legs and my hair crazy from the wind when I walked in—only to discover they were all there to see me. They looked at me as if I wore nothing but overalls with the pant legs rolled up, my feet bare, and a frog in my hands. My only saving grace was the sweater I had on over my sugar-stained polo."

He laughed and put the plate down in front of me, along with a glass of iced tea. It smelled good, and I dove right in as Rex leaned against the bar from the kitchen side. "I'd love to see you in nothing but overalls."

I glared at him, but couldn't respond because I'd taken a big bite of the sandwich. After I swallowed, I continued. "Frances got them all checked in, and Mom glared at me over her shoulder as they all went up to their rooms. Oh, you'll love this, it seems Uncle John—"

"Your mom's brother?" he asked.

"No, Uncle John is married to my mom's sister, Aunt Ginny. He's great, by the way. You'll really like him. Don't ask me why he married into my uptight family."

Rex winked at me. "Love works in mysterious ways."

"Hmm." I took a forkful of the best potato salad I'd ever eaten. Yep, I made the right choice picking this guy. I swallowed. "Anyway, Uncle John knew we didn't do the full-service butler routine. He arranged with the porter to have someone come into every room with a family member and hang up their clothes."

Rex roared with laughter.

"Yeah, I'm embarrassed, but I did see a twinkle of humor in Uncle John's eye."

"Are they here for two whole weeks?" Rex asked when he became sober again.

"On the island, yes, but they will be off to 'better' accommodations tomorrow. They only stayed here to show support for my 'little' business."

"That's good, right?" He rested his forearms on the bar top and snatched a bite of my sandwich.

"Hey," I said and pretended to pout.

As I finished my dinner, I told him about my mom's horror when she saw I didn't have a proper pedicure and still wore sandals. And that Mom had wanted me to show the family around and go to dinner with them, but decided it was better if I didn't.

"And you took Mal for a long walk to hide from them," he concluded. I drank my tea without looking at him. "And that's when you went back to the murder site," he said with a shake of his head.

I set the glass down. "In my defense, um, Mal dragged me there."

He looked down at Mal, who was currently begging to be picked up. "She's blaming you, bug." He picked her up. "Yeah, she does that a lot." He and Mal looked at me expectantly.

"Fine, it was me," I said and walked around the bar to put my empty dishes in the sink. Then I turned to face them both. "That said, both Mal and I found evidence that may have been overlooked."

"How?" Rex asked, a perplexed look on his face. "Shane is very thorough in his collection methods, and both Charles and I walked the scene as well, looking for anything he missed."

"Did anyone look on the other side of the bushes? The side nearest the library?" I asked.

"Why?" he asked.

It was exactly as I thought. He didn't remember that part of my eyewitness account. Instead, all they concentrated on was the fact that I held the murder weapon in my hands. I stepped out of the kitchen and grabbed the message from my mom. She'd written it on stationery, for goodness' sake.

"What?" he asked and put Mal down. "What did I miss?"

"If you read my account, you'll see that I mentioned seeing someone on the other side of the bushes."

"Huh."

"Go check your little notepad." I plopped down on the couch, and Mella jumped to the back of the couch and into my lap, giving Mal the stink eye, which usually meant, "I dare you to try." Rex sat in the chair beside the couch, and Mal jumped onto the chair and sat next to him.

"What you're saying is, the killer could have been watching through the bushes."

"Or an accomplice," I said. "As soon as they saw that I'd spotted them, they pulled back into the bush. You know, they say killers like to go back to the scene and watch."

"That's what they say." He eyed me. "You looked on the other side of the bushes."

"I did."

He tilted his head, his gaze curious. "And?"

"I found footprints where someone stood and looked between the bushes. There were also footprints headed away."

"Any heading to the bush?"

I shook my head. "None that I could find. They must have walked on the grass to get there. I mean, they didn't appear out of thin air."

"Unless it was the killer, who stepped behind the bushes to hide and watch," Rex said, thoughtfully.

"I don't know," I said and frowned. "The footprints faced the bush, not the other way. If it was the killer, they would have taken a very long step through the bush to avoid the dirt around the bushes. And, if they did, why leave footprints facing the other way?"

"I suppose they could have hurried around the bushes and then stopped there to watch." He ran his hand over Mal's head without thought. "Were they men's shoes?"

"If he's a very small man," I replied. "I used my foot for scale. The sneaker was smaller than mine."

"You mean tennis shoes, right?" He grinned at me.

"Fine, the shoe print." I was a bit annoyed. I hated it when he corrected me.

"That might be interesting." He tilted his head, trying to place that into the story in his head. "You took photos."

"Yup," I said and kept stroking Mella, as she purred. "I stopped by the office, and you weren't there, so I gave them to Charles. Oh, and I almost forgot, Mal sniffed out a piece of fabric stuck to a bush. It looks like the shirt that Richard wore. I gave that to Charles, too."

"I would have been there, but I had an appointment for the final fitting on my suit for the wedding," he replied.

"Booker told me."

"Have you called Esmerelda back to get yours?"

"Not yet," I replied. "But that doesn't mean anything. My relatives threw me for a loop coming when they did. I swear, I don't know how I'm going to entertain them for two weeks and get ready for the wedding and run my fudge shop."

"I thought Roxanne Jones was ready to step in for occasions like these," he said.

Roxanne was my new assistant fudge maker. She was fully trained and very good at the demonstrations. "She is," I said. "But we didn't plan for her to work two weeks by herself."

"Is your family into hiking or biking? We have a lot of places for that," he said. "That would help get them out of your hair."

"Sporting is only for high school and college." I heard my mom's words come out of my mouth.

"Huh," he said. "What are they going to do?"

"Uncle Wade brought his yacht," I said. "They'll probably spend most of the time out on the boat to avoid the crowds of tourists. I won't tell you what they really called them."

"At least they have something to do that's up to their standards." Rex reclined back into the chair and looked at the note in my hand. "What's your mom say?"

I opened the note. "Shoot."

"What?" Rex asked and lifted his chin up and down fast as if to say, read it to me.

"Allie, tomorrow is mother/daughter day. I've booked the salon all day to make you presentable. I've also reserved it for the day of your wedding. Marissa assured me she's great at wedding hairstyles. Bring your veil, and we'll see what she has to offer. See you at nine a.m. Love, Mom."

"Make you presentable?" Rex lifted an eyebrow.

"I told you she was horrified by my appearance today," I said.

He glanced at his phone. "It's really late for you to be up on a normal day. Do you want me to do anything to help?"

"I'm going to have to text Roxanne," I said with a sigh. "Let her know she'll be doing both demonstrations tomorrow and why."

"Can you get all the rest of the fudge made and be dressed for your mom's thing in time?" He looked concerned, came over to the couch, pulled me over, and tucked me under his arm. He brushed my arm in a very soothing, if not sexy, way. Then he kissed the top of my head.

I looked up at him. "I'm going to have to get up and go a couple hours earlier."

"You mean three a.m. instead of five a.m." He frowned. "Your mom's been here enough times to know better than to do this to you."

"I agree, but I've already given her a hard talking to about showing up with no notice. As she would say, she 'only wants to spend more time with her daughter.' Plus, she's counting on me being on my best behavior."

"And meanwhile you're going to investigate that murder, aren't you?" His tone was calm, but lying beside him, I could feel his worry.

"Irma asked me to," I said.

"Irma should know better, too," he sounded grumpy. "You're two weeks away from your wedding."

"I'm not going to try too hard to solve it. I'm only doing it to keep Carol and Irma from doing it. I promise to keep you apprised."

"You'll have to, since I live with you." He seemed pleased by that statement.

"Um, as for that . . ."

"Now what?"

"Mom would have a fit if she knew we lived together," I said, not taking my gaze off his beautiful blue eyes rimmed by black lashes.

He drew his eyebrows together. "I didn't realize she was that religious."

"She's not really," I said. "But she is mired in tradition, and the rules of the tradition are—"

"No living together before the wedding," he interrupted and rolled his eyes. "I didn't realize I would be subjected to these silly rules, too."

I gave him a big kiss. "That's it, I promise. Your shift starts at six a.m. tomorrow, and Mom won't be up and out before then. Please stay."

Chapter 6

"Did I see Rex going down the back stairs from your apartment this morning?" Mom asked. We were at the Lighthouse salon with our feet soaking and a mimosa in our hands. "You know the rules."

I gave her the side eye. "Why were you looking out your window at five a.m.? I know what room you're in. You had to have the window open and half your head outside to see my stairs."

She sniffed. "I thought I heard a noise, and with all the crimes you've encountered since you took over the McMurphy, I needed to ensure it wasn't a thief or a murderer." She took a sip of her mimosa. "You're lucky no one else noticed."

"Aren't you taking this a bit too far?" I asked. "I happen to know you and Dad did the same thing."

"That's beside the point," Mom said and picked out

the nail polish she wanted from the ones the cosmetologist held.

"And, if you must know, I wasn't in the apartment at the time. I was in the fudge shop making fudge starting at three a.m."

"Heavens, why would you do that? Not getting enough sleep will ruin your complexion for the wedding. Looks like I will need to have Jean Paul come up and take the photos early so that he can retouch them. I also suggest you don't allow cameras at the ceremony."

"I don't need your photographer," I said. "We're giving everyone disposable cameras to take photos from their point of view. That will be a memory for us and our attendees."

"What? No!" Mom said it so loud that the mimosa in her hand sloshed and everyone in the salon stopped and stared at her.

The manager came running over. "Is everything alright, madame?" His French accent was thick. "Is your service not up to par?"

"Oh, everything's fine," she said, with a wave of her hand at the cosmetologists. "Not as good as mine at home, but perfectly appropriate for"—she gave me a look and noticed the disapproval on my face—"this island. I was exclaiming about the fact that my one and only child"—she pointed toward me—"is not having a professional photographer at her wedding. It's completely inappropriate, don't you agree, whatever your name is?"

"Monsieur Louis Dupont," he provided and gave me a look of disapproval. "Indeed, it's highly inappropriate. Even more so if she is getting married on this beautiful destination island."

I gave him the stink eye, and his expression did not change except for a tick around the corner of his mouth. I'd met Louis at a Chamber of Commerce meeting. His accent was so slight that you had to really listen for it. But with all the money Mom spent in the salon today, he gave her the full treatment. I mouthed that he was uninvited to the wedding, and I could see his eyes dance in humor.

Louis cleared his throat. "I do know a very talented photographer in Mackinaw City who may be available. He was selected to be an assistant with Ms. Lange in New York."

Mom raised a newly waxed eyebrow. "Really? I would love to see his portfolio." She told him that he could find her at the Grand. "The front desk will let you up."

"Certainly, madame." Louis snapped his fingers, and our cosmetologists came right over. Taking their seats in front of us, they gently rubbed oil onto our feet.

"I told you I don't want a professional photographer," I said. "Don't make me have to tell you again."

Mom took a sip of her mimosa, watched Louis, and leaned toward me. "Do you think he's related to *the* Dupont family?"

"Sure, why not?" I muttered and downed the rest of my mimosa. A young woman arrived immediately with a tray to take my glass. "Another mimosa, mademoiselle?"

"I prefer a gin martini," I said dryly. Everyone knew I didn't drink unless the occasion called for it. Alcohol and sugar didn't mix.

"You know better than to drink hard alcohol before lunch," Mom chided. "Now, about the color you picked for your toenails."

By the time we left, it was nearly five o'clock. Every part of my body was waxed, massaged, trimmed, and coated in either lotion or hair spray. I felt like there was no way I could walk without my hair catching on fire. Mom had insisted that they show us what makeup would be good for the wedding. I was contoured, smudged, and lined to within an inch of my life. I didn't even recognize myself in the mirror. In fact, I wasn't sure Rex would recognize me.

"Well, there," Mom said, as we climbed into a carriage taxi. "That is how you should look. We have dinner at eight with the family at the Grand. I expect you to be as well dressed as the rest of the family."

"Mom, I have an important meeting I cannot get out of tonight," I said.

"Surely you cleared your calendar for the wedding." She gave me a look of reprimand.

"Of course," I said. "I know the protocol. You taught me over and over."

"Then what's the problem?"

"The problem is, Mom, you and your family are two weeks early. I didn't clear my calendar for that. In fact, I have many details left this week to clear my calendar for next week. Because you didn't give me any notice, I'm certain I'll not have a lot of time to visit."

Mom frowned at me.

"Careful, you'll get wrinkles," I said, quoting her mother, Grandma Rose.

"You will clear one evening for us this week," Mom demanded. "We arrived early to spend time with you before the big day, and I'm glad we did. No professional wedding photographer." She shook her head in disbelief. "What are we, working-class now?"

"If you haven't noticed, both Rex and I are working-class," I pointed out.

She shook her head. "I'll never understand how you could give up your trust fund for this. And that—" she paused and waved her hand as if she couldn't bring herself to say the words.

"Police officer?" I answered.

"Yes, that policeman, when you have someone like Harry Winston in love with you. Do you know what his net worth is?"

"That police *officer*'s name is Rex, and I love him. Harry is a good friend, Mom, that's all," I said for the millionth time.

"And you decided to be this policeman's—"

"Rex, Mom, and he's the lead police officer on Mackinac."

She sighed dramatically. "I'm having trouble understanding why you decided to be the third wife of a man who is a public servant and makes less money than my butler."

"I'm not in love with your butler," I said. "Now stop it, or you won't see me again until the wedding."

"Fine, I'll stop, but now I want two nights for dinner, one with you and the family. And one with your police," she paused, "officer."

"Mom!"

"I must insist. Your father is coming in at the end of the week. We can have the one with you and your fiancé on Friday. But the other is Wednesday at nine. Since I've told you early enough, you won't have any excuses, and you'd better not be late. In fact, I'll be knocking on your door at eight p.m. Now let's look at your wardrobe. You should have something decent to wear."

I rolled my eyes and sighed. "I already know I have nothing that fits the family's expected deportment. We might as well go shopping."

"On the family tour yesterday, I didn't see any stores on the island with outfits that would work for a formal dinner." Mom's mouth pursed tight in disappointment. "I know! I'll fly in my stylist, Andrew." She looked me up and down. "You don't eat, do you? Well, that's a good thing. It keeps you slim. I'll have Andrew bring sizes that should work for you."

"It's Tuesday. Won't it be difficult to get him here in time for dinner tomorrow?"

"Clearly, you've forgotten how tenacious I am when I need something. I'm sure he'll be fine. Now, I've been talking to the senior manager at the Grand Hotel. They have an intimate space open where we can have the wedding and cocktails with dinner. He suggested a nice three-piece chamber group. There will be the usual cake and an open bar. Then we'll move to an outdoor space for a live band and dancing."

"Mom," I said as calmly as I could. "We already have everything planned. You need to talk to Jenn. She's my wedding planner."

"Hmm, yes, I've heard about this insane idea of inviting the whole island with, of all things, a potluck reception in a park." She wrinkled her nose as if she smelled something horrible.

"Mom, all the planning is done. I have other things to do, like make fudge and manage the hotel."

"No, certainly not," she said in her crisp Mom voice. "You are not going to ruin your nails."

"When are you going to accept it's what I do? Enjoy your time at the Grand. I'm sure it's more to your taste."

I didn't get into Mom's carriage. Luckily, the Grand was in a different direction than the McMurphy and only a few blocks away. I stormed in the door as Frances finished her work for the day.

"Well, hello," she said looking up. "You certainly look . . ."

"Ridiculous?" I asked.

"I was going to say something different."

"This is what Mom thinks my makeup should look like for the wedding."

"Hmm," she uttered, trying to find something nice to say.

"And Mom has already talked to the senior manager at the Grand about an intimate wedding there. She's insistent, no matter what I say." By this time, Mal had greeted me, and I picked her up. She licked my face once and turned her head. "I know, baby," I said. "It's awful."

Frances couldn't help but chuckle at Mal.

"How'd the demonstrations go today? I trust Roxanne, but it was her first time, and it can be a little intimidating."

"She did a great job," Frances said, and compliments from her were rare. "She drew a nice crowd and sold a good amount of product."

"Great," I said. "One less thing off my shoulders."

"I heard about the murder. Seriously, this time you have to let it go for the sake of your wedding." Frances never said I shouldn't investigate, and it brought tears to my eyes.

I blinked them back fiercely. "I have to do what I think is right."

Rex walked in, and I ran straight into his arms in tears. I'm sure the layers of makeup dripped down my face, and later I would apologize for staining his uniform, but right now, I didn't care. He held me tight. "What's going on?"

"It's Mom."

He restrained himself from saying anything about my face. "Come on, let's go upstairs, and you can tell me everything."

Thank goodness, he always seemed to understand. We walked up the stairs hand in hand, as Mal raced ahead of us.

I was afraid of what Mom would do next. She was like a bulldozer when she wanted to get her way, destroying everything in front of her as she went.

Chapter 7

Peanut-Butter-Filled Chocolate Cupcakes

I love making these simple cupcakes to impress my friends.

Ingredients

Cupcakes

1 cup of flour
1 cup of sugar
½ cup of cocoa (I prefer Hershey's)
½ teaspoon of baking soda
¼ teaspoon of baking powder
¾ cup of buttermilk (regular will do in a pinch)
¼ cup of melted butter
1 teaspoon of vanilla
1 egg

Peanut Butter Filling

¾ cup of softened butter
¾ cup of peanut butter
1 teaspoon of vanilla
A dash of salt
5 cups of powdered sugar
5 tablespoons of heavy whipping cream—
or milk, in a pinch

Frosting

¾ cup of sugar
6 tablespoons of cocoa
3 tablespoons of cornstarch
A dash of salt
¾ cup of boiling water
5 tablespoons of butter
1 teaspoon of vanilla

Directions

Cupcakes

Preheat the oven to 350 degrees F. Line two 12-cupcake tins with cupcake liners.

In a medium bowl, add the flour, cocoa, sugar, baking soda, and baking powder. Stir to combine. Add the buttermilk, butter, vanilla, and egg.

Beat for 3 minutes until thick and light. Using a quarter-cup measuring cup as a scoop, fill each cupcake liner ¾ full. Bake 15–20 minutes until the cupcakes bounce when tapped or a toothpick comes out clean. Cool completely.

Filling

Beat the butter and peanut butter until smooth. Add the vanilla and salt, beat until combined. Slowly alternate adding the powdered sugar and the heavy whipping cream until the mixture is smooth and creamy.

Remove the centers of the cupcakes, carefully preserving the tops. Fill each cupcake with peanut butter filling and return the tops to cover the cupcakes. Refrigerate for 10 minutes and remove.

Frosting

In a medium pan, combine the sugar, cocoa, cornstarch, and dash of salt. Add boiling water and stir. On medium heat, stir until thick and shiny. Remove from heat, and add the butter and vanilla. While warm, frost cupcakes.

Let cool and enjoy! Makes 24 cupcakes.

"Allie!" Carol said when she opened the door. "We were worried you couldn't make it. Come in, come in." She studied me with a frown. Even though I'd washed the makeup away, which took me fifteen minutes, she still commented. "You look," she paused to find the right word and finally settled on "lovely."

"My mom had me at the spa from ten until five," I explained.

"I'm sorry, dear," she said.

"Was it the Lighthouse spa?" Betty Olway asked.

"Yes."

"They are very good there," Judith Schmidt said. "But don't let them do your makeup. They're ridiculous with all that contouring."

"I agree," Laura Morgan piped in. "My granddaughter went there once, and she hated it, and she's a teen."

"Your hair and nails look nice," Barbara Vissor tried to placate me.

Carol cleared her throat. "Can I get you a drink or some cookies? We do have Mary's famous coffee cake and coffee."

"Do you have anything stronger?" I asked.

"Certainly," Carol said. "Sit, sit, we finally put the murder board together."

The book club was a disguise, of course. Oh, it'd started out as a book club and then over the years became a social hour. After news of my sleuthing became widespread on the island, Carol and the ladies thought they would have fun "helping me" solve cases. I met with them in part to ask questions, as seniors knew better than anyone what went on on the island. Betty turned seventy-eight years old this year, and I would be twenty-eight. Crazy, right? With my mom still treating me as if I were sixteen, I didn't feel like I was twenty-eight.

I sat, and Carol brought me a tall glass of white wine and a plate of coffee cake. "Thank you," I said. "It's a good thing I haven't had my final fitting for the dress yet."

"Look at you," Judith said. "You're all skin and bones. You need to put a little meat on you for the honeymoon." She winked at me.

I took a bite of the cake. It was warm, filled with cinnamon, and had a lovely, crunchy crumble top. She'd cooked it in a bundt pan, and the slices were well defined. I washed it down with the dry white wine and immediately felt better. After today, I needed to be a little indulgent. "Irma, Myrtle is your friend. Why don't you tell me about what you have on the murder board."

"Okay," Irma said and stood next to it. There was a pointer on the tray of the easel they used to prop up the foam board. "We have the fight you saw with Velma. This was verified by Audrey. She said she usually has to break up a fight between these two once a week when shared or new books arrive."

"I've seen it before, too," Betty said. "Those two loved the competitive drama."

"It's why none of us think Myrtle did it," Judith said, looking at me over the top of her bright purple glasses.

"Go on, Irma," Carol said.

I took another bite of the rich, buttery coffee cake and checked the clearly 1990s blue and kelly-green striped cushion of the couch for crumbs. Carol's home was immaculate. The last thing I needed right now was to feel bad about crumbs. Thankfully, my wine was on a coaster on the coffee table in front of me, or I would most surely have sloshed it.

"Allie, are you okay?" Irma asked.

I looked up and blushed. "Yes, I'm listening. Please go on."

Irma used the pointer to indicate pictures of Velma and Myrtle at the beginning of a string of yarn they used to connect the events in a time line. It started at the last time Velma was seen alive and continued until Irma and Carol arrived on the scene. Then there were pictures underneath. "We know these two were together in the library. Allie, you were there. Did they leave together?"

"No, Velma left first."

"Wait," Irma said.

"Velma left first?" they all asked at the same time.

"Yes," I said and drew my eyebrows together. "If Velma left first, how did Myrtle kill her?"

"I bet the cops think Myrtle lay in wait to ambush Velma and bash her with a rock," Judith said, making it sound sinister.

"But we know better," Judith added.

"Ladies, please!" Carol said. "Irma, go on."

Irma cleared her throat.

"Allie, can you tell us what Myrtle did after Velma left? Did Myrtle follow her immediately? Did she sit to look over her selections?"

"No, actually." I put the coffee cake on the table and took a sip of my wine. "I scrolled through the database, looking for any bridal magazine I may have missed. Then Myrtle sat at the carrel next to me. I presume to find something on the shared library database."

"Did she say anything to you?" Irma asked.

All the ladies turned to me and appeared to be holding their breath. I guess this was new information. "I don't know what she looked for, but I remember telling her that what she said to Velma was mean."

"What did she say?" Mary leaned forward.

"Velma said she bought all the good books on purpose so that Myrtle could never have them," I said, trying to remember as much as I could about what they said. "If I remember right, Myrtle replied with something like, 'When you die, your family will sell your books, and I'll buy them all and have them anyway.'" The ladies all gasped and looked at one another. I went on quickly. "I'm sure it was simply a comeback to goad Velma. I'm certain Myrtle didn't mean it."

The ladies started talking to each other when Irma clapped her hands. "Ladies! Let Allie finish answering the question. Allie, is that all that happened when Myrtle sat down?"

"No," I said, doing my best to remember. "She looked at the screen and, I think, shook her head. Then she said something about Velma being inconsiderate by not putting the computer back to the home screen. She went on to say how odd it was that Velma had been looking at the Social Security website and how anyone receiving Social Security should already know everything about it."

"She's not wrong," Judith said thoughtfully. "And was she certain it was Velma looking something up?"

"She was certain," I said and sipped more wine, letting the dry green-apple taste coat my tongue and throat. It had started taking the edge off of the day I'd spent with Mom.

Carol wrote on sticky notes. She handed two to Irma. One that said Velma left first, and the other that Myrtle said something about when Velma died, she'd get her books. The sticky notes wouldn't adhere to the yarn time line, so Irma stuck them above it.

"I wonder what that was about," Laura said. "Why would she look at the Social Security website?"

"That's a mystery we'll have to check out," Barbara said. "But most likely it has nothing to do with the murder."

"Do you know what Myrtle looked up?" Mary asked me.

"No," I shook my head and put my wine glass on the end table and picked up my coffee cake plate, which had one bite left.

"Then what happened?" Irma asked.

"I think Myrtle checked out and left." I said, enjoying the last bite of cake before exchanging the plate for the wineglass which was almost empty. I'd be a little wobbly when I went home.

"You think Myrtle checked out and left?" Barbara asked.

"I was busy with the database," I said. "I thought I heard her check out and leave, but I could be wrong. All my concentration was on what I had or hadn't read, to see if there was any more information on weddings."

"Allie," Carol sat next to me and patted my hand, "your wedding is going to be lovely. I'm sure of it. Have faith in your own decisions, and trust that Jenn will help you fulfill your dreams in a tasteful way."

I finished my wine. "My relatives arrived two weeks early, and Mom has hijacked the wedding. It's not what she wants 'for her baby.' And no matter how much I put my foot down, she continues to take control of everything, right down to my hair, nails, and clothes."

"This is the first time I've heard her get this extreme," Irma said with a frown.

"Her brother and sisters are here, and she doesn't

want me to embarrass her," I said. "My family has expectations. I grew up with them, but 'ran away' when I left for college to learn how to take over the McMurphy."

"I see," said Laura. "My mom's family was the same, except she thumbed her nose at them all and trusted herself to be who she was."

"Allie, it sounds like this is your mom's problem, not yours," Betty said wisely. "She's the only one who can solve it. In short, be true to yourself."

"Thanks," I said and stood. "That's great advice." Then I looked at Carol. "I need to go. Before I do, I'll put these in the kitchen. You prefer the sink, right?"

"Yes, please," she said. "I like to load the dishwasher myself."

"Okay," I said with a gentle smile and went into the kitchen.

Carol followed. "Are you alright, dear? Did we insult you somehow?"

"What? No." I put the dishes in the sink, and washed then dried my hands. "It's been a very long and exhausting day in a string of long, exhausting days." I sent her a wry smile. "I should get home."

"We heard that Rex moved back into his cottage. Are you two OK?" Carol asked. She was clearly worried, her gaze taking in my slightest expression.

"We're okay. In fact, Rex is the only reason I can make it through days like today."

"Why did he move out?" she asked, clearly confused.

"Another one of my mom's family expectations. It's bad enough that I thumb my nose at most of them. But I need to do better. They're family, even though I haven't seen them since my debutante debut when I was sixteen."

"Wait, you were a debutante?" Carol asked, and I could feel the heat of a blush rush over my face.

"Don't tell anyone I said that. I don't want anyone to think I'm a rich snob. I've worked too hard to be a part of the island. Trust me, I ditched my trust fund long ago when I didn't go to the right college or marry someone of my 'station.'"

Carol confused me with her loud laughter after what I said. She walked me into the living room, where the rest of the book club sat with confusion on their faces. "Ladies," she laughed until tears ran down her cheeks, "Allie thinks . . . hah . . . Allie thinks that . . . hahaha . . . we wouldn't like her . . . haw!" She laughed so hard that everyone laughed, too.

I nervously laughed because everyone was and, well, heck, if I was going to lose my friends, I might as well do it with laughter.

Tears ran down Carol's face as she tried to speak. "If we discover—"

Everyone continued to laugh, and my abs protested. Carol sobered long enough to spit out the rest. "She was a debutante."

At that, they laughed even harder, but I sobered, confused. "Did I miss something?"

Carol bent over, trying to catch her breath. Then she asked, "who here was a deb?" The laughter became a roar, and one by one, they all raised their hands. "And who here has a trust fund?" Everyone but Betty raised their hand.

"Does it count if I inherited the family wealth instead of a trust fund?" Betty asked. "My father said trust funds only made the lawyer richer."

I was stunned. "Anyone go to an elite private school for girls?" I asked. I figured if none of them did, I would keep that secret to myself.

Everyone raised their hands as they sobered, though their eyes still shone with humor. Betty passed around the box of tissues.

"Most of the seniors have—well, at least the girls. I doubt the boys went to a private girl's school, even though they would have loved to do that." Laura shook her head.

"But you've talked about going to high school together." I was so confused.

"We did," Barbara said. "Just not here."

"You see, Allie," Carol said, after wiping her tears and blowing her nose, "the only reason most of us are here is because our families have been wealthy for the last one hundred years. They're the ones who built the Victorian cottages to get out of the heat and smell of the cities."

"Then everything was passed down, generation after generation," Mary added. "That includes all the traditions and showmanship of wealth, like with your mom and her family."

I sat down on the edge of the couch. "But I thought . . . everyone's homes are so modest."

"Haven't you figured it out, dear?" Barbara asked. "The only way to keep money is to not spend it willy-nilly. We have nothing to prove. Besides, we all love our homes. None of us wants a place so big it would take days to clean."

"Huh," I blinked in confusion. "You're all?"

"Just like your mom, dear," Irma said. "We've simply either outlived the family traditions or thumbed our noses at them."

"We all know exactly what your mom's gone through," Judith piped in. "And now it's your turn to thumb your nose at all that silly 'proper deportment' nonsense."

Carol helped me up by the elbow. "I think we've taken up enough of the bride's time tonight. Thank you for coming, Allie. We'll keep you apprised of our findings. Oh, and feel free to bring your mom to the next meeting on Thursday. You might find that she actually likes investigating."

"Oh, I highly doubt that. Not after the last time. Besides I haven't told her about the murder and my involvement in the investigation. She'd kill me if she knew."

Betty smiled softly. "You won't know she'd react that way until you try, my dear. Now go on. Seriously, we'll be fine without you."

"Good night," I said and turned so they couldn't see the confusion on my face as I put my spring coat on. It might be June, but it was still cold at night.

Carol gave me a quick hug and saw me to the door. "Next time you're alone with your mom, try asking her why this is important to her. You might learn a thing or two."

"I'll consider it," I said. A glance at my watch told me that, once again, I was out late. And I still had things to do: Mal needed a quick walk and Mella a few good cuddles. I couldn't forget my babies during all this.

When I got home, Rex was on the couch with Mal and Mella, the two vying for his attention. He stood and grabbed me as I entered and gave me a huge warm, welcoming kiss. I leaned into him. If anything could sustain me from the onslaught of my family, the wedding, fudge shop worries, and the recent murder, it was Rex and his kisses.

He put his hands on my cheeks and touched his forehead to mine. "You look exhausted."

"Thanks?" I asked.

"You're welcome." He gave me a quick wink. "Let me take your coat and shoes. Go sit on the couch. I'll bring you a glass of wine and rub your feet, and you can tell me all about your day."

I chuckled. "I've already had far too much wine, and I'd rather hear about yours."

"Fine," he agreed. "Now go sit down."

Chapter 8

The alarm went off, and I reached for Rex, but there was no one but Mella, who slept on my head, while Mal cuddled near my thighs. I sat up. "Rex?"

Then I remembered. He'd gone back to his house to please my family. I got out of bed into the cold of the room, then hurried to the bathroom. When I talked to my mom, again, I needed to talk to her about this ridiculous tradition of the bride and groom staying apart before the wedding. No matter how scandalized the family would be, I knew that none of them had followed this tradition. The family enjoyed whispering everyone's secrets.

Dressed in my fudge-making uniform, I took Mal out. Mella came with us, stopped on the landing, and jumped up on the railing, making herself comfortable. I scratched her behind the ears and then walked Mal down the stairs. We headed left, as we always do. It was dark this early in the morning, and I was glad I'd stopped to grab my coat and knitted hat. This early in June, the air was still crisp, and temperatures ranged from the low forties warming up to the high sixties in the afternoon.

The cold didn't matter to Mal.

It struck me, all of a sudden, that an outdoor wedding in less than two weeks could be chilly. My dress had long sleeves, but was all lace. I'd have to discuss what to do about the chill with Esmerelda. Thankfully, I'd made my final fitting appointment for tomorrow after my last demonstration. Mom wanted to be there, and I'd said yes. I hoped that wasn't a mistake.

I let Mal choose the path as long as it wasn't too far. She went straight for the library, her nose to the ground. "We were here yesterday," I said.

She kept sniffing, took me behind the library, and kept going until we were near the water's edge. I stopped her when she reached the fence line of the lovely home next door. It was still dark, and I wasn't going to walk around someone's home in the dark.

"Come on, Mal." I pulled her back. "I have to make as much fudge as I can before Mom makes me stop to try on dresses for tonight." I rushed her home and got her safely in my apartment with a treat for both Mal and Mella. Then I hurried down the stairs almost twenty minutes late. Luckily, Roxanne was setting up ingredients.

"Good morning," she greeted me with a smile.

"Thanks for covering for me during the demonstrations yesterday," I said as I put on my chef's coat and a fresh paper hat. "Frances said you did a wonderful job."

"Thanks. It was my first time doing them on my own. It's harder than I thought." She laughed at herself. "I'm used to both of us here pouring the candy."

"It is a large pot," I agreed and added the ingredients to the copper pot. "As Papa Liam got older, he didn't want to work with an assistant, so he added the hydraulic lift-and-pour system. It's not as much fun as when two candymakers lift and pour the pot together, but it gets the job done."

"People think the system is fun to watch," Roxanne said. "They seem mesmerized by the process. I tell them what you tell them: that it was made in the eighties. The kids look at the parents and say it was built in olden times. It makes me laugh."

"Me, too. Papa told me. It's a fun story."

We chatted through seven batches of fudge, stopping only to say hello to Frances and her husband, Douglas, my grumpy handyman, when they came into the McMurphy.

Mom walked in at ten o'clock, just in time for the first demonstration. She ignored the crowd gathered around to hear me tell Papa Liam's stories. Instead she made a sign telling me to hurry it up. I ignored it. When the demonstration was done, I left Roxanne to pass out samples and ring up the purchases.

"Good morning, Mom," I said. "How was your night at the Grand?"

"It was wonderful," she said pointedly. "The staff is impeccable."

"I'm sure they are," I said. "It's also nearly three times the price of staying here. More, if you consider you stay here for free."

"As it should be," Mom said.

I held back my retort. "Mom, why are you here early? I thought we agreed on three p.m., after my last demonstration."

She waved away my concerns. "I'm sure your assistant or whatever you call her can handle the rest of the day. My stylist is arriving in an hour, and I knew you would need a shower before we met with him. Do take off that hat. You're ruining your hair."

I did as she asked. "Mom, where are we meeting your stylist? And why is he coming today?"

"We have my suite at the Grand. I have the Musser suite. It has a nice, raised area in the bedroom." She tucked a wayward hair behind my ear.

"Of course it does," I muttered. "And the stylist?"

Mom took my arm and looped hers through it. "Never mind that. Let's get you to that shower."

"I need to let Roxanne know," I said as Mom walked me firmly to the stairs.

"Oh, I'm certain she'll figure it out."

I turned to Frances, who I hoped had heard the entire exchange, and mouthed, "Tell Roxanne I'll pay her double."

Frances nodded, stepped away from her desk, and moved toward the fudge shop. At least I could count on Roxanne to take care of things.

Chapter 9

"Darling, how wonderful to see you," a perfectly dressed, thin man said as he came out of the bedroom on the left, past the wet bar. He gave my mom a kiss on both cheeks.

"Andrew, you're such a sweetheart to do this for me," Mom replied, holding both of his hands.

"Is this your daughter?" Andrew asked.

"The one and only," Mom replied and used her hand like Vanna White to point to me.

"Oh, honey," Andrew said as he walked around me, looking as if he'd never seen anyone more in need of a makeover. "Well," he turned toward Mom, "I'm certain I have the sizes right. Now, let's do a little magic and make her shine."

I followed them into the bedroom, hating that they both talked about me as if I weren't in the room.

Andrew had a clothes rack set up next to Mom's bed. There, he had hung at least twenty garment bags. I sighed. How many dresses was I going to have to try on?

He walked to the rack. "You have a dinner tonight where the men have to wear suits and ties. Thank goodness for a hotel with taste. Now, darling," he addressed my mom, "what color, texture, and length are you wearing?"

My mom smiled and batted her eyes.

What? I thought. Is she flirting with this guy?

"I'm wearing the Armani, the red pleated cocktail dress," Mom said.

Andrew glanced at me once again, taking in my jeans, long sleeved T-shirt, and casual shoes, then went to a garment bag, unzipped it, pulled out a cocktail dress, and held it up to me. He addressed my mom, "What do you think about this green Dior?"

"Oh, it's perfect," Mom gushed. "It's innocent, yet brings back a time of glamor. Have her try it on."

When I reached for the hanger, he snatched it away from me, then took my hand and pulled me behind a dressing screen set up on the platform that was the bedroom sitting area. He stood there with the dress. "Well, get out of those dreadful things." He shooed me with his free hand.

"Mom!" I called and stuck my head out to glare at her. "Do I have to do this with him here?"

"Oh, darling, it's nothing," he said and pulled me back inside. "I've seen a thousand women in their underwear or less. I'm assessing for fit. Come on now, get those things off."

"Turn around then," I said firmly. "My fiancé is a police officer. One text from me, and there's nothing stopping him from coming in here with his gun."

"Oh, for pity's sake," Mom said. "Undress so we can try on gowns sometime before dinner."

"Dinner's at eight," I said. "That's nearly eight hours from now."

"Exactly," Mom answered.

I motioned for Andrew to turn around. He sighed and did what I asked. I got out of my clothes fast before he decided to turn back.

"Don't forget those awful shoes and socks," Andrew said as he stood away from me.

I glared at his back and took them off, too, then I folded my clothes neatly over the arm of a stuffed chair.

"I'm turning around," he said and unceremoniously unzipped the gown at the side. "Hands up."

I did what he asked, but muttered something mean under my breath about no longer being three years old. In a blink, the dress came right over my arms and head and settled around my shoulders and waist. The material wasn't as smooth as I thought. It had tiny nubs.

"It's raw silk," he explained as he zipped the side zipper easily. "And as usual, a perfect fit." He took my hand and pulled me out to face my mom. The master and only bedroom in the suite had this step-up private sitting area that looked out on the lake. It was brilliant to have me up there. It was like being in a salon. Now my mom could see all of the dress at once. There was also a full-length mirror for me to see myself—that is, if Mom would let me.

"It's quite lovely," Mom told him. "Allie, turn slowly for me."

I did as she asked, but it was hard to be treated like a teen again.

"The fit is nearly perfect," Mom said to Andrew. "She almost looks like a woman about to get married."

"That's because I am a woman about to get married," I said and turned to the mirror. The gown made my hazel eyes look particularly green. It had a portrait collar and three-quarter-length sleeves. The bodice nipped in at the waist, and the skirt was A-line. I was glad not to have a pencil skirt. It would be hard enough going to dinner with the relatives without having to worry about ripping the skirt on a designer dress. "It's lovely," I said and gently brushed my hands down the skirt. I'd forgotten how designer garments feel and fit. I was far from a sample size, but even I looked good in them. Still, after tonight, where would I ever wear this?

"And," Andrew said to my mom, "accessories, of course. A kitten heel in tasteful nude with an accent of matching green. He put the shoes in front of me and helped me slip them on.

"Perfect," Mom said.

"Plus, lovely emerald and diamond earrings and a necklace from our private collection." He handed me the earrings, and I put them in my pierced lobes. I rarely wore earrings and he was lucky my holes hadn't closed up. They hadn't because my mom would kill me if I let that happen. For a few days a week, I wore small studs. "*Et voilà*." He showed me off like some living doll.

"Do you like it, dear?" Mom asked, as she crossed her left arm and drummed her fingers on her chin. "Hmm." She gave Andrew a charming smile. "Don't you think we might look like Christmas ornaments, my red and her green?"

"Yes, of course," he said and contemplated me as if I were a mannequin. "Perhaps for dinner with the fiancé?"

"Perhaps," Mom said.

This ritual went on until I was numb to Andrew standing next to me in my underwear. Mom finally decided on vintage dresses for both dinners. For tonight, I'd wear a navy blue, three-layer chiffon, swirl-print cocktail dress by Christian Dior Haute Couture, from the early 1980s. Both Mom and Andrew loved that the dress had a deep V in the front and the back, knots at the top of each shoulder, and a side zipper with snaps. I was glad it wouldn't be hard to wear. Also, I doubted I'd eat anything that might ruin a vintage haute couture dress. Thanks, Mom. I sighed, but the dress was lovely. They wanted kitten heels; thank goodness, I didn't have to try to balance on anything higher.

And for the Friday dinner with Rex, I would be wearing a vintage silver-and-gold, floral-print cocktail dress by Ceil Chapman, from 1950. This one had short sleeves, a scoop neckline, and a high, fitted waist.

My only concern was that I'd be freezing in both since lows here in June could dip into the 40s, a temperature where everyone preferred to wear jackets. Mom pooh-poohed the idea of a jacket, and after that, Andrew came to my rescue with appropriate cover-ups.

"Now," Mom said, "Andrew, please bring out the pièce de résistance."

"Yes, of course," he said with a smile.

I was tired. "Mom, please, you're exhausting me. We already have the two dresses and accessories."

Andrew pulled out three bags. "Okay, love, back into the dressing room."

"Mom." I looked at her suspiciously.

"Come along," Andrew said.

I sighed and knew perfectly well what she was doing. "Close your eyes and raise your arms," Andrew ordered.

I frowned. "Fine." I did what he said and felt toile slip down over my arms to my waist, where he tightened it. He did this three times. I know because I counted. It's just as I suspected. Petticoats and a dress that would make me look like a giant marshmallow.

"Now, one more," he said. Four petticoats, really? "Take your bra off."

"What?" My voice was an octave or two higher than usual.

"Take it off," he said and sighed. "Really, love, I'm behind you. I promise not to look at you until the top is on."

"Great," I muttered as the heat of a blush rushed up from my neck and hit my cheeks. He had already undone my bra strap. Wait until Rex hears about this. I slipped my arms out of it and held the bra out. He snatched it before I could change my mind. At least the mirror was on the other side of the screen.

"Hands up!" I obeyed and felt satin run down my

arms. "Wonderful, now, put your hands down." When I did, I felt more toile. Great, I'll be an even bigger marshmallow. Where was Jenn when I needed her? Oh, right, her baby was sick, and she'd stayed home. I didn't blame her. To take on my mom, she would need to go toe to toe, quite literally. Today was not that day.

Andrew pulled the straps up. Thank goodness, it had straps. I'd be even more uncomfortable if it was strapless. I'd be constantly fiddling with it to ensure it stayed up. Then he zipped up the side. I needn't have worried. The dress was snug enough to keep the top up, even with no straps. Would I be able to breathe for the ceremony? Thank goodness, Esmerelda was coming tomorrow to fit my true dress.

"Perfect," he breathed. "Open your eyes now."

What I could see of the dress was that the top had a deep V in front and was satin covered in sequined flowers. The toile-covered skirt spread out in a circle around my toes and over a yard behind me. The same tiny, sequined flowers draped halfway down the skirt, with long pointed ends like a cake with a dripped frosting overlay. He gave me elbow-length satin gloves to put on, which I did, because Mom would have had a fit if I didn't. The color of the gown wasn't white. It was a soft, light gray, which I found odd. With one fluid motion, he took hold of my hair, twisted it, and put it up with a clip. Then he pinned a tiara on the top of my head, grabbed a long piece of satin with a fringed bottom that matched the dress, and tucked it in as my veil, then pointed the way.

I stepped out, trying not to squish the dress. It puffed out enough to hit the wall or knock down the screen.

I'd never seen my mom this happy. "Turn, dear, slowly." She looked at Andrew. "I knew the vintage Dior couture dress was perfect for her."

Vintage Dior Haute Couture meant it was handmade in Paris by some of the finest seamstresses in the world. "Shouldn't this be in a museum?" I asked. I managed to get a glimpse in the mirror. As pretty as the dress was, I was terrified to even sit in it for fear of ruining it.

Mom waved away my concerns. "It was in a private collection. Now it's ours."

"Oh, and the final touch," Andrew said and brought the dress rack over. I saw it was a long wrap with sleeves. "This will keep you quite warm."

"It's exactly like the pictures," Mom said.

"How does it fit?" I asked. "I'm not a sample size, and I know that even my bones are bigger than they were when this was designed."

"The previous owner went to Paris and had the Dior atelier alter it. We're lucky she was your size."

I was confused. "Did she wear it for her wedding?"

"Oh, no, no," Andrew said. "She wore it for a fashion show she sponsored for her charity."

"Oh."

Mom looked at me as if I were crass. "There is no way I'd have my baby wear a used wedding dress, no matter what designer hand stitched it."

"Mom, please, this is wonderful and all, but it's not appropriate for an outdoor wedding where everyone is invited and the reception is a potluck. What if I spill something on it?"

"That's why I planned an intimate wedding at the Grand with a sit-down dinner with six courses," Mom said. "There will be no need to stand or carry food around as people try to hug you."

Andrew nodded. "That is precisely what this dress is made for."

"But that is not what Rex and I want," I stressed.

"What would Rex know? This is his third wedding. There's no need for a full island wedding," Mom said. "Now, Andrew, will you be able to come back the night before the wedding?"

"Most certainly," he said.

"Then I would like you to take the dress with you. I don't want to take any chances with it. The other two we'll keep, of course."

"Of course," he said, waving me back to the screen, where he carefully peeled the bodice off, allowed me to put my bra back on, then stripped me of the dress and hung it on the hanger in the black bag. I slipped out of the petticoats quickly. At least there wasn't a hoop. Knowing Mom, if she hadn't been on this vintage kick, she would have found a dress that needed a hoop skirt. I took off the shoes and jewelry and quickly got dressed. Andrew took down the dressing screen, deftly added it to its rolling case, and packed up the dresses that we hadn't picked. Finally he carefully tucked the wedding dress back into three black hanging bags. Was it bad of me to wish something would happen to the dress so I wouldn't have to wear it?

"Thank you for coming out on a moment's notice," Mom said to Andrew and gave him an air kiss on either side of his face. "I don't know what we would have done without you."

"I have to go," I told her. "Thank you, Andrew." I gave him the required goodbye with air kisses.

Then I headed toward the door as fast as I could. Escape was so close I could taste it. In fact, I'd opened the door and had one foot out before Mom called for me. I stayed where I was and waited.

"Allie, I made an appointment with the salon tonight at six thirty. We'll have your hair whipped back into shape before our dinner."

I rolled my eyes and rushed out of the room, down the stairs, and straight outside. Some would have called it running away, but I wouldn't. When it comes to my mom, I've always had an escape plan. Now all I had to do was figure out what that plan would be this time.

Chapter 10

Taking a cue from Carol and Irma's power walk, I got away as fast and as far as I could, until I was too far for Mom to call after me. It was nearly five in the evening. I couldn't believe Mom had taken that much of my time. (Come to think of it, she had ordered a tray of cheeses, crackers, and fruit.) I'd been too busy trying on dresses to even notice the time. I hid in an alley where my mom wouldn't find me and texted Jenn.

You will not believe my mom. Not only has she rearranged the wedding to her liking—a room at the Grand—but she bought a couture vintage Christian Dior wedding gown. It's gray. I added a pukey face emoji. *Oh, how's Benjamin?*

Jenn texted back. *He's doing much better. It's a little tummy issue and a cold. That's what the doctor tells me anyway. Quick question: what kind of gray is it?*

The stylist said dove gray. It was Dior's signature color. I texted back.

And it's vintage couture?

Yes, I texted. *But that's not the issue.*

Wow, I would love to have a look at that dress.

I added a frowny face emoji. *I don't care if the dress is beautiful or not. It isn't the dress I want.*

There was a pause as three dots worked, letting me know she was typing an answer.

Of course, she texted. *I promised I'd take care of your mom, and I won't let you down.*

You'd better hurry. I texted. *Or Mom will have everyone thinking her wedding ideas were actually mine, and they should all allow me to have what I truly wanted.*

But everyone knows that isn't true.

Mom can convince someone who's drowning that they're in the middle of a desert. That's why she came here two weeks early, to start her campaign to convince everyone the wedding she wants is what I've wanted all along but didn't want to hurt anyone's feelings, so I settled.

Surely she's not that devious.

Have you met my mom?

Yes, she typed. *She may be clever and have a gorgeous vintage Dior couture gown . . .*

I sent her an eye roll emoji.

But, Jenn continued, *when it comes to convincing people, she's run up against the master.*

I texted a laughing emoji.

Do you doubt me? she texted.

Not one bit. I typed back.

I still want to see the dress . . .

I sent another eye roll emoji, then sighed and texted again. *It is lovely, but I'm afraid I'm going to ruin the dress. I would never be comfortable or able to move.*

I see your point, although I doubt you would do anything to hurt it.

Esmerelda is coming tomorrow to fit my actual dress. I won't be able to keep Mom away. Please come. I need you.

I'll be there. Shane can take a day off. It's his turn to watch Benji anyway.

I hoped Jenn would be able to handle Mom because she was my last defense. If she couldn't do it, then I would end up with the wedding of Mom's dreams. No matter how much I put my foot down.

I looked both ways at the mouth of the alley to make sure Mom hadn't tracked me down. When there was no sign of her or Andrew, I hurried to the McMurphy, where I could hide out in an empty guest room to think. I called Frances on the way there.

"Hello?"

"Frances, it's Allie. I got stuck in one of my mom's pushy schemes. I assume you're leaving if you haven't left already."

"We were on our way out. We have dinner plans for our anniversary."

"Oh, I'm sorry to bug you. Did Kaylee show up?"

"She's at the front desk now."

"Good, good," I said. "It seems my mom won't quit until I've lost two whole weeks of work."

"Don't worry, dear, we've got you covered. We all

suspected something like this was going to happen. I'm surprised you didn't."

"I didn't want to think about it." I sighed and rubbed my forehead in surrender. "Is Roxanne okay? I know she's not used to handling the copper pot by herself yet and telling the stories. That's why I got out Papa Liam's hydraulic pot lifter."

"She'll be fine," Frances said. "It's all going to be fine."

"Is that Allie?" I heard Mr. Devaney say in his gruff manner.

"Yes," Frances answered.

"Here, give me that phone." The phone rustled at the handover. "Allie, it's all going to be fine," he grumbled. "Now, go do what you have to do."

He hung up, and I wanted to scream.

Some part of me hoped for an emergency so that my staff would need me there.

"Oh, no! My babies!" Mal and Mella had only gone outside once today. Plus, they needed feeding. I hurried down the alleyway toward my back steps when my cell phone rang. It was Rex. "Hi," I answered.

"Hi, yourself," he said. The sound of his voice in my ear always made me warm inside. "Your dress shopping with your mom went late, didn't it?"

"Yes." I shook my head, knowing he couldn't see it but would understand. "The stylist was a man, and he made me take my bra off."

"Do you want me to kill him for you?"

"No," I said. "Maybe rough him up a bit."

We both laughed.

"She wants me back at the salon to quote fix my hair unquote."

"Didn't you have it done yesterday?"

"Obsessive, that's Mom's middle name," I said. "I think she wants them to do my makeup, too. She's dressing me like some kind of doll. And guess who insisted I try on a couture Dior wedding dress from the 1950s."

"Oh, no," he said, but I could hear the humor in his voice.

"It's not funny." I pouted. It really wasn't.

"You know you're going to have to stand up to her."

"I've tried. She doesn't listen, or she says I'm having a tantrum. As if I were eight years old and not twenty-eight." I was nearly to the McMurphy.

"I'm sorry, honey," he said.

"Now I have to face the relatives again." I rounded the corner into the alley and told Rex I had to take care of Mal and Mella. "They must think I've abandoned them."

"That's why I called," he said. "I was there and walked Mal and fed and watered them. They should be good to go until you get home from dinner."

"Thank you," said. "That was very thoughtful."

"You're welcome. Now quit looking for things to distract yourself and enjoy this time. It will never come again."

"One can only hope," I muttered, and he chuckled.

"Seriously, try to enjoy yourself."

"You can say that. You get to work the next two

nights. Wait until you have to have dinner with them on Friday. You'll change your tune."

"Speaking of work, I've got to go," he said. "Bye, and I love you."

"I love you, too," I said, with a grumpy tone in my voice.

No longer needing to walk Mal, I slowed and realized I needed to focus on something other than my mom's schemes. Thinking back to this morning's walk, I suddenly realized what it was that bothered me about Richard. He had had a fishing pole in his hand, but no fish. Then there was the small portion of beach behind the house next to the library. The wind had the waves higher than usual that day, so how come Richard didn't have waders on? And why were his pant legs dry? Exactly where was he fishing?

Okay, I told myself. Maybe he'd only gotten down to the water and heard the noise, then run back up. But then he should have beat me to the scene. Then again, he could also be friends with the neighboring homeowners and been allowed to cut through their lawn, which would have made him farther away. But then how could he have known about Velma? As far as I knew, no one screamed. I would have heard them first. Perhaps he was house-sitting and had access to the gate where the beach was wider. It did seem like he'd been fishing. Although if he were house-sitting, then wouldn't his wife be there? All those questions and more ran through my head as I walked down the alley to the McMurphy. I suppose Richard's wife, Julie, could have been doing anything from visiting with a friend to shopping, although she didn't have a shopping bag with her. But even then, she could have bought something small.

Before I could think about it any longer, I heard a voice behind me call my name. I turned to see Mr. Beecher.

"Hello, Mr. Beecher. My goodness, it's been a while. Are you doing okay?" Mr. Beacher always walked two times a day and usually cut down the alley behind the McMurphy.

"It certainly has been a while," he said while I waited for him. He always dressed very dapperly, and today wasn't any different. He wore a cream shirt under a brown and cream plaid waistcoat, a tweed suit coat with patches on the elbows, and matching brown pants. As usual, he used a fancy wooden cane. His way of speaking always reminded me of Burl Ives when he voiced the snowman in *Rudolph the Red-Nosed Reindeer*.

"I hope you've been doing something fun," I said.

He grinned. "Sheila and I took a monthlong cruise to the Caribbean."

"Wow, I bet that was fun."

"It was," he answered. "Say, where's your little friend? Is she alright?"

"She's fine," I said. "I had assistance today on walking and feeding. My mom and her brothers and sisters came in two weeks early, and she has been running me ragged ever since."

He shook his head and smiled. "Mothers tend to do that when their only child—and a girl child at that—is getting married. I bet she has grand ideas."

"Too grand for me," I said.

"I'm sure she wants only the best for you and believes she knows better what that is. How is the rest of your family? Are they enjoying the island?"

"I'll find out tonight. My mom has insisted I go to dinner with them, and she brought her stylist in to ensure I wore the right thing."

Mr. Beecher laughed and looked at his pocket watch. "When is your dinner?"

"Eight," I said. "But Mom wants me to meet her at the hair salon at six thirty."

"Well, dear, I won't keep you then. It's five thirty."

"Oh no! I've got to go. Nice to see you, Mr. Beecher. I hope you will be able to attend my wedding, not my mother's."

"Good luck," he said and tipped his fedora.

I did a quick calculation in my head. I would have to shower and change first, or I'd be late. Darn it! I rushed upstairs, greeted my babies, and spent at least five minutes showing my love. That's when I heard the key inserted in the front door of my apartment. Mom had come to check on me. I put my pets down and raced to my bedroom, stripped, and popped in and out of the shower without doing my hair. No matter what I did, the salon would redo it, so why bother?

Chapter 11

Mom sat on my bed. "You're running late as usual. Do you have a slip?"

"Do people still wear slips?" I countered, as I put on underwear and dug through my closet for something to wear to the salon and then inside the Grand to get to my mom's room, where my dress for the evening hung.

"Allie, I've taught you to always have a nice slip in your drawer." Mom got up and went through my drawers until she found what she wanted in the back of the bottom drawer. She pinched the bridge of her nose in disappointment, careful not to mess up her makeup, and handed it to me. "Put this on."

"I don't have anything in my wardrobe that works with a slip," I replied.

"Right, you don't," she muttered. "Put it on, you're going to need it. I should have dressed you here, but I didn't want your dress to smell like horses. Their droppings are everywhere on the street. Just think of what would happen to those beautiful shoes."

"We're taking a carriage to the Grand," I pointed out while I tossed the slip over my head.

"Of course," she said. "But a carriage is very different from walking the streets. Although you do sit right behind two horses."

"They keep the roads very clean, and no one smells like horses after riding in a carriage." I knew she wouldn't care.

She gave me a stern look, then handed me a dress Trent had bought me when we dated, before he had to go to Chicago and I started dating Rex. "Mom, that's—"

"What you're wearing. My goodness you are a stubborn girl. You had a decent dress all along, and yet you traipse around in a clearly inappropriate outfit for this weather. And sandals—I can't begin to tell you the horror I felt at that. Now where are those pumps I had you wear last year? You obviously still have them. It seems you keep everything. All these cheap clothes." She shook her head in disgust.

I put on the dress and bit the inside of my mouth to keep from explaining to her that they weren't inappropriate. But I know she would say I was being difficult and would add that sigh of hers.

She shoved the ridiculously high stilettos at me.

"Hurry. We're going to be late, and we're going to need every minute at the salon. I can't believe your hair looks this bad when we had it done yesterday. Did you use the silk nightcap I bought for you?"

"I did," I said, and pointed to it sitting on my bed.

"Then I don't see how your hair is this bad. Oh, you

put a hairnet on and made fudge this morning, didn't you?"

"It was a chef's hat," I said.

She turned her back on me with a long, put-upon sigh. "Of course it was. I don't even see a decent coat. All you have is this puffy thing. You're going to have to wear it. At least until we get safely to my room."

"It's too warm for that," I said. "I have a sweatshirt I can wear."

"Oh no you don't. You can't wear a sweatshirt to the Grand after five. Whatever are you thinking?" Her disappointment grew. She, of course, had a lovely lightweight coat that matched her dress.

"Fine, I'll go without. We'll be there quick enough."

"Speaking of quick, I've ordered a carriage to be ready the minute we get downstairs. Let's go." She pushed me toward the door. "Don't let your cat and dog touch you. We don't want hair all over you."

"Mom, you've gone too far." I let my anger into my voice.

"I have not," she said crisply. "Out you go." She pushed me out the door. "Go, go, go. I'll lock the door."

I glanced at the stairs. Usually living on the fourth floor didn't bother me, but I could barely walk in the pumps without falling. Unfortunately, the elevator was for guests and stopped on the floor below. I faced the fact that I would have to cling to the railing to get down to the third floor. I had carefully gone down three steps when Mom brushed past me and waited for me to make it down to the elevator.

"For goodness' sakes," she said. "Now you are purposely delaying everything."

"Would you prefer I slipped and fell or twisted my ankle? Then I would have to go to the clinic and not be able to make tonight's dinner. It would be such a shame after all the work you've put into it."

Mom crossed her arms and gave me the stink eye. "Fine, take the shoes off if it means we'll only be ten minutes late."

I kept a neutral expression as I took off the painful shoes and hurried down the stairs. She pushed the button and brought the elevator right up. Once we crossed the lobby and stood at the door, she said. "Put the shoes on. I won't have anyone see your bare feet."

I did as she asked, and the carriage driver stepped out to open the door for us. It was Sean O'Malley. "Mrs. McMurphy," he said with the tip of his hat. "Allie, here let me help you." He bent both arms for Mom on one side and me on the other.

"How thoughtful," Mom said with a bright smile.

"Yes, how thoughtful," I agreed. And Sean winked at me. Once he had us safely stuffed into the carriage, it was a short ride to the salon. Again, Sean escorted us to the door, and Mom gave him a nice tip. Thanks to him, I was able to arrive safely inside the salon.

While Mom and Louis both exclaimed over the mess of my hair and planned my makeup, I sat in the salon chair with a big, black plastic cape over me.

As they droned on, without even once asking me how I felt about it, Louis worked on my hair. I pulled my arms out of the cape and texted Carol. *Busy?*

What's up? Carol texted back.

I can't remember if Richard wore waders when he arrived at the crime scene, I wrote.

I can't be certain either, she texted and added a thinking emoji.

If not, then were the bottom of his pants wet? I texted back. *He had been fishing, right? He had a fishing pole and came from the lake side of the bushes. He should have had one or the other.*

That's a very good point, she texted. *I will put it up on the murder board and ask Irma and the other ladies if they remember.*

Thanks. Oh, and do you know if Richard or Julie know the people in the house beside the library?

No, but I can find out.

Thanks, I continued to text.

Why are we texting? Carol asked.

Mom, was all I needed to reply.

Ah, Carol answered. *Text me again if you need me or find out anything new.*

Thanks.

An hour later, my feet now in much more manageable shoes, I made a quick note to myself to throw those horrid stilettos away and have at least one pair I could walk in whenever Mom was on the island.

"You look exactly like I pictured you in that dress," Mom said. "The family won't be able to say anything snarky now."

"Why do you worry about them?" I asked as I handed her my phone. "Please take a picture, and I'll send it to Rex."

She took a quick photo and handed my phone back to me. "I'll never get used to using such a vulgar thing as a phone camera to take pictures. What happened to actual cameras and Polaroids? I know they didn't ring and disrupt a picture." We walked out of her room and down the stairs to the smaller, more formal dining room. "Why do I worry about what my family thinks?" she asked. "This is why. Gird your loins. We're going in."

We both plastered smiles on our faces as Uncle John, Uncle Wade, and Uncle Edmund stood and greeted us both with a kiss on the cheek.

"Ann, gorgeous as ever," Uncle John said. "And, Allie, you look lovely. Where's that fiancé of yours? Has he seen how beautiful you are? The spitting image of your mom."

I sent him a grateful smile, knowing I looked nothing like my mom. At least Mom and I had seemed to come to some sort of truce, if only for tonight.

The waiters pulled out our chairs and pushed them back in once we sat, then took our napkins off the table and laid them in our laps.

"You're late," Aunt Felicity said. Her golden hair was pressed smooth, and her chin-length bob swung when she moved, then returned perfectly into place. It looked like a sheet of silk. It was hard to believe we were related. My hair was thick and wavy and completely unruly. She wore an understated black dress with a necklace of gold and diamonds, and diamonds dripped from her ears. Not only was her makeup perfectly done, but she sat like a woman who had grown up trained in deportment. In other words, her back was perfectly straight but relaxed. She sipped from a delicate martini glass with an elegance generally seen only in a movie set in the nineteenth century.

"I see that you didn't wait for us," Mom replied.

I sat between my mom and Uncle John. He winked

at me. It seemed that more people caught on to my mother's manipulations than I thought. A waiter arrived and pulled a bottle of chardonnay from the silver bucket next to Uncle Wade and poured us both a generous glass.

"I hope you don't mind," he said. "I ordered a white for the table."

"Thank you, Uncle Wade," I said.

He stood and lifted his glass. He looked from his wife, Felicity, to the table. "To our dear Allie. May marriage make her happy for the rest of her life."

"Hear, hear," they all said and touched glasses before taking a sip.

"As long as it lasts," Aunt Felicity said, before finishing her martini in one gulp.

"Madame, may I bring you a glass of wine?" the waiter asked. Even I knew it was polite to drink wine with your food, especially an expensive wine shared at the table.

"I'll take another martini," she said, and Uncle Wade frowned at her.

Aunt Ginny cleared her throat and turned to me. "Allie, how brave of you to become a businesswoman. Is it difficult to both manage a business and make fudge?"

"At first," I said. "But my two degrees work well together to support the business."

"I understand you have a Bachelor of Fine Arts in Confections and an MBA in hospitality," Uncle Edmund said. Uncle Edmund and his wife, Celeste, had arrived this morning. Turns out they'd been delayed by a trial that went on longer than expected. Uncle Edmund was about six feet tall with wide shoulders and a slim physique. He wore a black velvet dinner coat and a crisp white shirt with a lovely, light blue silk tie. "Impressive, my dear."

"Thank you," I said.

"Do you find it fulfilling?" Aunt Celeste asked.

"I do. Every day brings something new," I replied.

The waiters brought a tray and set it up before distributing a single hors d'oeuvre. "This is a broiled oyster with parmigiano and 'nduja. We have the oyster topped with a teaspoon of 'nduja, followed by a lovely sausage from Italy, and finally Parmigiano-Reggiano, then broiled delicately. The cheese will make the oyster juice creamy, and a bit of sausage will add to the dish. Bon appétit." He bowed and removed the tray. At least Mom had taught me how to use a full set of silver. Without a second thought, I picked up my oyster fork, collected the appetizer politely, and popped the whole thing in my mouth at once. It was the perfect bite of crispy cheese, spicy sausage, and oyster.

"My goodness, that was delicious," Aunt Celeste said, as she daintily patted the corner of her mouth with her napkin. She was a small woman with copper-red hair that fell in curls down her back. Her pale skin and a smattering of freckles were deftly done to look as natural as possible. She wore a simple but finely cut green velvet shift dress and a long string of pearls.

"It was, wasn't it?" Mom said.

"Allie, what is your professional opinion?" Celeste asked, leaning forward a bit to look at me around Uncle Edmund.

"Good grief," Aunt Felicity rolled her eyes. "The

girl has a degree in sugar. I'm sure she knows as much as we do about the dish."

"She knows a great deal, actually," Mom said, looking down her nose at her sister, as if daring her.

Surprised, I turned my head to look at Mom in wonder. I had no idea she even cared enough to know what classes I took. She was the one who gave me the ultimatum to go to an Ivy League school and study a "real" subject or lose my trust fund.

"Allie," Mom said, without turning away from Aunt Felicity. "Give us your professional opinion."

Great, how the heck was I getting out of this fight?

"See, the girl doesn't even know," Aunt Felicity downed the rest of her martini and raised the glass, signaling the waiter to bring another.

Uncle Wade gently pushed her arm down and took the glass. "That's enough for now. You're making a fool of yourself."

"I am not," she protested and fought him for the glass. He held his arm out of her way, and a waiter deftly snagged the glass and took it away. "There's nothing wrong with a martini for dinner. At least there shouldn't be."

"Go on, Allie," Uncle Wade said as he pushed the goblet of drinking water toward his wife. As if on cue, the waiter showed up with a coffee cup and saucer for her.

"Allie," Mom nudged me.

"I thought it was an excellent bite," I finally said. "Chef Jules is known for her modern classic cuisine."

"I thought so as well," Aunt Celeste said.

"I would add something a little saltier to elevate the dish," I finished.

"Why ever do you work in a fudge shop and not a prestigious place like this?" Aunt Celeste asked.

"To me, it's not a fudge shop. It's my family heritage. Your heritage moves from generation to generation. The McMurphy is that for me."

Two waiters came out carrying small bowls of cold avocado soup and placed a bowl in front of everyone, while another discreetly poured Felicity a cup of coffee. Everyone at the table pretended not to see. Coffee was usually served with dessert.

The conversation stayed subdued and polite while the dishes were taken away and the waiters came around to refill wineglasses with the white. I put my hand over mine without touching the rim and said quietly, "I have an early morning."

"I understand, Ms. McMurphy," he said.

My family certainly gave the island gossipmongers plenty to talk about. Well, good, I thought. It will take people's minds off of me and the investigation.

Aunt Felicity frowned when Uncle Wade gave a slight shake of his head to the waiter who served the wine, and the waiter withdrew without serving her. Then she stood and left her napkin on the chair. "Excuse me. I've got to use the powder room."

Drawing our attention back to the table, Aunt Ginny addressed me. "I understand that you have a bit of a sleuth in you," she said. "You've caught thirteen killers, or is it fourteen?" Her forest-green eyes sparkled at the idea.

Mom kicked me under the table. "Those stories are simply rumors the locals like to tell. It gives them something to spice up the poor dears' lives."

I looked at her. "Mom, they're not—"

Aunt Felicity arrived back at the table as they served the fish course—a small slice of smelt, lightly fried on a single radicchio leaf topped with a teaspoon of herbed yogurt.

But no one even took a bite. The real display was what went on between Uncle Wade and Aunt Felicity, who had another martini in her hand.

Aunt Ginny gave me the side eye and lifted one eyebrow. I tried not to laugh and hid my reaction with a soft cough.

"Felicity, please," Mom said. "You're embarrassing yourself."

She took a purposeful gulp of her drink and looked Mom straight in the eye. "Not as much as you have. You raised a daughter who prefers to live on this godforsaken island, run a creaky old hotel, and spend her days talking to tourists, while making fudge, of all things. Just like a half a dozen other shops do. For goodness' sake, she gave up her trust fund for"—she waved a perfectly manicured hand—"this. The only thing I can think is that she despises you so much she'd rather do this than be a proper member of this family."

Chapter 12

I sat very quietly, angry to the bone. How dare she insult me and the island this way. Tension at the table grew. Meanwhile, Mom and Aunt Felicity were on the verge of a knock-down, drag-out fight. And I knew neither of them thought about me or the time I'd sacrificed to be here with them.

"That's enough!" Uncle Wade slapped the table, drawing the eyes of all those in the exclusive dining room. The men frowned. Meanwhile half of the women looked appalled, while the other half seemed to be enjoying the show.

"Excuse me." I stood and left the table. I couldn't believe the tension in the family. No wonder Mom didn't want them to visit when I was younger. And no wonder she wanted to impress them so badly that she turned me into her own dress-up doll. As I walked straight to the door, I texted Rex that I was leaving, retrieved my wrap from the coatroom, and walked out onto the lovely front porch. The views were beautiful at night. The Grand's claim to fame was that it had the longest porch in the world. Day and night, people would sit on rocking chairs, Adirondack chairs, and benches and watch the lake, admire the thick green lawn, and smell the lilacs and other flowers that had been carefully planted.

It was cold tonight, and I shivered. Rex may not have read the text yet. When he worked on a murder case, it took up all his time. I could have taken any number of carriages home, but I was so angry that I needed all the fresh air I could get. Plus, my low-heeled shoes were comfortable. I decided to walk, if you can call it that. It was more like I stormed off until I no longer wanted to scream.

The hill down from the Grand was quite steep. I decided to take my shoes off. Comfortable or not, they weren't made for going down steep hills. As I took them off, I wished once again Mom hadn't insisted I bring a very small, glittery evening bag. While it was lovely, it was impractical. My cell phone barely fit inside, but the bag did have a long silver chain that I slung over my shoulder, allowing my hands to be free. The sidewalk grew colder by the minute, and I practically ran down the hill.

Stopping at the bottom, I put my shoes back on. They were much more comfortable now that my feet were numb. Striding on before anyone thought to come after me, my anger cooled, and my thoughts wandered to the murder. It was very clear that Myrtle hadn't murdered Velma. When I got there, Myrtle had looked stunned, her face white, as if all the blood had run to her feet and she was about to faint. She was on her knees with her hands around her waist, as if she'd crumbled to the ground. Tears poured down her cheeks. Yes, there was a longtime rivalry, but they were like my mom and Aunt Felicity—no matter how hard they fought, in the end they loved each other.

The thought brought me back to my anger at my family. Aunt Felicity and Mom, I don't even know why they all came early. It seemed like this was the last place any of them wanted to be.

I checked my phone. No text from Rex. The cold air seemed to seep into my bones; the wrap Mom insisted I wear was little more than a decorative addition to the dress, and I needed a distraction. I decided to call Irma and see how Myrtle was. A quick dial, and I crossed to the other side of Cadotte Avenue with the phone to my ear.

"Hello," Irma answered.

"Oh, goodness, I didn't wake you up, did I?"

"No," she answered. "Carol and I were sitting here trying to figure out who might have had it in for Velma."

"Do you remember if Richard had waders on or if his jeans had wet hems from wading?"

"Let me ask Carol, hold on."

"But I already—"

It was too late. She'd covered the receiver with her hand. I could hear them discussing it through the muffled receiver. "Allie?"

"Yes," I had to work hard not to shiver. The temperature dropped the closer you got to the lake.

"Frankly, neither of us remember. We were distracted by Myrtle's tears and Richard's anger."

"I remember he wore a fishing vest and hat and a flannel shirt," I said, doing my best not to let on that my teeth had begun to chatter. "But now that I think about it, he had work boots on when he kicked the rock, not waders."

"Do you think he's a suspect?" Irma asked, with a touch of excitement in her voice.

"I don't know." I bit my bottom lip to keep the shivers out of my voice. "What would be his motive? They've been divorced nearly five years, and he has a new wife."

"Carol and I can do some snooping. If he had a motive, someone would know. Are you shivering?"

"I'm walking," I said, brushing off the question. "I called to ask how Myrtle was doing."

"Poor thing's beside herself. She keeps repeating that she shouldn't have said the things she did the last time she saw Velma alive."

"But that was their thing, right?" I asked. "The fierce rivalry?"

"Yes, but many people think it's a solid motive," Irma said. "She may have had enough and couldn't wait any longer for Velma to die and get her hands on Velma's collection of books."

"But you disagree," I pointed out.

"Of course, Myrtle is my dear friend. It was such a shock for her that she's been behaving irrationally lately. Even impulsively. Poor thing."

"Maybe she should see a doctor," I said, concerned.

"I've heard that something as simple as dehydration can cause erratic behavior."

"Yes, Brian tells us she's got an appointment to see her doctor in a few weeks."

"In the meantime, is she alone?" I asked worriedly.

"Oh, no," Irma said. "We've been taking turns staying with her when Brian goes to work. But I have to say, she's certainly not herself, and it's not all tears. Sometimes she talks about what happened as if it weren't real and simply a big joke. She even thinks Velma will pop in any moment and laugh at her for worrying."

"That sounds bad. Perhaps she needs to go to the clinic tomorrow," I said, this time unable to stop my teeth from chattering.

"Allie, where are you?" Irma asked with concern in her voice.

"Walking," I reminded her, trying to keep the cold and anger out of my voice. "It's a lovely night."

"Without at least a warm sweatshirt?"

"How'd you know that?"

"Why else would you be shivering? Where are you? We'll come get you."

"No, no," I said, trying not to sound too cold. "I'm headed for the police station to see Rex. I'm almost there. I'll be fine."

"I still have to scold you for not having your jacket. What were you thinking?"

"I had dinner with my mom's family," I explained. "And I've had enough. They were making quite a show. I'm sure you'll hear all about it soon."

"Ask her what happened," I could hear Carol say.

"I'm not going to pry," Irma told her.

"Well, I will," Carol's voice became clearer.

"She's outside and freezing. Let her get home before we—"

The phone scratched, and it was clear that Carol had taken it from Irma. "Allie, where are you? Are you alright?"

"I'm fine. I'm on my way to see Rex."

"And you walked from the Grand? Without a coat? At least tell me you have warm shoes on," Carol scolded.

"I . . ."

Carol sighed. "You don't," she assumed, and she happened to be correct. "Why the heck didn't you take a carriage?"

"My family gave people enough to gossip about. I didn't need to add to it."

"Why would taking a carriage home make people gossip?" Carol asked innocently.

"My so-called family insulted me and Mackinac Island," I said. "I'm spitting angry and thought I should leave before I made things worse. If I'd taken a carriage, I wouldn't have been able to keep my mouth shut. Either way, the whole mess with my family will be at the top of the social column. Afterward, we'll be frowned at by the cottage owners and watched like some reality show by everyone else. Not that I blame them," I said. "If I hadn't been there, I would have loved to see this kind of drama."

"What exactly happened?" Carol asked. "Don't you make me wait until morning to hear the gossip. If I hear it straight from you, then I can quell any rumors that aren't true."

"Um," I said not wanting to tell the story while I was still so angry. Luckily, my phone beeped. I looked down; someone had called, and it wasn't my mom. "Listen, Carol, I'm going to have to call you back. I have another call."

"But—"

I made the switch to end our call and pick up the other. "Hello?"

"Oh, good, Allie." I would know Aunt Ginny's voice anywhere. "It's Aunt Ginny."

"Hi," I said.

"And Aunt Felicity," said another voice.

"Oh." Clearly, they were away from the table. There was no way a six-course meal would be finished already.

"Where are you?" Aunt Felicity demanded and slurred her words a bit. "You're embarrassing your mother, disappearing like that."

"I'm certain my mom is not the only one who was embarrassed tonight," I said, remembering that they were not the only Chases on the island now. Mom's maiden name was Chase, and she never let me forget that I was one of them, too. Chases had backbone if nothing else. "I'm not going to make the rest of dinner. I have other things I'd rather do than watch you get drunk and bicker with my mom. You've ruined a beautiful meal. A chef's tasting meal. One that she worked very hard to prepare for us."

Aunt Felicity gasped, but Aunt Ginny remained quiet. "Are you insinuating that we've embarrassed you so much that you refuse to finish dinner with your aunts? Aunts you haven't seen in over ten years?" The phone radiated her insulted attitude.

"I'm not simply insinuating it," I replied, cool as a cucumber and egged on by my anger.

"Well, I never!" Aunt Felicity was so drunk I was certain she wouldn't remember this conversation, but I would.

"Also, ten years of not seeing you is not reason enough for me to waste my time being insulted a week and a half before my wedding. After all, you could have called any time and come to see me during those years. Or, at the very least, invited me to dinner."

Aunt Felicity sputtered, and Aunt Ginny piped in. "You're absolutely right. I'm afraid I let my fear of insulting Felicity and your grandmother, God rest her soul, keep me from trying to keep up our relationship."

"She's the child," Aunt Felicity said, as if I wasn't on the phone. "It's her duty to contact us. Allie, do you understand how hard we've all worked to help your mother reach her social potential? You hurt the social standing of the entire family when you spent your summers in those awful play clothes. Our friends vacationed on Mackinac, and they loved to talk about what a shame, what a pity it was that your parents clearly didn't show you how to wash and brush your hair and couldn't afford to keep you in nice clothes."

"Then you don't have very nice friends, do you?" I replied, anger making me forget how cold I was. "Picking on my parents and their child. They all knew I was in the right private school. I attended all the deportment classes, like their daughters, and we all debuted at the same time. What did it matter how I looked in the summer? Maybe instead of, quote, helping my mom's social standing, unquote, you should have shamed them all for even thinking something like that. I thought you were a family who had more manners and grace than other people. If I've embarrassed you so much that you felt you had to insult me, my business, my home, and my friends, feel free to leave early and not stay for my wedding."

"No one has ever spoken to me like that!" Aunt Felicity said in her most insulted tone. "Apologize immediately!"

"I will not." I was so angry that my teeth quit chattering. A few blocks away from the police station my phone beeped, interrupting Aunt Felicity, telling me Mom was on the other line. I hit decline.

"After all I've done for you—"

"Oh, you mean not supporting my career choices and ensuring I'd lose my trust fund if I didn't do things the family way?"

"Well! I won't stand here and be treated like this."

There was a long pause before Aunt Ginny spoke. "Good, she's gone. I always knew you had the Chase backbone. Only a true Chase woman could put an end to such nonsense. Forgive me?"

"I need some time," I replied.

"I understand," she said. "Please let me take you to breakfast."

"I get up at five a.m."

"I'll be there."

Chapter 13

I was in a full-on shiver when a carriage stopped me. "Allie!" It was Sean O'Malley. "What are you doing walking out here without a jacket and warm shoes? You look frozen. Get in, and I'll take you home. You should have waited for me. Your mom paid me to take you home, but I figured it would be much later."

"Oh, no thank you, Sean, I'm fine." I replied. "I'm headed to see Rex at the station." I pointed to the large white building half a block away.

"You still should have at least texted me. I would have been there in five minutes tops."

"I'm sorry. I didn't know she'd hired you, and I simply had to leave before they found me and dragged me back to that horrid dinner party."

"Fine," he said. "But don't blame me if you get pneumonia right before your wedding." He reached in the back and withdrew a blanket. "The least you can do is put this blanket around your shoulders."

I took it from him. "Thanks."

"Wait, did you walk all the way from the Grand?"

I couldn't make eye contact.

He shook his head, clearly disappointed in me. "You knew I drove tonight. Seriously, call me next time, okay?"

"Okay," I said, as I draped the blanket around my shoulders. It was warm, and I almost cried.

"Stop being stubborn," he said. "You do have friends here, you know?"

"I know," I said. "I'm sorry."

"Humph," he straightened and clicked, getting the horse to continue on to where he was going.

Great, I'd walked so I wouldn't get caught fleeing, and now I was going to make the news for stupidly trying to freeze to death. I felt a wave of self-pity begin under my anger, but stopped. It suddenly occurred to me that Mackinac Island was a small community of regulars. Why didn't anyone see Velma being murdered in broad daylight? Or did they?

I was too stubborn for my own good, and I was colder than I thought I would be when I'd started out. Doubting it was cold enough to get frostbite, I also didn't doubt that Rex would be upset with me. I walked with purpose to the station door, swung it open, and stepped inside.

Officer Trainee Booker Ashbury stood at the sight of me in a blanket, with my makeup most likely smeared and my nose and cheeks chafed from the wind off the lake. "Ms. McMurphy, are you okay?"

"I'm fine," I lied. "Is Rex in?"

"He and Officer Brown are on the case, interviewing a few people at their homes. I think they're close to an arrest. Do you want me to call someone?"

"No, don't," I said. "I'm fine really. But I will stay for a bit and warm up, if that's okay." In the warmth of the station, the shivers came in waves, and my teeth rattled no matter how hard I tried to stop them.

"Of course," he said. "Rex would have my head if I let you go back out there without thawing a little first. You should sit." I did what he asked and moved toward the chairs, and he picked up the phone receiver, turned his back to me, and spoke quietly enough that I couldn't hear anything he said. "Okay." Then he hung up the phone and turned back to me. "I'm going to get you something to drink to warm you up. Do you prefer coffee or hot chocolate?"

I shrugged and turned my hands palms up and said, "Hot cocoa?"

"I'll be right back." He eyed me before he left. "Don't leave or I'll be fired, and I can't be fired."

I nodded. He had effectively guilted me into staying, and I hoped my mom wouldn't think to look for me here.

He was back in a flash with a paper cup with a brown paper ring to hold so it wouldn't be too hot. We had the same thing, also with lids, in our coffee bar for guests to take up to their rooms.

Right on his tail was Officer Lasko. Megan and I had struck up a wary friendship once she'd admitted her reasons for treating me with hostility. She was a tall woman with a face that was not only feminine but gave off a "Don't mess with me" vibe. Her police uniform was always pressed and the creases neatly crisp. "Wow, hi, Allie," she said with a look of concern in her eyes. "Why don't you come with me, and we'll find you something warm and sensible to wear before Rex gets here. Okay?"

"Okay." I stood, took the offered hot chocolate, and let Megan put her arm around me. I noted a slight nod of her head to Booker as she ushered me through the door straight to the women's restroom.

"Why don't you stay here until I find something for you to wear," she said. "I'm going to bring you a chair so you can sit comfortably." She left for a moment to grab me a chair.

One look in the mirror and I understood why they were concerned. The thick mascara that Mom had insisted on ran down my cheeks from my eyes watering when the cold wind hit my face. My cheeks were red, chapped from the wind, and the contouring makeup was smeared. My hair was half up and half down. All that teasing and hair spray made me look as if I'd stepped out of a horror film. My cold feet, scuffed shoes, and blanket for a coat must have made me look like a crime victim.

Suddenly, I was embarrassed I'd come to the station and let them see me like this. I was glad Rex wasn't here. It was only a ridiculous dinner with my family.

Megan entered, pushing a wheeled office chair with soft seating rather than one of the usual small plastic, white chairs. "Sit," she said softly, but with enough force that anyone would know better than to not obey her. "Tell me what happened."

I shook my head at my stubborn need to get away as fast and as far as I could. Now I had scared everyone.

She grabbed a soft towel from a pile in the cabinet under the sink. "Did someone attack you?"

That made me laugh, and I began to cry.

She concentrated on getting my feet warm by taking my shoes off, running the towel under hot water, and wrapping my feet in it. Then she stayed squatted down and looked at my hands, which were blocks of ice, and I had the absurd thought that at least my manicure was still okay. I laughed again as tears ran from my eyes.

"Allie," she said gently, as she rubbed my hands between hers to bring back a stinging rush of blood, "what happened?"

"I didn't mean to scare everyone," I said. "I had to get away."

"From whom?" She looked up at me.

I grabbed the tissue box and blew my nose, then wiped the mascara-stained tears and makeup off my face. I shook my head. "It's all so stupid. I'm being a total idiot."

"Allie," she insisted. "Who did this to you?

"My mom's family."

Chapter 14

Caramel No-bake Cookies

Ingredients

1 cup of white sugar
1 cup of brown sugar
½ cup of butter
½ cup of milk
1 teaspoon of vanilla
½ cup of peanut butter
3 cups of quick-cooking oatmeal

Directions

In a medium pan, combine the white sugar, brown sugar, butter, and milk. Cook on medium heat, stirring often until boiling. Boil for 1 minute and remove from heat. Add the vanilla, peanut butter, and oatmeal. Stir until combined. Using a soup spoon, drop onto parchment paper and let cool. This recipe yields twenty-four cookies.

Megan listened and gently washed all the makeup off my face, while I started from when Mom arrived and continued until the events of the evening. She nodded and softly murmured, "That's horrible. How could they do that?"

"The worst part is that I know the wait staff and the maître d', and everyone there heard them arguing like that about me and Mackinac. After all I've done these past few years to fit in, and her family—my family—undid it in less than two hours. Such disdain for the things I love. I'll never be able to get back what I had." This time the tears were no longer from laughing.

"Okay." Megan stopped and rocked back on her heels. "Allie, you're not giving the people here enough credit for knowing that having idiot relatives doesn't mean you're like them."

"If those people show up at my wedding"—I shook my head—"I'm going to tell them all not to bother and to go home, where they won't embarrass me!"

"There you go, girl." She smiled at me. "Now, I have a police-issued T-shirt and some sweatpants that I think will be a lot warmer and might keep Rex from killing you." We both chuckled, and I removed the lovely but impractical dress Mom had bought for me. Megan refused to let me put the shoes back on and put both carefully in an evidence bag.

"That's all I have," she said. "I promise you can take them with you. We have enough of your wardrobe."

"This is much warmer, thanks," I said, and I put on the clothes, which hung on me. I rolled up the sleeves and the bottoms of the sweatpants, glad they had elastic at the ankle because it helped hold up the legs.

"Let me go get you socks and shoes," she said.

"Where are you getting those?" I asked, looking at my painted toes barely sticking out of the pants.

"Hey, you're the one who was stupid enough to wander off without using a carriage." She walked out.

I guess I deserved that. Before she got back, the door slammed open. Rex stood in the doorway, and he looked angrier than I'd ever seen him. He had his feet spread wide and his arms crossed. His chin was up, and there was fire in his blue eyes. I refused to be intimidated. Let him use that on any kids we might have, but I was a grown-up and didn't have to take it. I mirrored his posture, chin up, and raised an eyebrow at him.

"Yes?" I asked him. "Are you going to stand in the doorway of the ladies' restroom?"

Without a word, he rushed to me and grabbed me hard. My face was smashed on his chest. "Rex, Rex, I can't breathe."

He stopped holding me quite so hard. "When they said you came in half-frozen and looking like you'd run from something, the first thing I could think is that you were in the hands of another killer. I couldn't let that happen. Not now, not ever." He took a step back, his hands gently on my upper arms as he looked me up and down. "Are you sure you're okay?"

"I'm fine," I said, with one more chatter of my teeth and a shiver down my back. I grabbed him and pulled him closer. He was so warm.

"Lasko says your family did this to you? Made you run without thinking about yourself?" he asked as he rubbed my back to help me feel warm. "I'm going to go up there and give them all a piece of my mind. They need to get the hell off my island."

I laughed again. I swear, laughing and crying was my thing tonight. "I told Megan the same thing," I said. "First thing in the morning, I'm telling them that they aren't invited to my wedding and to leave and never come back. See? You don't have to save me. This is my family, and I'm going to do it."

I could feel the low chuckle in his chest, his heartbeat strong underneath. "That's my girl. That's the woman I am going to marry. Now tell me where you were running to? Home?"

"You," I said. "I was running to you."

"And I wasn't here," he sounded upset with himself.

"But your team took good care of me, and you're here now," I said.

"Now, with your permission." He looked down at me and pulled my chin up with a gentle touch until I could see his face fully. "I'd like to take you home and make sure no one, and I mean no one in your family disturbs you the rest of the night."

"Speaking of that," I said and smiled at him, "I want you to come home. My family's sensibilities can go out the window as far as I'm concerned. Come back where you belong."

"Yes, ma'am," he said with a devastating smile.

When we left the restroom hand in hand, Megan stood waiting by the door. "I have warm socks and shoes."

"Perfect," Rex said. "Thanks, Lasko, for taking good care of Allie."

"Allie and I are friends," she answered. "I'd do it for any of my friends."

"Don't make me cry again," I said and hugged her tight. "Thanks for being my friend." When I pulled away, I swear I saw tears in her eyes. Megan wasn't one to tear up at all, especially at work. I took the socks and shoes from her and turned to Rex as he led me to the chair by his desk. We did it on purpose, to let her get a hold of herself and maintain her dignity. I knew she would never forgive herself if she didn't, and friends wouldn't let that happen.

Chapter 15

The next morning, Rex made us breakfast. I'd missed that the last few days. He'd been doing it since we became engaged because he worried that I would forget to eat, what with everything going on. I teased him that at this rate I wasn't going to fit in my dress.

Speaking of dress fittings, Esmerelda would be here at three this afternoon. I'd asked Frances to show her to my apartment and let me know the moment she got here. I felt bad asking Esmerelda to come all the way to the island, but she said it was her decision, not mine. She also refused to let me pay for her trip. She was an amazing woman, and Rex and I decided to add a third of her bill as a tip for her talent alone. She deserved it.

I got downstairs and turned on the fudge shop lights at five, when there was a knock on the front door. I looked over to see Aunt Ginny wave at me. Unlike me last night, she had on a proper coat and hat. I opened the door. "Aunt Ginny? Come in, come in, out of the cold."

She did as I asked with a big smile. "I'm here to take you to breakfast," she said, rather proud of herself. Then she leaned toward me and put her hand to the side of her mouth as if someone listened. "You should have heard the big brouhaha that happened after you left last night." She straightened. "Good for you!" Her eyes twinkled at me.

After everything that'd happened last night, I couldn't help but smile.

"I'm sorry, I forgot about breakfast," I said. "Rex made me something already."

"Good man, that fiancé of yours," she said and looked over my shoulder at the fudge shop. "This is where the magic happens?"

"It is," I said. "Want a tour?"

"Oh, yes, please! I've never been inside the actual fudge maker's part of the hotel."

"You'll have to wear an apron and a hairnet," I warned, certain that would change her mind.

"Yes, of course," she said. "Where can I put my coat?"

I gave her a quick tour, then sent her out to get coffee from the coffee bar while I made the first batch of the day. She grabbed a chair and started chatting. "Now, I heard there was a murder the day we arrived. Is it true?"

"It's true," I said, surprised by Aunt Ginny's information. "But I can't talk about that right now. I'm measuring ingredients, and I can't be distracted."

She kept on anyway. "Tell me everything. I've been

keeping up on your life on the island. I receive the newspaper, too. And you amaze me. You've caught so many killers." Aunt Ginny sounded excited. "I want to do that, too. Even if it's only once."

Confused, I stressed, "It's very dangerous to try and find a killer."

"Nonsense, I'm a Chase woman, remember?" Aunt Ginny said a little too enthusiastically. "Tell me, are you investigating this one, too?"

"Um," I tried to think how to answer that.

"I knew it!" she cackled. "You haven't told your mom, have you."

"She'd kill me," I said.

"Even better," Aunt Ginny giggled. "Now tell me, when's this book club of yours meet again?"

Lucky for me, Roxanne arrived at six a.m., with Frances not far behind her. While Aunt Ginny introduced herself to Roxanne, I moved as quickly as I could, turning hot fudge with a long-handled paddle. There was no time to ask Frances why she was here early. She always came in at eight a.m. on the dot, with Douglas by her side.

Roxanne entered the fudge shop and put a sturdy apron over her black pants and pink-and-white-striped McMurphy polo with our logo on it. "Good morning, Allie," she said and grabbed a short scraper, as I changed from long to short, and helped me to fold in the fruit and nut fillings that made each fudge different.

"Good morning," I said and glanced at her to see if her expression showed that she knew anything about

last night's family drama. "Esmerelda is coming this afternoon around three," I reminded her.

"Don't worry, I have you. I love doing my part of making fudge, demonstrations, and selling. It's fun. Besides, I know how weddings can be, all the preparations and appointments and the family." She paused and glanced at Aunt Ginny, who was now talking to Frances. "I heard last night was a bit of a whopper."

"Yeah," I said as I cut pound pieces from the loaf of fudge, placed them on a tray and slid them into the candy counter. "They made quite a show of themselves and did nothing but disrespect the food, the chef, the Grand, the island, its people, and me. I couldn't sit there any longer, and I left."

"I heard you practically did a Cinderella, running from the ball without proper warm garments and good shoes. How are your feet feeling this morning?"

"A little tender," I admitted, while we made another batch of fudge. Roxanne mixed and cooked the base, while I chopped the fresh ingredients. This one I called peach pie fudge. It was white fudge with chopped-up peaches, cinnamon, and nutmeg. It had become a summer favorite.

"Then the rumor says that Rex practically carried you in his arms the whole way back to the McMurphy." She sighed. "I don't think my husband was ever that romantic. Even when we first got married."

I glanced at her. "Did you ever tell him you'd like a bit more romance?"

She laughed and waved me over to help her pour more fudge onto the freshly cleaned table.

"When you've been married as long as we have, romance comes in a different form. Things like a foot rub, making a nice meal, doing the dishes, or simply sitting on the couch together watching a program you both like can be very romantic."

We moved around the table, flipping the hot fudge with our long-handled paddles. "Do you have any idea why Frances is in early," I asked and motioned with my chin toward the reception desk.

"I think she's worried about you. I'm pretty sure the whole island is worried about you."

"That's very sweet," I said, my heart pounding and my thoughts running. Was it worry from my friends here or disgust?

As soon as we switched to short-handled fudge paddles, my mom stormed into the McMurphy. I wiped the sweat from my brow. She looked every inch the well-polished woman about town, from her matching jacket and skirt to her tucked-in shirt and perfectly pointed collar, her long legs highlighted by elegant shoes, and her matching pocketbook.

"Allie!" she said sternly and tried to open the fudge shop door. Thankfully, it was locked to keep my clever pets out. Mal stood beside Mom, her tail wagging, as if to say, "Oh, let me in if you're going in." Mom knocked. "Allie Louise, open this door right now."

I ignored her and grabbed a tray to cut thick one-pound slices and fill the tray.

"Are you going to let her in?" Roxanne asked. She was older than me and had kids.

"Normally, I'd be a good girl and jump the moment she said to, but not today."

"Oh," Roxanne said, her mouth making an O shape. "Was she part of—"

"Last night's petty squabble? Yes," I went back to chopping the filling for the next fudge batch, while Roxanne cleaned the copper pot.

"Allie!" My mom stood right in front of me on the opposite side of the glass, Mal beside her wagging her tail. I'm certain my pup thought this was a wonderful game. "We need to talk about last night and the way you behaved."

Out of the corner of my eye, I saw Aunt Ginny approach Mom and say something. Mom brushed her off.

Then Frances touched her arm and walked my mom over to the coffee bar to get a cup of coffee. Frances spoke to her low enough that we couldn't hear anything on our side of the glass. Aunt Ginny stood with them at the coffee bar. It looked like their discussion was quite animated.

"Don't you need to talk to your mom and clear the air?" Roxanne asked as she started the base for a milk-chocolate and peanut-butter fudge.

"Frances and Aunt Ginny are doing fine with her. Besides, we're working, and she can wait," I said, not paying any attention to Mom's antics. I could tell from the corner of my eye that she was worked up. She made hand gestures to punctuate her words, then pointed toward me and went back to gesturing. Well, now I know for certain where I got my bad habit of talking with my hands.

Somehow Mom had gotten away from both Frances and Ginny, who most likely had given up. I know I would have. There was no one more stubborn and self-righteous than my mom, not even me.

Roxanne was a sweet woman and a wonderful mom. "She's trying to catch your eye."

Mom had walked straight to the shop to face us as we waited for the batch to reach the right temperature. "She's clearly asking me to let you know she's there."

I continued to work, checking the fudge, and when the temperature was right, grabbed the pour handles and, with Roxanne's help, poured it onto the cool marble slab. Fudge making was fun and creative, but it was also hard work with all the lifting and stirring and folding.

"I really don't want you to get involved," I said. "You're a good friend, and I want to keep it that way. My mom is nothing if not manipulative." I could feel Roxanne becoming more and more uncomfortable as we lifted and folded the fudge to add air to it as it cooled. I didn't want that either. A distracted candymaker was a burned candymaker. And I knew I had to make my mom stop. "Fine, go ahead and keep turning the fudge. I'll be right back."

I saw Roxanne's shoulders relax and patted her on my way out. I didn't mean for my mom's ridiculousness to upset Roxanne.

Stepping out, I locked the door behind me to keep Mal from accidentally bumping into the door and entering the fudge shop. I needn't have worried. Mal was happy to run to the coffee machine with me, my mom on my heels. "Would you like another cup of coffee? Diet sweetener and no cream, right?"

I ignored her as I poured two cups of coffee, adding

cream for me and sweetener for her and pushed the plastic top on mine, leaving hers free. She hated plastic tops.

"Allie, I swear—"

"Have some coffee, Mom." I handed her hers and sipped mine. "When's Dad coming? Friday, you said?"

She took the coffee without thinking. Now she was stuck with a cup of coffee in each hand, one from Aunt Ginny and one from me. It made it difficult for her to get too worked up when she couldn't move her hands. I leaned against the coffee bar.

Even this early in the morning, she had her makeup perfectly set. If I didn't know better, I would think she slept with her makeup on. But I watched her most mornings of my childhood, taking forty-five minutes every morning to put on makeup and fix her hair. She must have gotten up very early.

I glanced over at Frances and Aunt Ginny, who quickly turned and tried to look as if they weren't interested in what was going on.

"Don't think that I didn't speak to your father about all this. He's coming in today, and he'll have something to say about your rude behavior."

I tried not to smile at the "Wait until your father gets home" bit and kept my expression as neutral as possible. That way, when she ranted and raved, she would only embarrass herself. "It'll be nice to see him," I blew on my coffee. "I understand he's been working on a large contract bid that has been accepted." And I took a sip. "I want to tell him congratulations and that I'm proud of him."

Mom narrowed her eyes. "Don't act all innocent

with me. We both know you ruined last night's dinner after I bought you that gorgeous dress and shoes and had your hair done. What were you thinking?"

"Rex has moved back in with me," I announced. "And he will stay until the night before the wedding."

Mom gasped. "The family would never allow—"

"With any luck, the family won't be here after this morning." I finished my cup and tossed it in the recycle bin, then headed back to the fudge shop.

"What do you mean, the family won't be here after this morning? What about the wedding?"

"They're no longer invited."

"You can't do that," Mom sputtered.

"I'm an adult, and it's my wedding," I said with a casual shrug. "I can do it. They were extremely disrespectful of me, you, and, most importantly, this island and all the people I care for. They have proven to the islanders that I am nothing but a wealthy outsider only here to insult them, after all my care and work to show them that I love this island, its people, and the McMurphy. Like I said, they're no longer invited, and might as well take their yacht and go home."

"Well, I never!"

"Seems to me that phrase runs in the family, and it's about time you all experience something you never have before. It's called growth, Mom. Don't worry, you don't have to tell them. I'm calling them promptly at eight a.m. and letting them know. See? I do have the Chase backbone." I walked away, gave Mal a squeeze, then told her to go lie down.

"What about your Aunt Ginny?" Mom said. "She came all the way over here to apologize."

"She's invited. Oh, and I'd be careful, if I were you, or you won't be." Then I unlocked the fudge shop door and went to work, leaving Mom to sputter. She tossed the coffee cups into the trash, grabbed Aunt Ginny, who waved goodbye, and stormed out.

Rex stopped by after my ten a.m. demonstration. I stood beside the registration desk, helping Frances with the check-outs, while she tagged the luggage for the porters. She then put them in the back room, where we kept our coats, boots, lunches, and purses.

Rex came through the front door, holding it open for a couple who were eager to hit the souvenir shops on their last day, then removed his hat. My heart skipped a beat at his handsome face, those intelligent blue eyes. He smiled at me as he strode through the lobby and waited for a lull.

"How'd it go?" he asked, leaning against the registration desk absently and giving Mal a pat on the head when she stretched her two front paws out on his leg. "I would have texted, but I didn't want a condensed answer like you usually give."

"She was impressive," Frances said when she went back to work on her computer.

"Hello to you, too," I said and kissed him lightly. Then I took his hand and pulled him into the back amid the luggage and the small employee kitchen and lockers, and gave him a proper greeting.

"Nice," he said and held me tight. "But you're not getting away without telling me everything. Do I need to go up to the Grand and forcibly remove them?"

I giggled. "No, I think they got the point. I flat-out told them they were rude and embarrassing to me for how they treated me, the people of the island, my father, and his family. And that I wouldn't stand for it. They were no longer welcome at my wedding and should leave."

"Ouch," he said. "But I'm proud of you."

"I won't have it," I said, my anger still raw. "I won't run away again. It's hard for me to properly express myself in the moment. I always need to come back later and address the issue."

"You did it perfectly. If you had done it at the table last night, you would have only added fuel to their ridiculousness." He gave me a squeeze. "How'd they take it?"

"Aunt Felicity said, and I quote, 'How dare you! I won't stand here and take this from a child with the manners of a . . . a—' I finished the sentence for her: Chase?"

Rex let out a short laugh.

"Then I hung up on her.

"The next person I called was Uncle Edmund, who had his back up. I could tell by his tone. He said, "Your Aunt Celeste and I have come a long way for your wedding and we had nothing to do with last night. Still you're kicking us out?

"I explained to him, in no uncertain terms, that he did nothing when it happened. That was as much as agreeing with the rest of the group.

"So he finished with, 'I hope you enjoy your small

life on this small island.' As if that were a terrible thing."

"What'd you say to that?" Rex asked, his eyes flashing with humor.

"I told him I most certainly would and hung up on him."

"Good for you. isn't there another aunt and uncle? How'd they take it?"

"I let Uncle John and Aunt Ginny stay," I looked up at him. "They apologized, even though they weren't the ones making a scene. How could I not?"

He kissed the top of my head. "You're amazing."

"Thank you," I said and kissed him, then took a step back. "Oh no, I didn't realize that even with my chef's coat and hat off, I'm still covered in fudge and sugar." I brushed off the front of his uniform.

He took my hand and gently kissed it. "It wouldn't be the first time I've gone back into the bullpen smelling like fudge." I felt the heat of a blush reach my cheeks at the thought that everyone in the police station knew exactly what we'd been doing and when.

There was a knock on the door, and Frances stuck her head inside the room. "Allie, Carol and Irma are here and want to talk to you."

"I need to get back to work," Rex said and gave me a quick kiss.

"See you later tonight?" I asked because, even though we lived together, our schedules sometimes meant we went days without actually having dinner together.

"Sorry, I'm still working the case," he said. "I'll most likely be home late."

"I understand," I said. "I think I might go to book club tonight."

He shook his head. "Don't get into any trouble before the wedding, please?"

I kissed him quickly and stepped out of the room as he held the door open for me and followed. "I'll try."

Chapter 16

"Carol, Irma," I said with a smile. "What can I do for you?"

Carol made herself a cup of coffee as usual. I swear that, since I'd opened the coffee bar for my guests, Carol hadn't bought a cup of coffee, except when she went to the Coffee Bean to meet her friends and get the local news firsthand.

Irma held my arm and watched Rex leave, before she said, in a low voice, "We realized that you're right. Neither of us remember Richard wearing waders or his pant legs being wet."

Carol blew on her coffee and took a sip. "The only problem with that is it's been proven that eyewitness testimony is susceptible to group thinking or poor memories."

"We don't know if we remember that fact or your

question made us think that we did," Irma said with a sigh.

"We've been asking around, but no one seems to have seen anything," Carol said.

"I wondered about that," I said. "Velma was killed in a very open park really close to Main Street. People come and go by there all the time. How was it no one saw anything?"

"Hmm, I'm certain there's a view from the Hotel Iroquois," Irma said thoughtfully. "What does that mean?"

"Do you think she was killed somewhere else and dumped there?" Carol asked.

"I wondered the same thing." I frowned. "But even then, someone should have seen her body being moved. It's not as if she were on a blanket napping."

"And your time line shows there wasn't enough time for someone to kill her and then dump her there. Right?"

I shook my head slowly. "I'm not sure. I wasn't paying attention to how long it was from the time Velma left to the time Myrtle checked out her books."

"It does seem like the killer cut it pretty short." Carol swallowed the last of her coffee. "Myrtle left the used bookshelves, sat down next to you to look something up, had time to complain about the Social Security research, and then checked out her books."

"And," Irma said, "how would they know for sure that Myrtle would find her first?"

"Maybe Myrtle wasn't supposed to find her first." I tapped my chin.

The doorbells jangled, and we all looked over at who it was. Usually, a glance will tell us if it's a fudge customer or a hotel guest, but instead it was Aunt Ginny again. "Allie, I'm glad you're still here," she said. "I left your mother at the Grand trying to figure out how to soothe the rest of the family."

"Aunt Ginny," I said. "This is Carol Tunisian and Irma—"

"You're one of Allie's aunts," Carol said, cutting me off. "I thought all of you left this morning."

"Oh, yes, well," Aunt Ginny looked at me.

"Aunt Ginny and Uncle John apologized and, frankly, were as astonished about yesterday's scene as I was," I said. "I told them they could stay, and it would be nice if they came to the wedding."

"I'm sorry about my rude family," Ginny said. "I'm sure everyone has heard how horrible they were yesterday. John and I happen to love Mackinac Island. Everyone from the wait staff to the store managers have been nothing but kind and welcoming. I have no idea what has gotten into my sisters." She shook her head, and her turquoise earrings swung from side to side. "I hope you'll forgive me for being there and not saying anything. I always get tongue-tied when people get rude and start to fight. I hate conflict."

"I suppose if Allie has accepted your apology, then we can, too" Carol said. "Don't you agree, Irma?"

"Certainly." Irma nodded.

"What brings you in again, Aunt Ginny?" I asked.

"Well," she glanced around, "remember, this morning we talked about the murder and how you might be investigating?"

"Yes," I replied.

"I'd still love to get involved. I'm quite clever when it comes to puzzles," she said.

"I don't know," I hedged. "You don't really know too many residents. Wouldn't it be difficult to help?"

"That's the thing," she said, with a wicked smile and a twinkle in her eyes. "As an outsider, I might be able to ask questions that could help you come to a conclusion."

"I'm not sure," I said and looked at the ladies, who seemed interested in what I thought.

"I heard your mom was being a momzilla," Aunt Ginny whispered. "I could help you corral her to make sure you get what you want and not what she wants."

"You can do that?" I asked, intrigued.

"Of course I can," she said and smiled wide. "She's my sister, and I'm her favorite. Besides, I heard she's already hijacked your dressmaker. And asked her to set up in her room, not your apartment."

"What? Why?" I could barely breathe. "I'm not about to wear the vintage Dior wedding dress she bought for me."

"She told the dressmaker that her suite had a raised sitting area in the bedroom and how that would allow her to get a good view of the fit and the hem."

"Esmerelda would ask me before she did what Mom asked," I said, my eyebrows drawn into a crease.

"Your mom also slipped the poor woman five hundred dollars to agree. Esmerelda should be calling you any second to suggest your mom's room."

I shook my head. "I never thought Mom would stoop that low."

"I contacted your wedding planner—what's her name again?"

"Jenn," I replied.

"I told her exactly what your mom did. Jenn promised to be there for your fitting. And I'll be there, too. Between the two of us, Ann will have to behave herself."

"You should let her do it," Irma said. "You wouldn't want to see Esmerelda lose a tip like that, would you?"

"I guess not," I replied.

"I agree," Carol said, then changed the subject. "Ginny, our book club meets tonight at my house. You're officially invited."

"Wonderful!" Aunt Ginny looked so excited. "I'll be there. What time do you meet?"

"Seven p.m." Carol said, then looked at me. "It might not hurt to get an outsider's point of view."

I sighed. "Okay."

"Thank you. I'm so honored," Aunt Ginny said. "Allie, I'll meet you here, and we can walk over there together."

"What will Uncle John say?" I had to ask.

"He'll say, what did you learn tonight?" Aunt Ginny said. She glanced at her expensive watch. "I have to go before your mom misses me and gets suspicious. I'm excited! I'll see you ladies tonight." She gave me another quick hug, waggled her fingers at the ladies, and hurried out of the lobby.

We all stared as she went out the door. "What just happened?" I asked.

"You have yourself an ally," Carol said.

"One who can help keep your mom in check," Irma agreed. "I see that as a win."

Then why did it feel as if I'd made a big mistake?

Chapter 17

"Good, she's here." Mom gave me a quick hug and a kiss on the cheek. "Come on, Allie, everyone is waiting for you."

"I had to get my undergarments on," I said. The bra and corset were tight, but not so tight that I couldn't breathe or sit down. The boning was uncomfortable, but I could do it for one day. Then I had to find something to wear to accommodate them while I got myself to Mom's room. All of which I could have done more comfortably in my own home. But Mom had called me and informed me that everything was set up in her suite, and it would be asking too much of poor Esmerelda to move it all to my place.

I gave in, knowing this was coming and glad Jenn and Aunt Ginny would be there.

Jenn set down a champagne flute, got up, and gave

me a hug. A year after Benji was born, Jenn looked amazing as always. Today she wore blue, wide-legged pants and a white T-shirt. Her blue, faux-leather jacket was folded neatly along the arm of the couch beside her. "How are you doing?" she whispered in my ear.

"Please don't encourage Mom's love of Dior," I whispered back. Jenn pulled back and winked at me.

Aunt Ginny got up next and gave me a big hug. "It's going to be alright."

"I certainly hope so." I hugged her back.

Esmerelda stood to the side, smiling her patient smile. She looked to be in her mid-thirties, but had confessed to me she was forty-five. Her short black hair was tucked behind her ears, and her makeup accented her copper skin. She told me once that she wore her hair short to keep from sewing it into a dress. I could imagine that image and was a little horrified. She'd laughed at me.

She came forward, and I gave her a quick hug. She wore her usual outfit of jeans and a T-shirt with her logo on it.

"Smile," she said. "This is a happy day. Relax and enjoy yourself."

"Thanks," I said.

"Let's impress your mom. Okay?"

"Okay." I nodded.

"Someone get this girl a glass of champagne," Aunt Ginny said.

Mom smiled, and I was certain her sudden happiness was because she had gotten her way with the fitting. She handed me a flute.

"To the bride-to-be," Jenn said.

"Here, here," they answered, and everyone lifted their glasses.

I swallowed half of my flute at once. "Let's do this."

They all clapped. That's when I noticed the small plates filled with finger food. Mom had ordered cheese and meat trays, hors d'oeuvres, a fruit plate, and a bowl of chocolate-covered strawberries.

There was no way I was going to eat anything before I put my dress on, no matter how much my stomach grumbled. Unlike Andrew with his screen, Esmerelda ushered me into the bathroom carrying a long, thick, black garment bag.

"Do you have your shoes?" she asked as she put the bag on the hook on the back of the door.

"I do," I held up the canvas shoe bag.

"Good," she said. "Get undressed and put your shoes on first."

I did what she asked, tucking my folded clothes on the towel rack. My shoes were silver, sequined flats. The bridal shop also had them in a tennis shoe. I would have happily gotten those, but I knew shoes were something my mom wouldn't compromise on. I believe her exact words would be, "Not over my dead body."

"Good," Esmerelda said. When I stood, I felt her intense gaze. "You've lost weight."

"I don't know how. Everyone keeps feeding me."

"Hmm," she replied and handed me the crinoline petticoat.

I slipped it on, and she took out the gown, careful not to let it touch the bathroom floor. The thought made me cringe. "Maybe we should put it on outside of the bathroom."

"I agree," she said, placed it back into the bag, and zippered it up. "I thought you would want a big reveal for your mom and friends, but this does not work." Then she opened the door. I grabbed it for her and held it open as she passed through.

It was odd to be wearing a bra and corset and crinoline. I had to push the petticoat down to go through the door and not snag it.

The ladies were distracted as they laughed and chatted. I grabbed my flute of champagne and downed the rest of the liquid courage. Also, I noticed the other black garment bag on the rack that Esmerelda brought. Disappointment, frustration, and a bit of anger rushed through me. It must have shown on my face because Esmerelda took me by the hand and helped me step up onto the raised platform. "Turn your back to them," she said gently, and I did. You could see the straits of Mackinac through the window, and I concentrated on the water, not my emotions. I heard the bag unzip. "Hands up," she said, as she stepped up beside me. I bent down to her height and raised my hands. She slipped the soft eyelet dress over my head and arms. It had a sweetheart neckline and three-quarter-inch sleeves. The waist nipped in when she zipped it. I could feel cool air on my back where it dipped in a V shape. I ran my hand over the thick satin ribbon at the waist and admired the white eyelet of the skirt. "Tip your head forward," she said, with my veil in her hands. Esmerelda was quite short, and even standing on her folding stool, she couldn't reach my head without my dipping down.

She stepped back a moment and adjusted the bodice, taking pins out of her wrist pincushion, and pinned.

"Tsk, tsk, tsk. Brides always think they have to lose a few more pounds to look good on their wedding day," she said as she adjusted the waist as well. Thankfully, the full skirt meant it didn't really matter if my hips had gotten smaller or larger.

"I swear, I'm not dieting."

"I'll see that she eats better," Jenn said.

"Come on, I'm an adult. I don't need to be coddled. I'm eating just fine."

"Okay, turn around," Esmerelda said.

I turned to face my friends and my mom.

"Oh, it's beautiful," Aunt Ginny said. "You're beautiful. You remind me of your mother on her wedding day."

"I love the eyelet for a gown," Jenn said. "It's lovely and perfect for a summery outdoor wedding."

Mom kept her mouth tight and disapproving. She looked at my dress, tilting her head one way and then the other, as if to find something, anything nice to say about it.

"Isn't it lovely, Ann?" Aunt Ginny tried to trap her, then grinned and sipped her champagne.

Finally, Mom let out a huffy sigh. "It's fine." She turned to Esmerelda. "Did you design this?"

Esmerelda didn't even blink at my mom's tone. "Allie knew what she wanted and brought me swatches of both the eyelet and the satin. We sat together as she filled in what she wanted for the design. Then I created the look that she wanted."

"And I love it," I said. "It's truly my dream dress."

"Yes, I can see that from the smile on your face," Aunt Ginny said.

Esmerelda had me step closer to the edge of the raised sitting room and then got on her knees and began to pin the hem.

"What about those eyelet holes?" Mom frowned. "A see-through wedding gown is not appropriate."

"I lined the bodice with satin," Esmerelda said. I swear this woman was unflappable. I bet she'd heard everything from mothers, brides, friends and even boyfriends. I know I couldn't do what she does, keeping everyone calm. If I were able, I would have done that last night.

"What if it's cold?" Mom asked. "I know that there are days in June when the weather is too chilly for eyelet. Like last night." She gave a pointed look that I chose to ignore. "Allie, what are you going to do if it's raining?"

"We thought of that," I said as calmly as I could. "There's a matching satin cloak." I pointed to the satin belt around the waist. "If it's chilly and if it's raining, they've already offered the Senior Center."

Mom shivered in disdain. "My daughter getting married in a senior center. Surely, there's a church with a rec center at the very least. And how are you going to accommodate all those people you invited?"

"Mackinac Island is a very popular place for a destination wedding," Jenn said. "The churches are already reserved for that day."

"With so many weddings that same day"—Mom's tone was icy—"and everyone at your wedding, who will be working the weddings and the shops?"

"We've already brought in waitstaff and caterers

from off the island, and the shops will be run by the summer staff."

Mom sighed dramatically. "I know you can't fit everyone in that Senior Center."

"How do you know that?" I asked.

"I've been to your Senior Center," Mom said. "I wanted to meet the people who take up most of your time and keep you from a normal twenty-eight-year-old life."

"We'll split everyone up. Whoever doesn't fit in the Senior Center will overflow to the McMurphy lobby. We plan on putting up a big screen showing the wedding live. And the potluck will be split as well. Everyone in the Senior Center will bring theirs, and everyone at the McMurphy will bring theirs. The caterers will take it from there."

"See, Ann," Ginny said and poured herself another drink. "They've thought of everything."

"I don't remember seeing that veil before." Mom swiftly changed the subject as Aunt Ginny refilled Mom's champagne and handed it back.

"Isn't it lovely?" I asked and touched the circlet of baby's breath and the satin-trimmed edges of a veil that fell to the bottom of the gown. "Carol let me borrow it."

That made Mom sit up straight and raise her chin. "You didn't ask to use my veil?"

I shrugged. "You never offered, and when Carol showed it to me, I knew it was a perfect match for my dress. It would be my something borrowed."

"I didn't offer because I expected to go dress shopping with you. But you were always too busy with your fudge shop and everything else you do that keeps you from visiting your mother." She took a tissue out of the box near the bed and dabbed her eyes. "Bridal dress shopping is important to a mother. It's an event we have in common, and you robbed me of it."

She gently blew her nose to emphasize how badly I'd hurt her.

I started to apologize when Jenn caught my eye and shook her head.

"Oh, please," Aunt Ginny said. "You eloped and didn't even tell our mom until you had that ring on your finger. If you're talking about denying a mother, you practically stuck out your tongue at ours and made a gesture we won't talk about here."

"Well, I—"

"That's right," Aunt Ginny cut her off. "You did that. At the very least, your daughter wants you to be at her wedding and this dress fitting. Isn't that, right?" Aunt Ginny didn't even look at me.

I glanced at Jenn, who subtly motioned for me to agree. "That's right, Mom."

Mom didn't answer. Instead, it was as if she realized she had a full flute of champagne in her hand and took a few sips.

"I love those shoes," Jenn said and ate a piece of cheese from a toothpick.

"Mom helped me pick them out," I said with emphasis. "I'd lift my skirt to show them off, but I think Esmerelda would kill me."

"Not kill you," Esmerelda answered seriously. "Poke you with pins, but not kill you."

Everyone laughed, and some of the tension left the room. I wished I could have another drink, but the gown was more important.

"Turn around and face the windows," Esmerelda ordered. I did. And she hemmed the back of the dress.

I could hear Jenn chatting with my mom, trying to get her on our side when it came to the wedding plans. Aunt Ginny stepped up and stood beside me as we both looked out the window.

"It's a gorgeous view, isn't it?" I asked. "I've never been in an upper guest room. I usually only see this view from the porch."

"The grounds are immaculate," Aunt Ginny said. "Isn't it amazing how private the grounds are? I mean, from the sidewalk or even a carriage, you can only see a bit of lawn."

"I think the way they designed the grounds lower on the hill and then surrounded the roadside with hedges really is wonderful," I said.

A thought occurred to me as Aunt Ginny went on to say, "Why, I could barely tell there was a pool."

"I hadn't realized that before," I said. What I didn't say was that might explain why no one saw Velma's murder.

Chapter 18

"This is Carol's house." Aunt Ginny and I headed up to the porch. We could hear the laughing and chatting inside, and Aunt Ginny grinned.

"What does Carol's husband think of this not-really-a-book-club book club?"

"He's fine with it," I replied. "It gives Carol something to do while he's away, and he is always on some outdoor trip or another. This week, he's fishing with a buddy down in South Carolina."

"With the wonderful fishing available in the Great Lakes, it's strange he goes all the way to South Carolina."

I shrugged and knocked on the door. We heard footsteps come our way, and Carol opened the door. "Allie, Ginny, you're finally here. Come in." Carol gave me and Aunt Ginny hugs. "Let me take your jackets." She hung them in her coat closet and welcomed us both into the living room. But first I took my shoes off, and, following my lead, so did Aunt Ginny. "Everyone, Allie's here!" Carol said. "And she brought her Aunt Ginny. I'm sorry, but I can't remember your last name."

"Olds," Aunt Ginny and I said at the same time, which made us both giggle.

"Hi, Ginny!" they all said together.

Carol waved for us to sit. "It seems Ginny isn't our only new member tonight. This is my niece, Mallory Smith. She's staying with me this weekend before she runs off to Paris for the summer."

Mallory gave us a little wave. Her light brown hair had beautiful blond streaks and she wore a cute blue floral dress with a forest-green sweater that made her eyes look blue-green.

"Next to Mallory is Judith Schmidt, and next to her in the blue wingback chair is Mary O'Malley. To her right is Laura Morgan, then Betty Olway, Irma Gooseman, and Barbara Vissor." All of the ladies wore cropped pants in various shades and matching patterned shirts. They looked like a fashion shoot for seniors.

Aunt Ginny and I took a seat on the couch, and I turned to Mallory. "Hi, Mallory," I said. "I'm Allie."

"Nice to meet you," she said politely. "I've heard so much about you. You are practically a celebrity."

"No, simply normal," I replied.

"Sure." Aunt Ginny laughed. "Even I know better than that."

"Can I get you ladies something to drink?" Carol asked. "I have red wine, white wine, coffee, hot tea, pop, or water."

"I'll have a white wine, please," Aunt Ginny said. "Can I help you get anything?"

"Oh, no," Carol replied. "Thank you, but I enjoy this part. Allie, what can I get you?"

"I'll have the same."

"There are snacks on the buffet." She pointed to the buffet in the dining room, which was open to the living room.

"It's really delicious," Betty said, leaning in. "She has a cheese plate, a fruit plate, and a vegetable plate. Later she'll serve homemade cookies and coffee."

"How wonderful!" Aunt Ginny said, with no snobbery or malice. "Shall we get a bite?" she asked, looking at me.

"Sure." I rose with Aunt Ginny and followed her to the buffet.

Aunt Ginny picked up a small plate and filled it with a variety of cheese, veggies, and fruit, as well as crackers for the cheese. "That Gruyere looks divine, doesn't it?"

"Yes, it does." As we filled our small plates, I asked. "What do you think of the ladies?"

"They seem very nice, and intelligent as well."

I had clearly underestimated Aunt Ginny, like she said. Then I began to wonder if all the family's hysterics were because no one wanted to show that they didn't live up to the impossible Chase family legend. Perhaps most of them, if not all of them, didn't even like that way of life. I needed to have a talk with Mom.

We returned to the couch just as Carol emerged with our drinks. The wine was chilled perfectly and tasted like butter on my tongue.

"Shall we start?" Carol asked and pulled out the murder board the ladies usually made to show a time line and suspects. "Even though we all know that Myrtle didn't do this heinous thing, the police think otherwise. At least they haven't arrested her yet. Poor thing, it would kill her."

"We're all certain she was set up to take the blame," Irma continued. "The murder weapon was a large rock that had blood and hair on it. It sat near Velma's dead body and, unfortunately, too close to Myrtle not to be noticed."

"Judith, you were to ask around and dig out any rumors about anyone else who might be very unhappy with Velma," Carol said. "Is there anything to report?"

"Yes," Judith said. "Velma was seen on her phone outside the Senior Center. Whoever she talked to must have been arguing, because Velma's free hand moved quite swiftly, and we all know she talks, I mean talked, with her hands."

"Oh, can we get her phone records?" Aunt Ginny asked.

"Unfortunately, no," I said. "Rex can, but he never reveals anything about his investigation."

"Not even to his bride?" Aunt Ginny asked.

"Especially not to his bride," everyone in the room answered in unison and laughed.

When I finished wiping the tears of laughter from my eyes, I explained. "Rex knows I investigate and worries that I'll get hurt, and frankly, I do sometimes."

"But she always gets her man," Betty said.

"Maybe we're looking at this all wrong," Laura said. "What if it's not Velma they hate but Myrtle. What better way to make her pay than to see her go to jail in handcuffs for the rest of her life?"

"That's a lot of hate," Mallory said. "I love Mackinac Island, and I sincerely doubt anyone here could have that much hate in their hearts."

"True, everyone who lives here is wonderful," Judith said. "But sometimes it gets like Peyton Place around here."

"Where?" Mallory asked.

"Okay, that's a little too old for you," Judith said.

"It was a book first," Mary said. "It made quite the splash in its day. Grace Metalious was a great writer."

"I haven't read it." Mallory looked at me for help. I shrugged to let her know I was as lost as she was.

"What about that one in the cul-de-sac. What was the name of that show?" Betty asked.

"*Knots Landing*," Irma said. "I used to love to watch that."

Mallory and I were lost again. "Oh, goodness, we forget how very young you are," Mary said. "What we're trying to say is that, even though we're like a big loving family, brothers and sisters squabble all the time."

"Sometimes things get out of hand," Judith said. "Then when you toss in the wealthy families who have been coming here to summer for generations, well, things can certainly get interesting. Especially if two or more of the families are business competitors."

"I'm sure they put any animosity down for a vacation," Mallory said.

"Hardly," Laura spoke up.

"Let's go back to the thought that Myrtle is the real target of hate. Why not kill Myrtle and dispose of the body in the lake? It was the closest place to hide a body," Carol said. "You wouldn't even need a rock. You could drown her, and no one would be the wiser when she washed ashore."

"Maybe Velma saw something she shouldn't have and ran," Aunt Ginny said. "The killer most likely couldn't catch her in time to keep her from talking. So they picked up the closest thing nearby and threw it to try and trip her. But when they chucked it, it hit her head instead and killed her."

"Yes," I said. "That could explain why no one saw her get killed. The killer could have been standing on the lake side of the bushes and couldn't be seen from the sidewalk."

"Like the lawn from the Grand Hotel," Aunt Ginny said. "You can't really see it, even though it's very large."

"I never knew it had a swimming pool," I said. "But the only time I'd ever been inside was for the Fudge Off contest. We didn't exactly have time to have a leisurely look at the hotel or the grounds."

"I worked there for ten years after I graduated from high school," Mary said. "It's actually quite beautiful, both inside and the lawns outside."

"I agree. We're staying there," Aunt Ginny said.

I took a couple of big gulps from my wine. "It feels like we're going around in circles. What we know is that Velma and Myrtle had a spat in the library about books. That doesn't seem to be unusual. Especially since the rivalry had been going on since high school. If one actually wanted to kill the other, they would have done it years ago."

"That means the other two theories are the most

likely," Irma said. "Not the only reasonable theories, but the most likely ones."

"That is, until we come up with something better," Laura said. Then she looked at Mallory and Aunt Ginny. "It does happen from time to time."

"What do you think happened next?" Aunt Ginny asked.

"Most certainly, the real killer was in the crowd watching the whole scene," Judith said.

"Myrtle was first on the scene, of course. Then Allie."

"Wait, what made you hurry toward the scene?" Laura asked me.

"I found Velma's and Myrtle's books on the ground. The ones they fought over. I thought it was really odd that both women would drop their books like a trail. I remember thinking, what happened? I ran in the direction of the books, which were on the other side of the bushes, and there was Velma, motionless on the ground, and Myrtle sitting right beside her, crying like her heart was broken."

"We were second on the scene," Carol said, pointing to herself and Irma.

"That's about the time a crowd began to gather. Someone must have texted Richard, because he came barreling around the corner, aghast at what he saw."

"I did see someone peeking at the scene from the other side of the bushes," I said.

"Oh," Aunt Ginny said and put a hand over her mouth. "Do you think you saw the killer?"

"Maybe," I said. "Or maybe it was a fudgie." I glanced at Mallory, remembering she was a visitor along with Aunt Ginny. "A fudgie is our fun pet name for tourist."

"Ah," Aunt Ginny said. "Because they come for the fudge and stay for the fun."

"Exactly," I said. "Anyway, what if it was a fudgie who heard the commotion and peeked between the bushes to see what was going on? Or they could have gone around the crowd to take video to put on their YouTube page or a selfie for their influencer page."

"Those kids and their selfies." Aunt Ginny shook her head.

Mallory and I looked at each other, rolled our eyes and shook our heads at the words "those kids."

"Did you see where one of them got hurt by a buffalo when they were taking a selfie?" Aunt Ginny continued.

"True," Irma said, "but there are a lot of people out there who would pay a pretty penny for an exclusive crime-scene video or photograph."

"Paparazzi here on the island?" Mary scoffed. "Seems ridiculous."

"Not as silly as you'd think," Laura said. "True crime is very popular right now. Remember those two video bloggers who followed Allie around? It's the same thing."

"Oh, you should have seen the paparazzi tromping everywhere on the island terrorizing everyone when *Somewhere in Time* was being shot here," Carol said.

"*Somewhere in Time*?" Mallory asked me.

I leaned toward her. "It's an old, romantic movie starring Christopher Reeve."

"Oh," she said. "That's the guy in the wheelchair."

"He was so handsome," Betty said.

Judith smacked Betty teasingly on the arm. "Snap out of it. You were too old for him, even then."

"I was not," Betty replied. "He was twenty-seven and I was thirty-seven. Well within the acceptable dating range."

"More like forty-nine," Laura said, and everyone laughed, including Betty.

"Well, ladies, I've got to go," I said. "Aunt Ginny, do you want to stay?"

She stood. "I'll go with you, Allie. Ladies, nice to meet you."

"You, too," they all said at the same time. You could tell they had grown up with each other.

"Oh, Allie, before you go," Carol said, "what do you need us to do next?"

I took a deep breath. What was I going to have them do? I didn't know myself.

Aunt Ginny winked at me. "Ladies, you know this island backward and forward, right?"

"Yes," they said in unison again, and it was kind of creepy.

"Do you think you could figure out where the killer might have taken her and killed her in the—" She looked at me.

"Fifteen or twenty minutes?" I said.

"Between the time Myrtle left and the time Allie found them. It had to have been close enough that the killer could see when Myrtle walked out of the library. Maybe they dropped Velma's books like breadcrumbs."

"Maybe Myrtle followed the books and then was the first one to find her," I finished and looked at her. "Except Myrtle's books were also dropped near Velma's."

"Myrtle could have dropped her books when she saw Velma, and the killer could have picked them up while Myrtle was distracted and planted them near Velma's," Mallory said.

"It could have been a ploy to confuse us," I replied thoughtfully.

"That's a good theory. See I told you I love to watch true crime and have fun with the puzzles in cozy mysteries." Aunt Ginny winked at me. "Ladies?" she asked.

"We're on it," Carol said.

"Good night, everyone." She took my arm and turned me toward the door.

"Good night," they said. This time not in unison.

Chapter 19

"You, okay?" Rex asked when he came through the back door.

"Yes," I answered, still stunned about what Aunt Ginny had said. My pets were in my lap trying to get my attention, but all I could do was absently pet them as I went over the conversation we had on the way home.

"You and I are more alike than you think," Aunt Ginny had said. "I love sleuthing."

"I didn't know," I'd replied. "Does anybody else know?"

"Oh, goodness, no. My mother wouldn't have stood for it. Besides, those were different times, when it truly wasn't safe for a woman to chase murderers."

"But you did?" I'd asked.

"Oh, I did," she'd replied with the biggest smile. "All I had to do was call in an anonymous tip."

"How did you collect any reward money if you were anonymous?"

"I didn't," she'd said. "Why would I? I had plenty. I asked them to donate it to a food pantry or a safe home for women."

"Are you sure you're okay?" Rex asked, drawing my attention back to the present. "You haven't changed your mind about your family, have you?" After securing his service revolver in the gun safe, he went to the fridge, grabbed a beer, and poured me a white wine.

"No, I haven't." I took the wine happily and drank a good quarter of the glass.

Rex raised an eyebrow, pulled me close to his chest, and kissed me until I felt warm and relaxed. "Now tell me why you're so distracted."

"I . . . I'm confused."

"About?"

"Aunt Ginny." I told him as much as I could about her, without giving away the fact that I'd rather be sleuthing than worrying about our wedding. I was afraid it would hurt him.

"I knew you couldn't resist," he said. "Even with the wedding getting closer every day, and with your mom and her family here."

"I'm under a lot of pressure," I said. "And when Irma asked me to look into it, it felt right."

"It gave you something to think about besides our pending wedding." He kissed my hand and put it against his heart. "We can still elope."

"Mom would never forgive us. She'd stop her visits altogether."

He chuckled. "Isn't that a good thing?"

That made me laugh, too. Then I sobered. "She moved my dress fitting to her room by slipping Esmerelda five hundred dollars, which she deserves, but that's unimportant. Mom's excuse was that her bedroom sitting area had a raised floor and it would be easier to pin the hem."

"Sounds like her," he said.

"After fitting my dress, Mom showed Esmerelda the Dior, and I saw how her face lit up. She looked from the dress to me, and I swear she said 'please' without saying a word. Even Jenn and Aunt Ginny ogled it. I gave in and put it on. Everyone sighed."

"Even Jenn?" Rex asked. "I thought she was there to stop your mom from pressuring you."

"She was supposed to be, but Jenn wanted to see it, too," I said. "Aunt Ginny wasn't much help either. Mom plied them with champagne the entire time. At least they made a big deal about my dress."

"It's been quite a day for you," he said, "hasn't it?"

I laughed. "Wait until tomorrow. You get to have dinner with what's left of my relatives. I hope you have a nice suit. The only saving grace is that Dad will be there this time, and he doesn't put up with any nonsense."

"I like your dad," Rex said. "I always have. He has a good head on his shoulders, and you always seem more relaxed around him. As for a nice suit, I have a couple. I picked up my blue suit at the cleaners this morning."

"Oh, that's right," I said. "You're wearing a gray suit at the wedding."

"With a lilac tie." He took my hand, pulled me up.

"It's late for you. Come on and get ready for bed. I'll tuck you in. Tomorrow will be a busy day."

It was then I noticed that my wineglass was somehow empty. I shook my head at myself. I don't normally drink, and suddenly I was having wine at least twice a day just to get through these demanding events. I put the glass down, and both Mal and Mella followed me into the bedroom.

I tossed and turned all night. It felt like my life was completely out of my control. From my mom's antics, to standing up to family, to the pressure of living up to the island's "wedding of the year." Not to mention that my sleuthing skills had been off so much that when Aunt Ginny stepped in, she did a much better job.

I was downstairs on time, but sluggish all morning, and finally Roxanne pushed me out of the fudge shop after the ten o'clock demonstration.

"Go. You're making me nervous around all this hot sugar," Roxanne said. "Besides, I've got this, remember? You've trained me to handle everything. I'm taking over the fudge shop until after the wedding. You're far too distracted to do any good here."

"I guess you're right," I said and took off my chef's coat.

"Of course I'm right," she said. "Now don't come back until after your honeymoon. You're exhausting yourself, and it'll show in your wedding pictures. Do you want that?"

"No," I said. "No, I don't."

"Hmm," Roxanne said with her hands on her hips. "And when was the last time you took a vacation?"

I frowned. "I'm not sure. I went to see my parents a couple times at Christmas, but I'm usually busy with Christmas orders and shipping and such."

"Uh-huh." She nodded. "And when was the last time you had a girl's weekend with your friends or even had coffee and a catch-up?"

"I keep meaning to."

"That's it. No more worrying about the business. I don't want to see you down here. I have the fudge shop, and Frances has the hotel. You have to trust us. And don't get any ideas. Frances will keep an eye out to make sure you don't try to sneak in here."

"Okay, okay," I said, my heart sinking. Maybe I wasn't as needed here as I thought.

"Don't worry, we do need you," she said as if reading my mind. "But this is an intervention, and Frances agrees. You need to start taking two days off a week."

"But—"

She held up her hand in a "stop" sign. "No excuses. Now sleep in. Eat something, and drink plenty of water."

I glanced through the glass surrounding the fudge shop. Frances watched and raised an eyebrow at me, as if daring me to try to change things. I had indeed been set up. It made me wonder whether Rex was involved in this, too. I had a feeling he had something to do with it.

Stepping out of the fudge shop, I looked back one more time, and Roxanne gave me a "don't even think about it" look. I sighed, then turned toward Frances.

"It's for your own good," she said.

Mal ran to me and slid the last few feet. It was something she loved to do. I picked her up and headed for the stairs.

"I'm going to change and take Mal for a walk," I said as I passed Frances, unsure whether I was hurt, angry, or relieved. Maybe I was all three. I realized that it would all sort itself out and that perhaps they weren't wrong. Plus, it would give me more time to find Velma's killer.

Chapter 20

Spiced White-Chocolate Bonbons

Ingredients

1½ cups of white-chocolate chips
1½ tablespoons of butter
2 teaspoons of cinnamon
½ teaspoon of ginger
¼ teaspoon of cloves
¼ teaspoon of nutmeg
½ cup of whipping cream
2½ cups of white-chocolate melting wafers

Directions

In a glass bowl, place the white-chocolate chips, butter, cinnamon, ginger, cloves, and nutmeg. In a heavy saucepan, heat the whipping cream; just as it starts to boil, remove from the heat. Pour into the glass bowl and allow to rest until the butter and chips begin to melt. Whisk until combined and smooth. Cover and refrigerate at least 2 hours until set.

Line cookie sheet with parchment paper. Scoop a spoonful of the white chocolate mixture into damp hands and roll it into a ball. (You can use a melon baller, if you prefer, but you must warm it in hot water every two or three balls and dry it completely before using it.) Place the balls on the cookie sheet and put it back into the refrigerator for 10 minutes.

Place the wafers in a microwave-safe bowl and microwave for 30 seconds at a time, stirring in between the 30 seconds until the chocolate is smooth. Using a fork, dip each ball into the melted wafers; use a spoon to ensure it is well coated and place it on the cookie sheet. Repeat with all balls. Allow truffles to set and store in the refrigerator. Makes 24 truffles.

I showered, dressed in jeans and a sweatshirt, put Mal in her harness and left through the back door of my apartment. While Mal did her business, I texted Rex. *Did you help stage this "stop working so much" intervention?*

He texted back. *It's not a bad thing. You need to take better care of yourself.*

I texted back a GIF of a scene from a horror movie in which the actor is screaming "noooo" in terror over and over. After a long pause, I texted. *Fine. It's strange to admit I need it and hard to let someone else take care of everything.*

I know. He replied. *We're looking out for you.*

What do I do now?

Rest your brain. Have lunch with a friend. If you'll remember, your friends like to hear from you instead of you disappearing on them, only to say hi in passing.

I'll try. I texted.

Why don't you start with Liz? I heard that Angus isn't doing well. He texted. *And when was the last time you saw Sophie?*

Now you're just guilting me. I texted.

You talk to Carol and Irma way more than your girlfriends.

I sighed. He wasn't wrong. *Be safe out there. Love you.*

Love you, too.

The first thing I did was walk Mal over to the *Town Crier*, our local newspaper. I was a little nervous going inside. Besides not seeing Liz in what seemed like forever, I'd only asked Jenn to be my matron of honor. Otherwise, I didn't have bridesmaids. Was Liz upset? There was nothing to do but bite the bullet and find out. We walked up to the door slowly. Mal wanted to make sure there was nothing interesting to smell before we went inside. Had it really been that long since our last visit?

"Come on, silly," I said and tugged on her harness. "Let's go see Liz." We stepped inside, with Mal in the lead. The bells over the door let them know someone had entered.

"Be right with you," I heard, followed a bout of coughing that had me concerned. Angus McElroy walked out from the back. "Well, look what the cat dragged in," he said. "Are you here to kill another old man? I still have my lucky rabbit's foot."

"Angus," I said with a wide smile and moved around the desk to give him a big hug. He always reminded me of Papa Liam. Two gruff old men with hearts of gold. "How are you? I heard you weren't doing well."

"Who told you that? I'm perfectly fine." He looked at me under bushy white eyebrows and then started coughing. I patted him on the back.

"You don't sound good," I said.

"It's only a bit of a cold," he replied.

"Hmm," I said.

"Enough about me." He brushed my concerns aside. "How're the wedding plans going?"

"Peachy," I said. "My family showed up two weeks early and made an ugly scene."

"Oh, yes, it made for good copy." He had a twinkle in his eye. "Especially when we heard you kicked them out and most of them left on their yacht the next day."

I closed my eyes and shook my head in resignation. "Family. Mom stayed, of course, with her own ideas for the wedding. None of which matches mine."

He laughed. "Sounds like a mom."

"Really? Then why wasn't she part of the planning in the first place?"

"Let me guess," he said. "She started planning, and you shut her down and didn't let her plan even one little thing."

He made it sound like this was my fault. "She wanted

the opposite of what I wanted—heck, what I needed—and instead of understanding, she arrived two weeks early to simply overrule me and get what she wanted anyway."

"What does she want that's bad?" he asked.

"She wants a quiet wedding with only family. The reception would be a six-course meal ending with the wedding cake. She scoffed at the idea of inviting everyone on the island and a potluck reception."

"And what's wrong with what you planned?" Angus crossed his arms.

"It's beneath a Chase." I imitated my mom. "Chase is my mom's maiden name. Never mind that I'm a McMurphy and so is she."

"Your mom is an interesting person," he answered. "Are you looking into Velma's murder? Anything new you might want to share?"

"You know I can't say anything. Didn't the police give a statement?" I said.

"They gave the usual 'the investigation is ongoing.' Yadda, yadda, yadda. There's really nothing to write about. They like to keep the details as private as they can." He frowned. "I don't know why they bother doing that. Nearly half the island is already involved in the investigation. Of the people the police didn't question face-to-face, they hope anyone with information will stop by the station. But as far as we can tell, no one has come forward."

"That's the part that keeps bothering me," I told him. "Why didn't anyone see anything? The murder took place in broad daylight in the park and as close to a sidewalk as possible."

"It does seem strange," he said. "If I remember correctly, it wasn't even rainy that day. Which means that whoever did it didn't care about being seen."

"Off the record," I said, "I don't think she was killed there. I think the killer did it out of sight and then arranged the body to frame Myrtle."

"That's an interesting idea," he said.

"You can't publish that," I said. "It's a thought with no substantial evidence to prove it." I didn't mention that it had to have happened within a few feet of the person I saw in the bushes. In fact, I didn't mention the person in the bushes at all. Why? Mostly because I didn't really see their face, and even if the footprints were small, at the time I couldn't tell if it was a man or a woman.

"I understand. Now, are you here to see Liz?" He coughed again, then gave me the stink eye, as if I should have been coming around more often.

"Yes, we keep missing each other, and I hoped she might be free for lunch," I said.

"I don't know her schedule, but she's in the back." He pointed with his thumb.

"Thanks." I went back and found her setting up the printer. "Liz?" I wanted to make sure I didn't startle her.

"Allie!" She gave me a big hug. "What are you doing here? Don't you have wedding stuff to get done and fudge to sell?"

"Nope," I said. "Jenn is conquering the wedding stuff, and Roxanne kicked me out of the fudge shop."

"Good, it's about time," she said. "I don't know how

you get everything done." Then she studied me. "Let me guess. You're also looking into Velma's murder."

"Irma asked me to."

"Shame on her! This close to your wedding! Irma should know better," Liz said.

"It's important to her," I said. "I came by to see if you wanted to get lunch. It's been a long time."

"It has," she agreed. "I figure you needed to spend any free time you had with Rex."

"He's the one who wanted me to check in with you and Sophie."

"Good," Liz said. "Sophie's super busy with her charter airplane business. This week she's flying in a really big group. They won't all fit in her plane and decided it'll be okay to split up into three groups."

"That's great! Good for her," I said.

"And when she's not working, she's with her new guy."

"Sophie's dating?" How could I have missed that? The island is small. I should have run into her on a date.

"She's dating Harry Winston."

"Harry? Really? No wonder he hasn't been around lately," I said with a soft smile.

"Been around?" Liz waggled her brows at me. "Did you two have a fling?"

"No, nothing like that," I assured her. "He wanted to, but I told him that, for me, he was a really good friend. I was in love with Rex, no matter how much my mom preferred Harry over Rex."

"Oh, this is good. Hang on. Let me finish setting up the printer, and we'll go to lunch." I waited until she checked the printer for the right copy and then started the batch. "Okay, good to go." We walked out together, arm in arm.

"What other gossip am I missing?" I asked.

Chapter 21

Catching up with Liz was great fun. She told me that she'd been poking into Velma's death, too. But had come up against a dead end. I would have exchanged notes with her, but I knew she wanted something to write in an article. I reiterated that I didn't have enough information to draw any conclusions. She didn't believe me, of course, but that didn't matter to either of us.

After we parted with a big hug and a promise to have lunch every other week, Mal and I went back to the scene of the crime. Or at least the staged scene. As I looked around and walked the bushes, I became increasingly certain the murder didn't happen here. Where did it happen?

"Allie," Aunt Ginny appeared from the opposite side of the hedge. She gave me a hug and a kiss on the cheek. Mal wanted in on it, and Aunt Ginny was happy to oblige.

"What brings you out here?" I asked her.

"The same thing that brings you out," she replied. "I don't know what I expected to find. How about you?"

"I hoped for some insight," I said. "If the murderer killed Velma somewhere else and carried her body to where she was discovered, they had to be pretty strong. Velma was small. But dead bodies can be heavier than living bodies."

"Hmm," Aunt Ginny said. "It could be a large, strong person or two people."

"It'd never occurred to me that there might be a second person." Although that would explain how they could have come from somewhere else, making it look like friends resting in the park as they staged the scene. Why go to the trouble of staging the scene? Was it to frame Myrtle? Or to give them time to hide the fact that they were the murderers?

"If you assume there was more than one killer, it would certainly change the direction of the investigation. Where do you think we should start?"

"Let's start at the beginning," I said. "Why would two killers plan to kill Velma and then stage the scene in the park? Why not bury the body in the woods, or take it out and dump it in the middle of the lake?"

"Good question," Aunt Ginny said. "The killers must have wanted Velma to be found in the park. What if it was a message to someone else that they would be next."

"That makes sense," I said. "That means the murder

was most likely premeditated. But how did they know Velma would be at the library?"

"Most people have a regular routine. You mentioned the new books on the shelf. Maybe she went to the library," Ginny said, "on the same day and time every week."

"Could be," I agreed. "What had Velma gotten into that she was killed as a message to others?"

"Was the book club looking into another crime?" Aunt Ginny asked.

"They would have told me the minute they discovered Velma dead." I tapped my chin. "Money is always the most likely motive, then anger, rivalry, and revenge. With all the new betting sites online, maybe there's a group on the island that pools their money to place bigger bets."

"And Velma could have not paid into the pool and still taken her share of the winnings. It could be why she was looking into her Social Security funds," Aunt Ginny said.

"We need to know who gains from Velma's death. Whether it was for money or revenge, something about Velma made her a target." My thoughts whirled with possible motives. Of our two unlikely suspects, what did Richard and Myrtle have to gain from Velma's death?

It struck me that Aunt Ginny had asked me a question. "I'm sorry, what?" I asked.

"Did Velma have any recent arguments besides the book stuff with Myrtle?" Aunt Ginny repeated.

"That's a good question," I said. "But why stage the scene if she was killed out of anger?"

"Maybe to throw the police off the scent?"

I stopped in my tracks. "I hadn't thought of that. If that's the case, who is the least likely person to stage the scene?"

"Everyone in the book club would know that burying the body provides a greater chance of it being found, and tossing it in the lake, with its currents, would mean there's a chance of it washing up on shore."

"Why not simply put it in plain sight," I said. "And lead the police on a merry goose chase. I struggle with the idea that anyone in the book club did this."

"That's because you're too close to them, and the killer might be counting on that," Aunt Ginny said. "Or it could be someone the book club ladies trust enough to tell about their investigations."

"Which means we've going to have to keep our investigation out of the book club while allowing them to continue helping," I said.

"Seems like that's a lot for a bride-to-be with a family to attend to," Aunt Ginny said. "Is there anyone you can trust to do your part of the investigation?"

Aunt Ginny was right, of course. But who could I trust? Mal took that moment to bark and wag her stump tail. I glanced over to see who she barked at. It was Audrey Davis, the librarian. I waved her down.

While Aunt Ginny filled Audrey in on what was going on, Mal and I went to visit Irene. She was one of Carol's closest friends, but I hadn't seen her in ages, and she hadn't been at any of the book club meetings. Maybe she knew something the others didn't. I knocked on the door and hoped that she was home this late in the afternoon and not off visiting her son.

Then I heard footsteps, and the door opened. “Allie!” she said and gave me a quick hug.

“Is now a bad time to visit?” I asked.

“No, no,” she reassured me. “Come on in. Hello, Mal.” She bent down to pick up my dog and scratch her behind her ears. There was nothing Mal liked better than to be picked up and loved on. From the expression on her little face she was in doggy heaven. I took off my shoes and entered Irene’s small ranch home, which looked a lot like Carol’s. The walls were painted a lovely soft blue that mirrored the sky. Her couch was a green velour, and her maple-wood floors were covered with an area carpet colored blue, green, and cream.

Irene was a lovely woman in her seventies, with long white hair that used to be red. Her eyes were blue and filled with intelligence.

I sat on the couch, and she returned Mal to my lap. “Can I get you anything to drink?” she asked.

“Don’t go to too much trouble.” I said. “Water would be fine.” I knew that if I said, “Nothing, thank you,” she would be insulted.

“Nonsense, I have some nice iced tea,” she offered.

“Oh, that does sound good.”

She left and was back with a tray that held a bowl full of water, two iced teas, and a plateful of cookies. She set it down on the oak coffee table in front of me, placed the bowl of water carefully on the carpet for Mal, and handed me a glass.

“What brings you over?” she asked as she sat next to me and took a sip of her tea.

"I haven't seen you in a long while," I said. "Have you stopped going to the book club?"

She gave me a small smile. "Thank you for missing me. I've been spending a lot of time with my sister in St. Ignace. She's doing poorly and had to enter a nursing home."

"I'm sorry to hear that." I drew my eyebrows together with concern. "Caregiving can take a toll on a person. Are you taking time to care of yourself?"

"I'm fine," she said. "I get a power walk in daily and do a little yoga."

"Are you getting time with friends? I've noticed you and Carol don't seem to be as close as you used to be."

"Carol and I had a bit of a falling-out." She sipped her tea.

I copied her. The tea was smooth, with a touch of lemon. "I'm sorry to hear that."

She shrugged. "We'll make up soon enough. This is something that happens when people see too much of each other. Think of us as siblings who fight. They still love each other, but there are times when there's a difference of opinion and it escalates until they decide to not be friends for a while."

"Would I be prying too much if I ask you what the argument was about?" I put my glass of tea down and leaned toward her.

"No, I suppose not," she said with a sigh and sat back. "I heard that Carol would rather spend time with Irma than me, but I dismissed it. Then I found out that Carol had a tea party and didn't invite me." Her grip tightened around her glass, and her knuckles turned white. I could see a flash of anger in her eyes. "I went straight to Carol and told her that I thought we were good friends. Why would she not include me in such an event? Her excuse was that she didn't want me to feel bad about turning her down because I needed to go take care of my sister."

"I see." I petted Mal without taking my eyes off of Irene. I really was concerned for her because I'd never seen her upset.

"Don't tell me I'm silly for letting this upset me," she said, not really looking at or talking to me.

"Who told you that?" I asked.

"Judith did," she replied, her anger spilling over to Judith. "As far as I'm concerned, Carol could have invited me and let me choose. I could have stayed for the party, if I'd known about it. Instead, she snubbed me, and like it or not, she did it intentionally."

I let Mal go. She bounced off my lap and into Irene's to comfort her. "You're right, that's very mean. I can't believe Carol would do such a thing."

"I spoke to Laura, and she told me that Carol had sided with Irma over something I'd said that she took the wrong way."

"But you're good friends with both. Why didn't you explain?"

"I did," she said. "But they didn't believe me, and, well, here it is until I apologize and they forgive me. I'm not going to apologize for something I said being misinterpreted, even after I explained what I meant. Irma and Carol are stubborn old fools."

I gave her a hug. "Keep me posted about this, please."

"And before you ask," Irene said, "Velma had a falling-out with her friend Tammy over something Velma heard

Tammy said about her. That Julie, you know, Richard's second wife, told Tammy about what Velma said, then went with Tammy to confront Velma. She told them they were wrong. She would never say such a thing, but Julie insisted she had. One thing led to another, and friends who loved each other vowed never to speak to each other again."

"Wow," I said. "Do you think Tammy would kill her over something like that?"

"I doubt Tammy would, but there are others who would," was her response.

"Any on the island?" I ask.

"Perhaps a few," she answered. "I can let you know if I hear or see anything."

"Thanks." I stood to leave. "Stay away from any killers, okay?"

"I'll try," she replied.

After we left, I made a mental note to text Aunt Ginny that Julie French was not only at the crime scene but had inserted herself into a conflict between Velma and Tammy. Maybe she was someone we should follow up on.

Chapter 22

"Don't forget, we meet for dinner in less than three hours," Mom said over the phone.

"I know, Mom. We're going to the yacht club this time, right?" I asked.

"Yes," she replied. "Wear that lovely dress I bought for you. What's Rex going to wear?"

"I don't know," I said, making her nervous on purpose. "I don't see why his police uniform wouldn't work. You and Daddy have already met him, and so has everyone at the yacht club. And you don't want to pick a fight or degrade the island and the people here, now do you?"

Mom started to say something when I heard my father clearing his throat very loudly. There was a pause. "Certainly not," Mom said. "Wouldn't he prefer to wear a suit coat?"

"You're going to have to trust me, no matter what he wears," I said, "Rex will be allowed in the yacht club."

"Okay, dear." She sounded disappointed. "Your father and I are looking forward to dinner. Please don't be late."

"Why? Uncle John and Aunt Ginny no longer need to be impressed," I said.

"Your father and I have preordered a special meal to celebrate," she said. "I would hate for you to keep the chef and his staff waiting. That would be disrespectful and rude, don't you think?"

Touché, Mom, I thought. "I would never dream of that."

"Good," she said. "Our hair appointment is in thirty minutes. Would you prefer I come pick you up or will you meet me there?"

I'd forgotten about the hair appointment. It was the third time this week. "Mom, I'm going to have to skip the appointment. Don't worry, I'll look appropriate for dinner tonight."

"But you really need help with your hair." I could hear the insult and frustration in her tone at the thought that I was ignoring her plans. She paused, and I could imagine Dad giving her a look to say that she was overstepping.

"Fine," she said. "Oh, and I made grooming appointments for both of your pets for a week from today."

"Okaaay . . ." I drew the sound out.

"Oh, I didn't tell you? It seems as though I did," she said. "Jenn told me that Mal and Mella are in the wedding party. Is that not right?"

"That's right," I said.

"I know you will be too busy and too stressed to take them to the groomer in Mackinaw City and back. Your cousin Babs and her twins will be here, and she has already agreed to take them and bring them back."

"Cousin Babs?"

"Surely you remember Babs," Mom said. "She's a little eccentric, but then her mom, your Great Aunt Cecil, never was able to control her."

"I don't remember inviting Babs," I said.

"If I remember correctly, you told me I could invite whoever I wanted."

"Mom, how many family members did you invite?" I tried to sound calm.

"You remember that my mother came from a family with eight children, and I had to invite them. Then her daughter, Peggy, had six children, and all the cousins had at least four kids, if not more. And then the grandkids. Maybe close to one hundred. I've lost track."

I took a deep breath and was suddenly glad the reception was a potluck. "What about your plan for a small intimate wedding and reception?" I asked.

"When you said the entire island was invited, I saw no reason not to invite the family."

"Mom," I warned, dismayed at yet another one of her tricks.

"Don't worry, dear. I imagine most won't actually come. They'll send gifts, and they should. After all, I certainly spent enough money going to their children's weddings, graduations, and baby showers."

"And for those who do come, where are they going to stay?"

"We've got this, dear," she said. "Your father and I have rented out two entire bed and breakfasts. One of them belongs to that handsome Harry Winston. I told him to bring his parents as well as his lovely plus one. I believe her name is Sophie or something."

Did everyone know about Harry and Sophie but me? "Is there anyone you didn't invite?" I had to work hard to keep the frustration out of my voice.

"I hoped to have a chat with Rex's mother and coordinate outfits. It's only polite. But I couldn't find out anything about them. I know Rex is a public servant, and when I couldn't find out anything about his family, I assumed they were, well, you know."

"No, Mom, I don't know."

She could hear the tone of my voice grow angry. "Your father keeps tapping his watch in that annoying way he does. I'll see you in—what—an hour and a half?"

"Mom, I swear—" but she had already hung up. What other surprises did she have in store? The closer the wedding day approached, the more I wished we'd eloped, like Rex suggested. I'd never thought I'd get married, but now that I was about to, I wanted the dress, the flowers, the cake, and everything that went with it. I have no idea what I was thinking.

"Why so nervous?" Rex asked, He leaned against the bedroom door and watched me get dressed. "It's dinner with your parents and your Aunt Ginny and Uncle John, who, surprisingly, seem really down to earth."

"I don't want a repeat of Wednesday's dinner." I put on the dress and slipped the kitten-heel shoes on.

"You're worried the others will show up uninvited

and there'll be another humiliating show." He zipped me up.

"Yes," I said and studied myself in the mirror, looking for any flaws my mother would complain about.

Rex put his arms around me and held me to him. He looked handsome in his dark blue suit. "See how good we look together? You're going to have people talking for months."

I turned into his arms. "Did you know Harry and Sophie were dating?"

"Everyone knows that," he said. "Why? Are you upset he isn't following you around like a lovesick puppy anymore?"

I pushed him, but he didn't move. "No, Sophie is my dear friend, and I didn't even know she'd met Harry. I feel like I'm losing touch with everyone who's important to me."

"Not everyone," he said and gave me a gentle squeeze. "Come on, you look absolutely heart-stopping." He took my hand. "I'm proud to be at your side."

Rex got my coat. Mal jumped up against me, and I lifted her up. She tried to lick my face, but I had done my makeup and couldn't let her. "Come on, let's get a treat." I put her down, and Mella, hearing the word "treat," jumped up on the counter for hers. I handed Mal hers, and she took it and ran to the couch to eat it. I put Mella's in front of her, and she looked at it, as if deciding whether it was worthy of her attention or not.

Rex helped me into the matching coat. "You look distracted."

Even though the yacht club wasn't far, we took a carriage to save me from hurting my feet in the shoes my mother picked out. Once inside, he put his arm around me as the horses clip-clopped slowly down the street. “Allie, tell me what’s going on. Maybe I can help.”

I turned toward him. “Why haven’t I met your family? We should have gone to dinner with them at least once before the wedding. I don’t remember you even inviting them. Are you embarrassed by me?”

He squeezed my hand. “Of course not.”

“Then your family?”

The carriage stopped in front of the club before he could answer. He helped me out. “Are you ready for this?”

“I’m ready,” I said, still worried that there was a reason I hadn’t met his family. Then I imagined my mom meeting them and thought maybe it was for the best.

Chapter 23

My fears were dead-on. When we reached the table, every one of my mom's brothers and sisters were there. I gave Mom the stink eye.

"They were still here after taking the boat out," she explained. "How could I not invite them?"

"Because they weren't invited," I said. I glanced at their contrite faces and sighed. If I kicked them out, I would be making as big a scene as they made at the Grand. Frustrated, I introduced Rex to everyone around the table. Then gave my father a hug and a kiss and whispered, "I can't believe you let Mom do this."

"Give her a chance," he said, soft and low. "I promise it's going to be alright."

Rex waved off the waiter, pulled out my chair for me, and then tucked me in before he sat down next to me. He took my hand and squeezed it, letting me know I had his support.

"Allie, before we begin, your aunts and uncles have something they want to say to you," Mom said.

Spurred on by Uncle John and Aunt Ginny, the others had the good grace to look ashamed for their actions and apologized one by one.

"We went back to the Grand," Uncle Edmund said, "and personally apologized to the chef, her staff, and the waiters. We were entirely out of line, and compensated all of them again and tipped them well."

"That doesn't make up for what you said about the people here. People I love and who are my dearest friends."

"We put a full-page apology in tomorrow's *Town Crier* and sent a generous sum to the island's school," Aunt Felicity said.

"You can't buy these people off," I said with frustration.

"We know," Uncle Wade said. "That's why we made a public apology. It's all we can do."

"You're important to us," Aunt Felicity added. "We hope we can attend your wedding."

Father gave me a kind look, and I reluctantly agreed.

"Best behavior," I said, giving them all the stink eye. "For goodness' sake, act like a true Chase, not some made-up one who looks at others with disdain."

"Thank you," Uncle Wade said.

After that, dinner was filled with pleasant conversation, in which Rex was gently grilled about who he was and why he deserved me. We held hands whenever we could. His strong confidence and impeccable manners comforted me, and at the same time, I realized he was better at handling them than I was. Toward the end, a couple came in who caught my eye. It was Sophie and Harry. I gave a little wave, hoping to catch their attention, but they only had eyes for each other. Something warm filled my heart. It was good to see my friends happy.

Before dessert, I politely got up to go to the ladies' room, promised I'd be back this time, and stopped by their table. "Sophie!" I exclaimed. "It's been ages since I've seen you."

"Allie!" She jumped up and gave me a hug. I'd never seen her in a dress, but she looked lovely in the peacock blue one she wore, far from her usual uniform of cargo pants and a polo. Her blond hair fell past her ears and down her back in gentle waves. I stepped back, our arms still entangled, and looked at her. "You look gorgeous," I declared. "I love that dress."

"And look at you," she said with a soft smile. "Bride-to-be, you look amazing."

Harry stood the whole time and finally cleared his throat. "Allie, nice to see you."

"You, too, Harry," I said. "I didn't mean to exclude you." We hugged, and I whispered in his ear. "You don't know how happy it makes me to see you happy." Then I added, "I expect you both at the wedding. It means a lot to me."

The two reached for each other. "Of course we will," Harry said, without taking his eyes from Sophie's face.

She finally looked at me. "We're excited for you and will be there no matter what."

In the restroom, as I washed my hands and checked my hair and makeup, Julie French stepped next to me to touch up her lipstick.

"Hello," I said. "How are you and Richard doing after the loss of Velma?"

She shrugged and didn't take her eyes off of herself. "Richard is beside himself, and it was all I could do to get him to go out to dinner tonight. Of course, it hurts to play second fiddle to Velma right now. But what am I supposed to do? I've had to plan the funeral, of course. It's next week Saturday at Trinity Episcopal Church," she said, knowing full well that was when my wedding was and that everyone who lives on Mackinac Island was invited. She patted her hair. "The funeral is at two, and I hope to see you there." As she walked out, she turned to look over her shoulder. "It would be a slap in the face not only to Velma but to Irma, her best friend, if you didn't show up."

A sudden surge of anger had me wanting to punch her, but I restrained myself. The last thing I needed right now was to have her press charges for assault.

Chapter 24

"I can't believe she did that," I said to Rex, as I watched him make eggs and sausage the next morning. I sat at the kitchen bar feeling uncomfortable in jeans and a T-shirt when I should be in my work uniform.

"Julie sounds like someone who desperately needs attention because everyone is focused on Velma, including Richard. She may feel as if she's disappeared from sight, and this is her way of getting noticed."

"That doesn't make it right." He passed a full plate toward me and came around to take the stool next to me and share breakfast. Mal begged beside him, and Mella watched us with keen eyes from the nearby cat tree I'd gotten for her Christmas. "I want to grab her and shake her."

He squeezed my hand. "Honey, you barely know her. Are you letting her become that important to you now, with everything that's going on?" He raised my hand and kissed the back of it.

I grumbled, ate what was on my plate, then reached for my coffee. Suddenly I remembered an important question I'd asked him the night before that he'd never answered. In fact, every time I'd asked, he'd avoided the issue.

"Alright," I said, putting the cup down. "We're days away from the wedding, and I need to know why I've never met your parents and why they haven't been involved in the planning. I know my mom's too involved, but seriously, no involvement? Come to think of it, you've never even talked about your family. You do have a family, right?" Why hadn't I pressed him on this issue years ago? I thought back. I had asked, and he'd always changed the subject. And I didn't want to pry, so I told myself he'd tell me when he was ready, but he never did. "Be honest with me."

He cleared his throat. "I've been meaning to tell you, but there was never a right time."

"We have known each other for how long now? And yet whenever I brought up the subject, you would sidestep the issue. Is it me? Or are they in jail? Did they murder someone?" I knew my questions were ridiculous, but the whole thing was baffling.

He laughed at the last one and took my hand. "Okay, here's the truth. I'm the black sheep of the family."

I narrowed my eyes. "Wait, family? You have siblings you've been hiding?"

He blew out his breath. "I have a brother, Roger, and a sister, Rose."

"Are you serious?"

"Yes," he said. "Let me get through this. It's the first time I've ever told anyone."

"Not even your first two wives?"

"Allie, please, just let me talk." I'd never seen him look so worried, and I squeezed his hand for support. "When I was sixteen, I rebelled against my parents and their lifestyle. I purposely hung out with the wrong kids, let my grades go, and missed curfew. The last straw was when I pawned a pair of my mom's earrings I knew she hated. When my father found out, he hit me and knocked me to the floor. I shook my head and stood, daring him to do it again. When he turned his back on me, I yelled as loud as I could that I never wanted to be like him. I was never going into the family business." He shook his head. "Dad had had enough. He disowned me on the spot."

I gasped as anger went through me. He raised his hand to let me know he wasn't done. "He threw me out and said he never wanted to see or hear from me again."

"You were sixteen, for goodness' sake," I said and held his hand next to my heart. "What did you do?"

"I couch surfed with friends, staying only a week, then moving on. A month later, my mom contacted me and asked me to go to lunch. I was relieved. I'd been scared, and alone. There was money in my bank account, but I had to save it to pay my private school tuition. You know how expensive that is. Who wants to change schools at sixteen? It didn't help that I didn't have an address or apartment. I knew enough to know that Child Services would put me in a foster home if they found out."

"What did your mom say? Did she tell you that your father was wrong, and they wanted you back home?"

"No, she always backed my father and always will."

I bit my tongue and didn't interrupt. No wonder he didn't ever tell this story.

"We met," he went on, "and instead of the hug I expected, she introduced me to Dad's lawyer. He'd drawn up a contract between me and my parents. They would continue to pay for my high school, but only if I went to a military boarding school. If I managed to get into college, they would continue to pay my college fees, including room and board. The catch was I had to send proof to the lawyer that I was indeed in school before, during, and after each semester. I would be on my own in the summers, and above all, I was to never contact anyone in the family again."

"What did you do?" I asked, fighting tears for the boy that he was and anger at the family who did this to him. Even my family, who'd taken away my trust fund, had never disowned me. Yes, though they were a pain, they still loved me.

"What could I do?" he said. "I didn't have that much money or anywhere to go. I simply couldn't believe this was happening. I didn't do anything worse than some of my friends had done. I looked at my mom. She stared at the table and didn't say a word." He paused to collect himself and finished with a shaky voice. "I signed the contract. She and the lawyer didn't even stay for lunch, but they'd paid for it, so I ate as much as I could. After I graduated with a social justice and law degree, I changed my last name. And went through the police academy. The rest you know."

"I want to give them all a piece of my mind!" I hugged him tight. "No wonder you didn't want to be like them. I'm proud of the boy you were then and the man you are now."

He held me until I could feel him relax. "I don't tell anyone because I don't want them to pity me or think of me as the guy with a sad childhood story. It's over, and I want to keep it over."

"It's no wonder my mom couldn't find anything about them online. You changed your name," I said.

He sat back, his expression two parts wondering and one part suspicion. "Why would she look?"

"She told me she thought it would be nice for the parents to meet, and if they couldn't, she wanted to keep your mom in the loop about what we were planning and coordinate their outfits for the photos."

"Hmm," he said with a small tilt of his head as if he understood.

"How did you end up here?" I asked. "You know how I did."

"There's family property here that's been handed down for generations, and, no, it's not one of the cottages. When I was fifteen, I worked here for the summer, and I loved it. It was natural for me to apply here after the academy. Apparently, the guy before me had retired and moved to Florida."

"He must've had enough of the snow," I said, and we both laughed, breaking the tension.

"Now that you know, let's not talk about this with anyone. I prefer to keep my private life private."

I kissed him. "This will go no further, cross my heart and hope to die."

"Don't go that far," he pushed a wayward curl behind my ear. "I don't want you to die."

"Then how about, if I ever say anything, I'll sell the McMurphy."

"Wow, well then," he looked surprised. "That is quite the guarantee. Everyone, including me, knows you love the McMurphy more than you love me."

"Hmm." I tapped my index finger on my chin. "Maybe I do." We laughed. "Thanks for telling me."

"You're welcome." He took my hand. "Enough about me. Let's celebrate that the dinner with your relatives is over and they behaved themselves."

"Yes!" I agreed. "After all, what worse could happen?"

Chapter 25

"Dinner went better than I thought," Aunt Ginny said the next morning as we stood in line at the Coffee Bean to order our coffees. She had called and asked to meet me. "I thought for sure you would throw them out on their ears."

I laughed. "Trust me, I was tempted, but I could see the newspaper headline: Bridezilla refuses to eat with family."

"Or Momzilla forces bride to include the family, who took away her trust fund," Aunt Ginny teased.

"It's weird that I was once a trust-fund baby. Besides my mom demanding that I attend the expected schools and wear the best clothes, neither of my parents ever talked about a trust fund. In fact, I didn't even know I had one until it was taken away. That's when I learned that, not only did my intention to be a fudge maker shame the family, but so did my running barefoot in the grass and jumping through the sprinkler." I shrugged. "After not knowing the trust fund existed, I really didn't care."

"It shocked the family that you wouldn't comply," Aunt Ginny said. "You should've heard them go on about it—for years—until they realized you were never going to come back and beg."

We got our coffees and sat in the back corner, as far away from prying ears as we could. Audrey saved us a table.

"We want to tell you about what we found out about the—" Aunt Ginny looked around to make sure no one heard her. "You know what? Audrey has some insight she wants to share. Audrey?"

"We hear a lot of gossip at the library. From what I've heard, Julie French is a nasty one. She seems to be in the middle of everything, and where she goes, conflict follows," Audrey said. "But I doubt she'd go as far as murder. She likes to ensure no one suspects her of any wrongdoing."

I took another swallow of my coffee. It was warm and bitter on my tongue, just the way I liked it. "But that doesn't mean she didn't manipulate someone else into doing it." I leaned forward. "Did you know she planned Velma's funeral for less than two hours before my wedding?"

"What?" Aunt Ginny leaned forward again. "Aren't they usually within a few days of the death? It should've been today or tomorrow at the latest."

"She seemed pretty happy with herself last night when she told me that."

"Don't worry," Audrey said. "I know someone who

can fix this." She stood. "I've got to go back to work. A librarian's job is never done. We'll talk later."

"Please be safe," I said.

"Don't worry, I will."

It was Aunt Ginny's turn to get up. She hugged me. "I'm going to keep looking into any connection Julie may have had with a member of the book club. I'm sure they are clever enough to stage that scene."

I couldn't worry about Aunt Ginny for the rest of the day. Jenn had me busy with the details of the wedding.

Chapter 26

"How's the investigation going?" Jenn asked.

"Slow," I said. "With Mom and the wedding, it's hard to have enough time to do a good job."

"I have a juicy tidbit. There were no fingerprints other than yours on the rock, and none at all on Velma. Whoever killed her had to have had gloves in their pocket."

"How did you know about the fingerprints?" I asked.

"I do live with a crime-scene investigator. And as I've said before, he talks in his sleep, especially when I'm up with Benji in the middle of the night."

"Hmm, come to think of it, a head wound means there was blood, a lot of blood. How did the killer disappear with blood all over them?" I asked.

"True," she said thoughtfully, as we moved on to our next appointment. This one was the final fitting of Jenn's matron-of-honor dress. She'd bought her dress from a local dress shop that offered tailoring. We went inside to find several shoppers perusing the clothes.

"Jenn, Allie, and sweet little Mal," Amy Zimmerman, the manager, greeted us. She was short, with a blunt-cut bob of dark-blond hair and a round face with blue eyes that spoke to her Dutch heritage. "Let's go in the back." We followed her through the employees-only door to see where the clothes were kept. In a corner was a three-sided mirror with a wide wooden platform.

"I can't wait to see it." I sat in one of the folding chairs to the side of the platform. Mal hopped up on my lap to get a better view. Jenn grabbed a black dress bag that hung nearby, along with a shoe box, and went behind the stacks to change. Mal decided she didn't want to wait and jumped down, tugged her leash out of my hand, and followed Jenn. I sighed. My dog would get to see the dress before I did. "You could change in front of me," I said loudly, while looking back to where she and Mal had disappeared.

"And ruin the surprise?" Jenn replied. "I think not."

"What are you going to do if I don't like it?" I asked, with laughter in my voice.

"Then tough biscuits for you," she replied back. "It's already bought."

I laughed even harder. "Whatever you wear, I'll like it," I said. "As long as you're there, that's all that matters."

"Close your eyes," she said as she came closer. I did as she asked and kept them closed, even when Mal unexpectedly jumped in my lap. "Don't open them until I say so."

"Okay," I said. I heard her climb up on the platform. "Now?"

"Now," she said.

"Wow!" Her dress was a lilac-colored goddess dress. It had a halter top and bands that crisscrossed around an empire waist; the rest of the gown had easy pleats that draped to the floor. "I thought bridesmaids weren't supposed to upstage the bride."

Jenn frowned and looked in the mirror. "It doesn't upstage you."

"I was teasing," I said, to comfort her. "I like it, and it will complement my dress."

"That said, your mom gave me that vintage dress to hold," Jenn said. "She said it was in case you changed your mind or something happened to your dress."

"Nothing's going to happen to my dress," I said, with a shake of my head.

"Not while I'm around," Jenn agreed. "I took it anyway, to make her happy and to be able to tell her no on everything else."

"I don't know," I warned. "Now that you agreed to one thing, she'll expect you to agree to everything."

"We'll see about that," Jenn said with a stubborn tone.

"Remember, you have Aunt Ginny on your side. She can help with my mom when things get crazy and you don't have time to deal with her nonsense. The only thing I can hope for," I said, "is that when the rest of the family arrives, they'll keep Mom too busy for her to do any further damage. As for me, I'll spend most of my time on the investigation and away from my family."

"Good luck with that." Jenn grinned. "They seem to all be as stubborn as you."

I shook my head and rolled my eyes. "I wish that wasn't true."

After the fitting, Mal and I said goodbye to Jenn, as she left to go home and see how baby Benji was. I decided to hide out at the Senior Center. My excuse was that I wanted to see what the ladies had discovered about who might have wanted to kill Velma. The day was beautiful and bright, but jackets were still in order due to the breeze off the lake. I told myself that my wedding would be beautiful as long as the weather warmed up a bit which was totally possible this time of year. I didn't want to look at the forecast. It's not always right, and if it was bad, Jenn had plan B ready and waiting.

Mal and I entered the Senior Center to find everyone sitting in a circle talking about a cozy mystery, *Death by Irish Whiskey*, by Catie Murphy. Laura Morgan read from a list she held in her hands, telling everyone why she loved the book; it was two pages long. Angus, Eli Hatfield, and Bill Stanislov had dozed off and snored softly. Barbara and Mary passed notes to each other.

"Allie, Mal!" Carol said quite loudly, cutting Laura off and getting the sleeping men's attention. She and Irma hurried toward me. "How lovely to see you." I let Mal off her leash. She greeted them first, then disappeared into the crowd for the glory and attention she thought she deserved.

Irma gave me a big hug. "Thanks for saving us."

Carol hugged me next. "I was never happier to see your face. We all love Laura, but she's nutso at the book circle. It's why we always make sure she goes last." Carol turned to face the group. "Everyone," Carol said very loudly, "there are cookies and beverages in the kitchen."

As they moved toward the kitchen, I saw Barb holding Mal, who seemed very happy. "Please don't give any cookies to Mal. She has treats at home." But somehow I knew she would be too full of cookies to eat her dinner.

Carol put her arm through mine and walked me over to the small reading area with a waist-high shelf filled with books. It had beautiful windows that were joined at the corner by stained wood that matched the bookshelf. We sat in three easy chairs gathered in a circle around a central coffee table.

"Tell me everything you know," I said. "I can't come to book club this week. I have family coming. Too much family, and that doesn't even include my father's family."

"I see," Irma concluded. "You're hiding."

Chapter 27

"Yes," I admitted. "I am. Now, what do you know so far?"

"Right now, our suspects are Tammy, who is still mad at Velma and refuses to come to the funeral. Oh, let me tell you about the funeral in a bit. Now where was I? Oh, yes. Our most likely suspects are Tammy, Richard, and whoever Velma had an altercation with on the phone," Irma said.

"Add Julie French to that," I said. "She was with Tammy when they confronted Velma, and she's married to Richard."

"Really?" Carol asked. "She doesn't look strong enough to move a dead body."

"I agree," Irma said. "That's why I never understood why the police thought Myrtle had something to do with it."

"We need to figure out who had the strongest motive to kill Velma, including who called Velma and why," I said.

"I know someone who may be able to hack into the records and discover what phone number called Velma at that time," Carol said.

"Is this the same person who got you access to the teens-only website?" Irma asked.

"I can't say," Carol answered.

"I think the crime scene may have been staged, and that means the murder was most probably—"

"Premeditated," Carol interrupted.

"The main motivator in a murder is usually money," I said. "Do you know if Velma owed anyone money or knew a secret they didn't want to get out? Maybe the killer was in the crowd at the crime scene."

"I was too busy with Myrtle to look at the crowd," Irma said.

"And I had my hands full with Richard," Carol said.

"I knew most of the people in the crowd at the crime scene, except for the two waiters up front. I think one said something to Myrtle. Irma, do you remember who it was?"

"If I remember right," Irma said, "it was Brian, Myrtle's son, asking her if she was all right."

"And we still need to figure out who you saw in the bushes," Carol said. "I suspect they're either the murderer or a witness."

"I'll take a closer look at Richard and Julie," I said. "You two try to dig out a motive. I get the feeling we're missing something."

"We're on it," Carol said and stood.

"Wait," Irma pushed Carol back down. "Velma's funeral has been moved up."

"Oh, yes, I almost forgot," Carol said. "We all got together and spoke to Lionel. He agreed that two large events on the same day would be disastrous, and since Velma's body was already embalmed, Monday is a better choice."

I blew out a breath I didn't even know I was holding. "Thank you so much." I hugged them both.

"It was a team effort," Irma told me. "Now, you go take care of your wedding details. We'll let you know if we find anything of interest."

"I will," I agreed and went to pull Mal off the lap of Erwin Jones, who was feeding her cookies by the halves.

"Come on Mal, it's time to go," I said. Erwin handed her over, much to the squirming Mal's sadness.

"Okay, let's go," I said and set her down. She tugged at her leash, gathered it up, and ran to the door. "Good girl." I opened the door and we headed out. But I wasn't ready to go home where Mom could easily find me. She told me earlier that quite a few relatives would be arriving to see the island and I should be there to say hi. I was in no hurry to do to greet all one hundred or more people Mom had invited. What was she thinking? At least the investigation was something I had more control of.

"Who else was at the crime scene?" I asked Mal. We walked until we ended up inside the library. Maybe there was a clue there.

"Allie," Alice said and gave me a quick hug.

"Is it alright if I bring Mal in with me?" I asked.

"We usually frown on dogs unless they're a service dog. But we have no patrons who will complain, and I think we can make an exception this once."

"Thanks," I said, and Mal agreed by licking Alice's hand.

"Audrey and I could not believe that a murder happened that close to the library." She looked horrified. "And to think we were the last people to see Velma alive. Now people have been coming and going, wanting a look at where Velma died. It's distracting, and I'm afraid it has kept our usual patrons away. Do you have any idea who would do such a thing? I heard they suspect Myrtle."

"True," I said.

"I don't think she did it," she said. "It's not like Myrtle at all. If she wanted Velma dead, she could have done it years ago."

"I agree," I said. "It doesn't make any sense to kill her now over a few craft books."

"Especially since new ones come in every week," Alice said. "I'm going to miss their little arguments." She looked at me. "What brings you here? Not still looking for more bridal books, are you? It's a little late for that."

"I'm hiding from my family," I said.

"I heard they were quite the handful."

"More like a wagon full," I said. "But, truly, I thought I'd come inside and replay what happened that morning to see if it jogs my memory. There has to be something I missed."

"Ah, a vital clue could be right here in our library."

"I certainly hope so," I said. "Let's see, I came inside that day and handed you a stack of wedding books and magazines."

"Oh, how are the wedding details going? I heard your mom has come up with wedding plans of her own."

"They're nothing like ours," I said. She wants a private wedding. But what doesn't make sense is then she went and invited nearly one hundred of her friends, family, and coworkers. Is she trying to kill me?"

Alice leaned in toward me. "Perhaps she's trying to test your resolve."

I chuckled. "Rex keeps telling me we could elope. I'm beginning to think that's a good idea."

"You do what you want and the heck with everyone else," she said. "But I'm certainly looking forward to the wedding and the potluck. I'm bringing my famous brisket."

"That sounds delicious," I said. "But we have caterers grilling."

"No one is going to complain if I bring my brisket," she said proudly. "Don't you worry. Now, go on and find a helpful clue, okay?"

I retraced my steps on the day of the murder. After dropping off the books, I went to the computer and sat to see if there was anything I'd missed. While I'd scrolled that day, the argument began. I remember Audrey going over to shush the ladies, but they refused to be quiet. Then I leaned over the desk to sec if I could get a glimpse of the fight. That's when I recognized Velma and Myrtle. I remember being distracted by their argument.

It suddenly occurred to me. Someone left by the side door during the argument. Hmm, did I or didn't I really remember that? As Irma said, memories are strange sometimes. Focus, I told myself, with Mal in my lap. Velma checked out and left, while Myrtle sat down next to me. She complained that Velma had left the computer screen on the Social Security site. Then Myrtle looked something up, returned the computer to the home screen, and left. What did she look up? Was that the clue I was missing?

Audrey walked by. "Did you find a clue yet?"

"No, but I do have a question. Would you happen to know why Velma would be looking up Social Security information? Did she ask you about it?"

"What do you mean?"

"Myrtle complained that Velma left the computer screen on the Social Security site," I said. "I wondered if you helped her with anything or saw her at the computer."

"Oh, no," Audrey said. "Myrtle was wrong. Poor dear is losing it. Velma didn't use the computer. It was Julie French."

"Huh," I said suddenly putting some pieces together. "Is she the one who left by the side door?"

"I assume so," Audrey said. "I was busy with Velma and Myrtle, but I never saw Julie check out."

"Thank you," I said and with a wave, I left with Mal. What did Julie want with the Social Security site and why did she leave through the side door?

Chapter 28

"Where's Jenn?" I asked when I could no longer find a reason to avoid the McMurphy and any family that might be waiting to pounce on me.

"She went home," Mr. Devaney said. "Shane called. He had a case and couldn't watch Benji."

"I'd better go check on her," I said and told Mal she couldn't go.

"Running away again," Douglas said, as he checked the lock on the office.

"As fast and as far as I can," I said and unlocked my apartment, well, our apartment now. Leaving Mal to sleep off the cookies, I hurried out the back door, hoping that no other family members lurked in the alley. Before I knew it, I was at Jenn and Shane's little bungalow that they'd remodeled before Benji arrived on the scene. Suddenly I felt safe enough to slow down and take a breath.

I knocked, and Jenn greeted me with open arms. "Are you okay?"

"Mom has so many relatives, and I don't need them popping in to see me."

"Here, sit." She grabbed a kitchen chair and pulled it out. I did and looked around. Her table was a warm rich maple, with turned legs and four chairs. She had a printed tablecloth covering it, with four matching place mats. "This is really cute," I said.

"The table is my mother's, and the tablecloth belonged to my grandmother. Let's get you something to drink," she looked at me. "And something to eat. Have you had lunch?"

"Not yet," I said, suddenly tired.

Jenn brought me a cup of iced tea and made me a ham-and-cheese sandwich. "You should be tired. You've been going like a crazy woman." She gave me the side eye. "And most of it is avoiding the relatives."

"Aunt Ginny is helping with the investigation," I said. "I see her a lot. It's a good thing I like her."

"Your Aunt Ginny is an interesting character," Jenn said. "Does your mom have dinner plans for you tonight? Is she going to force you into another hair appointment? I mean. How many times can you get your hair done in a week?"

"Right? I've got permanent hair spray now. I told her no last night, and I'm going to continue to say no until she gets the hint."

Jenn laughed. "You go, girl. Stay strong."

"I don't have to worry about her for a while," I said. "Now that so many relatives are arriving, she can't keep up with the dinners. Instead, she's planned a reception with cocktails and small bites for tomorrow. I wanted you to be there, but Mom insisted that it was for family only. Have you ever heard of such a thing? It's not like a rehearsal dinner, which is usually the bridal party only."

"I've not heard of such a thing, but when it comes to your mother, who knows what's going to happen? As for the rehearsal dinner, don't worry. I've got it all planned out, including security at the door ensuring that only the parents and bridal party will be there." Jenn picked up my empty plate. "How's Rex?"

"The case is keeping him busy. He usually tells me he can't discuss it. But he says that while Myrtle is still a person of interest, it's highly unlikely she had anything to do with the murder."

"Good. Now you can ease up on your investigation and think about your wedding."

I didn't really want to talk about the wedding. Right now, it was too much for me. I changed the subject and looked around. There was a high chair in the corner, and I noticed that Jenn's kitchen curtains matched her tablecloth. "You've really outdone yourself with the kitchen. Are the curtains also from your grandma?"

"Yes," she said. "Allie, you've been here a million times. What is really going on with you? Do you have cold feet? Because you can stop this whole thing right now."

"It's not that," I said. "How's Benji?"

"He's fine and napping. Now, no more stalling. What is really going on?"

"I don't know . . ." I said.

"Guess," she demanded, her gaze directed at me.

I took a deep breath. "There are all these people, and they have such family baggage. I haven't been able to make fudge and tell Papa Liam's stories for days now. Even my pets are out of sorts."

"You need to stay home and take a breather from it all for a day." She squeezed my hand.

"If I stay home, Mom walks through the door and drags me here and there. All the while, she's telling me—more like ordering me—about what comes next, which has nothing to do with the wedding Rex and I have planned."

"I can have Mr. Devaney change the locks so your mother can't pop into your apartment."

I laughed. "That would make her livid."

"But it would give you some peace," Jenn said pointedly. "I told you. I won't let her change things."

"Then why the whirlwind of dinners and cocktail parties and talking to people I either don't know or haven't seen in so long all I hear is 'My what a pretty girl you've grown into.'"

"Ouch," Jenn said.

I put my head in my hands and tried not to think about it. "And she keeps pushing new dresses on me for every event. I have no clue what I'm going to do with a closet full of dresses when this is over. And then there's the investigation."

"How's it going, by the way?" Jenn asked as she sat with me. "And why don't you leave it to someone else, like your Aunt Ginny?"

"There are very few suspects and, so far, no motive.

Plus, I worry that Carol, Irma, or Aunt Ginny will get themselves in trouble if I don't keep a close eye on them."

"Rex is perfectly capable of figuring things out. As for the other ladies, they aren't your responsibility. You're using it as a distraction," Jenn said, eyeing me with compassion. "And you're wearing yourself thin, literally. If you don't tell Carol and Irma that you can't investigate any more, then I will."

"Jenn, I don't want to give up on them."

"You're not," she was firm. "You need to think about yourself."

"But—"

"I mean it, Allie. And I'm going to have a talk with your mom today. The cocktail party tomorrow is not a bad idea. But she needs to stop the rest. You have four days until the ceremony, and you want to be glowing and happy, not wrung-out. I'm doing it whether you want me to or not."

I realized she was right and suddenly felt tired.

"I believe Benji wants to see his Auntie Allie. It's been a while."

"I know," I said. "After my family leaves, I'll have more time to visit and babysit."

She brought him out and heated a bottle, then gave it to him. "I'm cutting down on the number of bottles he gets," Jenn said. "He's eating more food, and the pediatrician says we should wean him by eighteen months."

"He's growing up so fast," I said and made a face at the still sleepy Benji. He giggled and waved at me with the nipple still in his mouth. I couldn't resist. It only took a minute to cross the room and take him out of

Jenn's arms. The baby always made me smile, no matter how my day was going. I sat on the couch as he finished the bottle. I bounced him until he burped before I gave him back to his mom. "I think the next part's yours," I said.

She sent me a wry smile. "He's like a goose. Food in and immediately poop out."

I hugged her and gently squeezed him between us, which made him giggle. "Thanks for everything."

"That's what friends, matrons of honor, and wedding planners do," she said as she got up to take care of a squirming Benji.

"Do you feel like you have a split personality?" I teased.

"Mom, wife, sister, and aunt," she said ruefully. "I'm totally a split personality. I will save my true self for Shane and you."

"Take care of yourself." I gave her another squeeze and left. The wind had picked up, making my hair whip around in the eddies and swirls. I hurried home to see what my mom had thought of next.

Chapter 29

Easy Dark-Chocolate Slow-Cooker Lava Cake

Ingredients

1 box of dark-chocolate cake mix
½ cup of oil
3 eggs
1 4-ounce serving-size box of instant dark-chocolate pudding and pie filling
2 cups of cold milk
2 cups of dark-chocolate chips

Grease the interior of a 6-quart slow cooker. In a large bowl, beat the cake mix, oil, and eggs for 2 minutes and pour into the slow cooker. In a medium bowl, beat the pudding mix and cold milk until thick. Pour the mixture over the cake batter, being careful not to mix the two. Cover with the dark-chocolate chips.

Put the slow cooker on low heat, and cook for 3 to 3½ hours until the cake is set but still soft in the center. Take the ceramic center out of the slow cooker, taking care not to burn yourself, and set it on a cooling rack for 30 minutes. Serve. The remaining cake can be refrigerated.

I ran into Aunt Ginny on our early-evening walk. The sun had warmed things up a bit, but I still had a sweatshirt on and Mal wore her favorite sweater. "Allie, darling, how are you?" Aunt Ginny asked. "I've been looking for you to see how you're holding up."

"Hiding from Mom. She's running me in circles."

"She does tend to panic when the family gets all together," Aunt Ginny said. "Poor thing."

"I wouldn't call her a poor thing. I think she knows exactly what she's doing," I said. Mal was so happy about an extra walk. Her little nose to the ground, she rushed ahead. But then she stopped less than a block away from the library and sniffed under a homeowner's thick hedges. She sat, waiting patiently for me to catch up, but when I kept going, she refused to budge. Mal was insistent. But when I moved to pick her up, she shied away from me toward the bushes. "Fine," I said, "what's under there." She wagged her bobbed tail and poked the bush with her nose.

I got down on my knees and looked. There, between the bushes, stuck to the rough bark of one of them, was what looked like cotton material. "What's this, Mal?" I said. I took out my phone and took two pictures, then set it down and turned on the video. I put on a pair of clear food-handling gloves, which I'd grabbed from the fudge shop and stuck in my pocket. This time, I had prepared before we walked, in case we found more clues. Under the bushes, I was careful not to block the camera, and I tugged hard on the bit of cotton. The dirt from the top flew everywhere until my eyes and my mouth were covered in bits of dirt and mulch.

"What is it?" Aunt Ginny asked, bending in as far as she could.

"It looks like it might be a T-shirt," I replied and tugged some more. "But it's nearly buried. It might have been here a while." One of the shirt's shoulders popped out. It was stained with red-brown spots. Then I backed out slowly from under the bush, pulling on the T-shirt, until the entire wadded-up shirt came out. It was stiff and stuck together. I got out from under the bush, and we inspected it.

"A bloody T-shirt," Aunt Ginny said. "Do you think it's connected to the murder?"

"It's hard to tell," I answered, as I gently pulled it apart. There was so much blood on the shirt that it was clear something bad had happened. Considering it possible evidence, I handed my phone to Aunt Ginny to hold as the video kept running.

Mal sat beside me, panting, her pink tongue hanging out and a look of satisfaction on her face. "Good girl," I said and gently pulled the stiff T-shirt apart until I revealed the whole thing. The work was slow and laborious.

The shirt was bigger than I expected.

"What's the size?" Aunt Ginny asked

I looked at the collar. "Size XL"

"Definitely a man large enough to carry a body,"

Aunt Ginny said. "From the picture on the murder board, it looks like it could fit Richard."

"Yes, it does."

"Allie!" I looked up to see Carol walking this way, still in her velour tracksuit, her face red and sweaty. "I saw you from the sidewalk and simply had to come see what you have."

"Carol," I said. "Where's Irma? Don't you two usually power walk together?"

"She's walking with Myrtle," Carol replied. "That poor woman. Irma went with her to see the doctor, who prescribed her bladder medicine, along with something to calm her, and told her to drink water. Finally, he pulled Irma aside and counseled her to set up more tests in Cheboygan to check for early-onset dementia."

"That's terrible," Aunt Ginny said.

"This whole thing is simply awful. Myrtle's a wreck. Brian's taken extra shifts to cover an hour a day of home nursing care. Meanwhile, Irma has been at Myrtle's house every day, taking care of her," Carol replied. "Now, what did you find?"

"A bloody T-shirt," Aunt Ginny said. "Allie carefully pulled it apart to see if we can figure out who it belongs to. I find this all exhilarating, don't you?"

"Yes," Carol replied. "It's why the book club helps investigate the murders." She stood over my shoulder and watched as I revealed the words on the T-shirt.

Carol read the words on the T-shirt. "'Sorry I wasn't listening. I was thinking about fishing,'" She looked at me and Aunt Ginny. "I know that shirt and I know who killed Velma!"

Chapter 30

"It belongs to Richard French!" Carol said excitedly. "It's our biggest break in the case."

"This is so exciting," Aunt Ginny said, as I removed a gallon-sized freezer bag from my pocket.

Much better than a poo bag, I thought to myself. I took another photo with my phone, then ever so gently slipped the shirt into the bag, along with the gloves I'd used. I held the bag up in the light. "It's definitely bloody enough to belong to the killer and close enough to the crime scene that they could have ditched it for a cleaner one. Since they would be part of the crowd, no one would be the wiser." I stood and brushed the dirt off of my now grass-stained pants.

"May I?" Aunt Ginny asked, with excitement in her tone. She took the bag and studied it.

Meanwhile, I texted Rex and Shane the pictures and

videos. I'd not only taken a video of when I pulled it out of the ground, but also one when I gently pulled it apart and slipped it into the evidence bag. I didn't want anyone to argue that the shirt was contaminated.

"Okay," I said. "I texted Rex and Shane everything. We need to take it to the station right away."

"I've done some sleuthing in my time," Aunt Ginny said and handed me the bag, "but nothing like this."

"How did you know it was there?" Carol asked as we headed down Market Street toward the police station.

"Mal found it on our walk," I said.

As we rushed down Market Street, we ran into Irma and Myrtle. "Where are you ladies going in such a hurry?" Irma asked.

"We have new evidence," Carol said. "We're taking it to the station right now. Do you want to come with us?"

"Can we?" Myrtle asked with tears in her eyes. "I can't go to jail for something I didn't do."

Irma patted her on the hand. "It's going to be alright. Allie will find the killer, just like I said she would. You'll see."

I felt like I had a parade behind me as we all finished the trek to the police station and stormed in. We were noisy enough to have Officer Elija Gray jump out of his chair at the front desk in a hurry and grab his phone. When he saw it was me, he held his heart and took a deep breath, then sat back down. "Allie," he said, "you nearly scared me half to death. I thought I had a riot on my hands."

"I need to see Rex or Charles," I said and held up the baggie.

"I'll call them," he said, not fazed by my evidence. He pushed a button on his office phone. "Officer Manning, we have some ladies here to see you. They have a bag of something."

"Yes, sir," Elija said and hung up. "He'll be right out."

We didn't even have time to sit before Rex opened the door. He looked curious at first as to why so many of us were in the lobby. Then his gaze lit up when he saw me. He strode over immediately and gave me a nice kiss that had the ladies twittering. "What can I do for you, ladies," he asked, not letting go of me.

"We have evidence," Aunt Ginny said, with pride in her tone. "Allie and I found it." When Mal went to her and jumped on her leg, Aunt Ginny laughed and picked her up so that she could see what was going on. "Oh, and Mal, of course."

"And the rest of you?" Rex asked, with a quirk of his eyebrow.

"I was there and identified who it belonged to," Carol said proudly. "Oh, and it's covered with blood. We know for sure who the killer is. Now you can stop harassing Myrtle, who clearly didn't do it."

"I see," Rex said, and he hid his chuckle until he turned to me. "What evidence are we talking about, and where did you find it?"

I handed him the overstuffed baggie.

"I ran into Allie as she walked Mal," Aunt Ginny said. "Then Mal stopped at a hedge and wouldn't let us take a step farther."

"I looked under the hedge and found a small bit of

cloth sticking to the bark," I said. "I texted you and Shane the images and videos."

"I saw the text." he said, gave me a look that said we'd talk later, and then studied the big shirt stuffed into the small bag.

"Here's the video, in case you haven't watched it yet." I let him watch it, and you could hear me say, "It looks like it might be a T-shirt. But it's nearly buried. It might have been here a while."

All the ladies leaned forward and listened, wanting to know firsthand how it'd all happened. Since they hadn't seen me actually take it out of the ground and carefully pull the dried-blood-soaked shirt apart, listening was the next best thing.

Rex stopped the video and gave me the stink eye. "You pulled it apart?"

"Yes, gently. You can see how careful I was." I pointed to the frames of the video below.

"Not only are you wanting to take my job, but Shane's?" He gave me his flat cop stare. He hadn't done that in a while, no matter how much trouble I managed to get myself into.

I gulped. "No, I don't want your job or his. I simply wanted to see if I could find anything that made the shirt easy to identify."

"And we did," Aunt Ginny said, pointing to the evidence. "It is a size extra-large, perfect for a man big enough to carry a dead woman. It says, 'Sorry I wasn't listening. I was thinking about fishing.'"

"I knew the T-shirt right away." Carol paused for drama.

Rex closed his eyes, then shook his head while taking a big breath. "Let's hear it—your theory of who this killer is."

"That shirt belongs to Richard French," Carol said with certainty. "I knew he was behind this! All that crying and kicking the evidence into the lake. He put on quite the show, didn't he, ladies?" Everyone agreed, their voices echoing through the lobby.

"Calm down, calm down," Rex said. "This might be a shirt like his. You don't know it is his. If you go around telling everyone he's the killer, it becomes a witch hunt. Do you want to be responsible for harming a possibly innocent man?"

They all hung their heads as he chided them. Tears fell to the floor as Myrtle hung her head low. I could tell Rex had become an old softy. He stepped toward her and put a hand on her shoulder. "How could you point a finger at a man after others did the same thing to you?" he asked, then he handed her a tissue from the front desk.

She dried her cheeks and blew her nose. "Ladies," she croaked and cleared her throat, "he's right. Richard is under the same suspicion I am, with no way to prove otherwise. Simply because we found a T-shirt, if it even is his shirt, doesn't mean he's any more guilty than I am."

Irma hugged her and turned her toward the door. "You're very brave. Come now, let's all go to Carol's house and get some coffee and cookies. That always makes you feel better, right, Carol?"

"Of course," Carol said and put her arm around Myrtle.

"You defused that expertly," Aunt Ginny said to Rex when they left. "How clever."

"Clever only because I know these women very well, and I knew if I didn't stop them, they'd have the whole island up in arms," he said. "Now, about this evidence."

Chapter 31

"Allie, it's wonderful to see you. My goodness, you're all grown up. Where does the time go? This is your cousin . . ." I heard the refrain over and over again, until my face hurt from smiling and welcoming Mom's family and my parents' friends. Mom made us stand in a reception line and greet everyone in the room. The next thing they would say was, "And you must be Allie's Rex. Aren't you handsome?"

When the last person went through the welcome line, Rex asked if I wanted a drink. "Please," I said. "I'll be over in the corner, trying to recover."

Dad winked at me and took Mom's arm. "Shall we mingle, dear?" He whisked her away.

There was a small table with four chairs that I'd been eyeing for a while, hoping no one would take it. I debated whether to sit in the chair facing the crowd, so that I could see anyone coming my way, or with my back to the crowd, where they hopefully couldn't tell it was me.

I took the one in the corner. It was darkest there and hopefully hid my face as much as possible.

"How are you holding up?" Rex asked as he set a glass of white wine in front of me.

I took a gulp before I answered. "I'm fine. Everything is fine," I said, taking a quote from a *Friends* episode. It meant I was far from fine. I adjusted the outfit Mom had bought me for the occasion. It was also vintage 1950s, this time in peacock blue with gold threads. At least this one had a slit skirt with matching stove pipe slacks underneath in a classic 1950s style.

Rex snagged two plates of the savory small bites off of a waiter's tray and placed one in front of me. "Eat something. You look like you're about to pass out from hunger."

"Jenn fed me the other day, too," I said and took a bite of a tiny bagel smeared with a thick coating of lobster and cream cheese. "Why does everyone feel the need to feed me?"

"Maybe because you look too thin," he said and took a swig of his beer. Then he glanced over his shoulder. "There must be close to a hundred people here. I thought your mom wanted us to have a small private ceremony."

"That doesn't mean she wouldn't throw a big party after," I said and grabbed a small slice of toasted rye bread with roast beef on top and an artfully placed touch of horseradish.

Rex raised an eyebrow. "This isn't a big party?"

I laughed and swallowed more wine. "This." I moved my hand like a waiter with no tray, "This is merely a cocktail party."

"You grew up with this?" he asked.

"Didn't you?" I asked sarcastically, followed by a laugh. Then I finished my wine. "Can I just go back to making fudge and enjoying my husband and pets?"

"Husband," he said and took my hand, planting a kiss on my fingers. "I like the sound of that."

"Alright, you two. You can't hide in the corner of your own party," Uncle John said and held out his hand as if to take me away. Darn, if I hadn't been distracted, I would have excused myself to go to the bathroom.

Rex got up to let me by, and Uncle John looped my arm through his. "I haven't had a pretty girl on my arm in a long time."

I gave him a look. "What about Aunt Ginny?"

"My Ginny is a beautiful woman." He grinned at me. "Not much difference, I'd say, but enough not to get me into any trouble." Then turned his head in time to see Rex sit down. "Oh, no, my boy. Come on. You need to go wherever your blushing bride goes."

"Yes, sir," Rex said, and the rest of the evening was a blur of people and hugs and handshakes and kids running around.

Even my aunts and uncles took to the dance floor to, as Aunt Ginny said, "shake our booties."

Rex and I preferred the slow dances where we could lean into each other and share the quiet together. "I can't believe all these people are your family," he said.

"My dad's family isn't here yet." I batted my eyes at him

"But I thought you said this would be all your mom and dad's family? Besides, isn't he an only child?"

"Let me clear this up. This is my mom's family and Mom and Dad's friends, plus a few garden club friends."

"I thought since you said your dad was an only child, and his parents were dead . . ."

"That he had a few aunts, uncles, or cousins in this group?"

He gently squeezed my fingers and lightly pressed the small of my back. "Yes," he said with disappointment in his gaze. "He comes from the island, right? The McMurphy came down from his family?"

"Yes, but Grammy Alice came from a family of eight. That means there are seven on that side, plus spouses, children, grandchildren, not to mention—"

"There's more?" He looked shocked.

"Well, they all have grandchildren and great-grandchildren. I'd say that, all told, there are nearly one hundred and fifty. One of my aunts alone has more than fifty between her children, grandchildren, and great-grandchildren."

Tiny beads of sweat popped out on his forehead, and I had to bite my cheek not to laugh. "Are there enough rooms on the island to accommodate the horde of relatives you seem to have?"

Poor guy. It didn't seem fair to wait until two nights before the wedding to tell him he'd now be related to half the state of Michigan, some parts of Chicago and

Florida, and a few stragglers in California and Tennessee.

The music stopped, and a fast song started. As Rex and I walked off the dance floor, Aunt Ginny came up, put both her arms through ours, and shouted above the music, "Follow along."

Chapter 32

"Where are you going with our guests of honor?" my cousin Babs asked. It was clear she was enjoying the free beverages.

"Are those your boys over there drinking beer?" Aunt Ginny pointed with her chin.

"They better not be," Babs turned and pushed her way through the crowd.

"Huh," Rex said, watching her go.

Aunt Ginny grinned. "Come on."

We were almost halfway to the door when Aunt Felicity sloshed our way. "Oh, no, you don't," she said, her words slightly slurring, though only close family would notice. "Ginny, what makes you think you can get away with hogging these two?"

"They want me to show them the best place to look at the stars from here," Aunt Ginny said and nudged me.

"That's right," I said, trying not to laugh.

Aunt Felicity looked at us suspiciously. "But they both live here. Why would they need you to show them where to see the stars?'

Aunt Ginny looked confused. "Whatever do you mean? Of course they live here. I asked them to show me the stars. Why did you think I wanted to show them?"

I swallowed my laughter and glanced at Rex. His blue eyes danced with humor.

"Wait, I thought—" Aunt Felicity blinked. "I thought you said you were showing them."

"Why would I do that?" Aunt Ginny asked. "They both live here, silly. Clearly, you need to eat something." Aunt Ginny tilted her head, as if to point. "There's a waiter over there."

"The lobster and cream cheese are to die for," I said.

Aunt Felicity walked away, muttering to herself. "I'm sure I didn't mix that up. Did I?"

"That was almost mean," I said to Aunt Ginny.

She shrugged. "She's my sister. I can have fun with her, right?" Rex shook his head as Aunt Ginny continued pulling us through the crowd.

We were at the door when my mom stepped out. I heard Aunt Ginny say, "Drat," under her breath.

Mom narrowed her eyes. "Where do you think you're going?"

You could tell Aunt Ginny was thinking quickly, trying one answer after another in her head. Mom was formidable. It would have to be good.

Rex spoke up. "Allie was hot and needed some fresh air. So, Aunt Ginny wanted to show us where the chairs are set up on the lawn. We'll be back in fifteen minutes when Allie gets cool enough. I don't want her to pass out from the heat with all the family and friends around. What would they think?"

I fanned myself with my free hand and knew it looked authentic. My face was red from dancing and the wine, and sweat-soaked bits of my hair that had sprung free of the hair-sprayed shellac of my updo stressed his point.

"Isn't the porch good enough to cool off?" Mom asked, her eyebrows pulled together, giving her two lines between the brows.

"Everyone is going to the porch. The kids wanted a moment of quiet for Allie to cool off and fix her hair." Aunt Ginny piped up and gave me a glance, and I nodded.

"We won't be long, Mom." I promised. "Besides, everyone is dancing and having fun. We'll hardly be missed for all of fifteen minutes."

She finally gave in. "Fifteen minutes," she said. "If you're not back by then, I'm sending your father out to get you, and if that doesn't work, I'll send your Aunt Celeste next."

The thought of Aunt Celeste crossing the lawn in her Armani cocktail dress and designer heels that would sink into the grass made me cringe. "We'll be back," I promised.

"You'd better be." Then she looked straight at Rex.

"You're responsible for these two. I expect you to not let me down."

"Yes, ma'am," Rex said with the look of a boy chastised by his mom. I'd never seen that look on his face before and found it adorable.

Aunt Ginny steered us out the door and across the porch, and as we stepped onto the lawn, she let out a big sigh. "For a minute there, I thought we weren't going to make it."

"I'm not sure our shoes will make it," I said wryly. "Mom will kill me."

"Take your shoes off," Aunt Ginny already held hers. "It's good for your soul to reconnect with the earth."

"Aunt Ginny," I said. "You amaze me every day."

"I might look like an uptight high-society woman, but I was a hippie in my day." She laughed and waited for me to remove my shoes. The ground was cold and wet. Come to think of it, I was swiftly losing the body heat that had felt so stifling in the ballroom.

The temperature had fallen since we arrived, and it wasn't that high to begin with. The outdoors smelled of dew and living things. The fragrance of trees and grass and flowers was everywhere, along with the breeze off the lake.

"I've been so busy lately I'd forgotten how wonderful it is to stand barefoot in the grass," I said.

"Come sit down," Aunt Ginny patted an Adirondack chair.

Rex and I sat. Aunt Ginny said. "You looked into the evidence we brought you this morning?"

Rex cleared his throat, "I can't discuss an ongoing investigation."

"I'm leaving in a few days, and Allie is your bride. How could we possibly do anything to sabotage your case?"

Rex shook his head and looked pointedly at me. "She'll decide we have the wrong person arrested and then go and find the 'real' one."

"Posh." Aunt Ginny pooh-poohed the idea. "You have a wedding in less than two days. Allie would never."

"Of course I wouldn't," I said. Rex coughed and cleared his throat. I felt a deep blush rush up my neck. "Well, not on purpose."

"You want to marry the boy, don't you?" Aunt Ginny asked.

"More than anything I've ever wanted in my whole life," I said and looked into his eyes.

"See?" Aunt Ginny said with determination. "Now the least you could do is tell us if the blood on the shirt belonged to our killer."

"I can't talk about—"

"You might as well give in," I said with a grin and a shake of my head. "Aunt Ginny's my mom's sister. She will never let it go. She'll hound you night and day."

Aunt Ginny innocently blinked at him, but didn't say a word.

Rex took a deep breath and glanced at the door.

"No one's coming to save you, dear," she pointed out. "And no one can hear what we're saying. Spill."

Rex muttered something low under his breath, and I had to work hard to keep my expression both neutral and expectant. If nothing else, I had learned from the best growing up. He cleared his throat again and gave in to two female gazes.

"I took the evidence you found—and keep in mind any good defense lawyer would tell the judge that you *allegedly* found it—because no law-enforcement persons were there."

Neither of us spoke in case he expected to distract us.

He ran his hand over his bald head and gave up. "I took it to Shane, who, by the way, said to tell you that if you don't stop doing his job and not allow him to do it . . ."

"I couldn't call him simply because I saw a T-shirt under a bush. And then it seemed silly not to look for something to help us identify a killer." That sounded reasonable. "Wait, if I don't stop, then what?"

"You can forget your invitation to their barbeques for the rest of the summer."

I laughed. "As if Jenn would ever let that happen."

Rex sighed.

"Quit stalling," Aunt Ginny said and loomed over him as well as a small woman could, her arms crossed and her toe tapping impatiently.

Rex bowed his head a little. "Yes, ma'am," he said again. "The blood was the victim's, but it was mixed with the killer's as well. The killer's blood was found near the sleeves. Shane estimated that when the killer picked up her body, he scratched himself as he rounded the bushes to carefully place it where Myrtle would find it."

Aunt Ginny's expression, lit by the light from the porch, seemed joyful. "Then you've caught the killer!"

"Hold on," he said. "I didn't say that. The killer's blood

was O positive, one of the most common blood types. It might take a while to identify the true killer."

"At least the T-shirt proved that Myrtle didn't do it, which was the entire reason I was investigating," I said, relieved.

"And all you have to do," Aunt Ginny said, "is look for a man who owns and wears the same size shirt who also has scratches on his arms. Voilà! Easy. We have practically handed you your case, Detective."

"Officer," he corrected her. "Of course you did. There's only one problem: that T-shirt is sold in three stores on the island, and there's no telling who bought this one."

"Oh," Aunt Ginny said. "And Richard?"

"We brought him in and questioned him again, but we had to let him go. Don't worry, we're very close to arresting the killer. We know who it is and are in the process of getting a warrant. As soon as the judge signs off, we'll have this thing wrapped up."

"That's encouraging," she said. "Let's get back to the party. I'm certain you'll have everything wrapped up in a neat bow before Allie's father's family comes in tomorrow."

"Right," he muttered, stood, then held out his hand for me and helped me out of the chair.

"I can't believe you told her all that." I know my expression looked perplexed.

Rex gave a little chuckle. "If she thinks it's almost over, then I can finish my investigation in peace."

"Ah," I said and took hold of the arm he held out for

me. Bending carefully, I put my shoes back on to climb the porch steps. "You are a very clever man."

"Isn't that why you love me?"

I couldn't resist his grin and gave him a kiss. Someone cleared their throat, and I looked up to see my mom on top of the stairs tapping her toe. "You're late."

Chapter 33

"Where were you today?" I asked, not trying to sound accusatory. "Mom's antics are escalating, and you know I love you, Jenn, but I hoped you'd help."

"I can't believe she invited a little over a hundred people to a cocktail party and more for a picnic today."

"Rex bailed on the picnic with my father's family with an excuse that he'd been called to work for an emergency, the coward," I muttered.

"I still can't believe she made you greet them all. That's terrible and devious," Jenn said, with a little too much awe in her voice. It was my bachelorette party. Since everyone on the island knew the party was tonight, they expected us at the bars. Instead, we all met at Liz's house for a slumber party. Jenn wore a pretty blue-flannel nightshirt with a pattern of little sprays of white flowers and a comfy pink robe and slippers. She was curled up on Liz's purple overstuffed couch.

I wore the striped, red-and-blue, footed pajamas the ladies had surprised me with tonight, along with my blue robe, and sat cross-legged on the floor nearest the coffee table full of snack food. "Jenn, what do you mean—devious?" I asked, waiting for an answer.

"She's making you so exhausted by people that you'll beg for an intimate wedding," Jenn said incredulously. "She told me it was a little cocktail party with her family and an intimate picnic with your dad's. I should have known better." She gave me a hug. "I'm so sorry."

"And then Rex set up an out by saying he had a police emergency? The rat," Sophie said from the other side of the couch, her long legs stretched out. She wore light-green silk pajama pants with a matching top. Then, to complete her outfit, she had on a matching robe and ridiculous mule slippers with the toes covered in feathers that matched the rest of her outfit.

"It's kind of funny, if you think about it," Liz said, with a chuckle. She sat in a matching comfy chair on the opposite side of the coffee table from me, wearing a flannel nightshirt in a lumberjack plaid, a blue fuzzy robe, and loafer slippers with a suede exterior and fleece interior. "She had to have been planning this for months to pull it off."

"I know," I said and took a gulp of my margarita, our drink of choice for the party. My friends wanted to recreate a scene from *Practical Magic* where they all dance to midnight margaritas along with enough food to feed an army. The coffee table held a plate of brownies, bowls of cheese snacks, and potato chips and dip.

On the dining room table were trays piled high with small sandwiches, cheeses, fruit plates, charcuterie, potato salad, coleslaw, nuts, mints, and a cake that had a bride figure chasing a groom with a dog and cat figure running behind.

"I can't believe I've never been to your home before," I said to Liz. "It's absolutely gorgeous."

Liz lived in a three-bedroom log cabin with a huge, two-sided lake-stone fireplace that currently roared with fire that warmed my back. The main floor was open concept, with big windows. The kitchen was separated by cabinets with enough space left between the top and bottom to see that her appliances were stainless-steel and state of the art. You could see French doors framing it on either side and a huge deck behind that with a firepit and, beyond it, the trees and forests of the island. The floors were gleaming pine topped with oval rag rugs.

"Thanks," she said and shrugged. "It's rare to have guests. Probably because all my friends live on the island with homes of their own."

"We should have a once-a-month get-together," Sophie said as she ate from her tiny plate full of chips and brownies.

"That would be fun," I agreed, as I snatched a brownie from the plate and ate it between sips of my drink. I was surprised at how good chocolate and lime tasted together. It was giving me fudge ideas.

"We could have it here," Liz volunteered. "It would be good to catch up with each other's lives."

Yes," I agreed, then turned to Sophie. "When did you and Harry start dating? And why didn't anyone tell me?"

"It's not like we were trying to hide it from you," Sophie said with the twinkle of love in her gaze and a sigh on her lips.

Liz teased me. "Oh, Allie, we all knew that Harry kept asking you to marry him, even though you were with Rex. He followed you around like a puppy with his gorgeous, Thor body, blond hair, and money. Nobody told you because we all thought you'd be devastated to lose one of your men."

"Jealous, aren't you?" Jenn teased, and I gave her the look, and she laughed until we were all giggling.

After tears of laughter, and with tissues handed all around and stomach muscles hurting, we all sighed.

I raised my chin and said, "I didn't even realize he hasn't been around lately."

Which made everyone burst into laughter again. "Come on, ladies," I said. "My face already hurts from the constant smile I've had to wear for the last two weeks."

When we settled down enough to finish our first drink and grab another, along with more plates full of food, Jenn asked. "Seriously, Sophie, how did you two meet?"

"I piloted his family in, and he waited to welcome them on the tarmac. I came around to block my plane—you know, place the blocks in front of the wheels—and then open the door, when I turned to see this extreme eye candy of a man, watching me with a stunned look on his face. I think I was a little stunned, too, because it took me a long time to open the door, and his family started knocking on the windows. I was embarrassed for them to see how unprofessional I was and broke eye contact, then opened the door, pulling down the stairs. Before I could help them out of the plane, which is a part of my service, he was there, right beside me. He smelled like spice and cookies and something else that I can't describe except to say it was an intriguing male scent that had my heart pounding. We both reached for his mom's hand at the same time. His hand covered mine, and I didn't know what to do. Then he put his other hand around my waist and gently pushed me out of the way, yet staying close enough that I didn't leave his side, then he helped his family out of the plane. After one more smoldering look, he walked away."

"That's romantic," Jenn said with a sigh.

"Anyone want another drink?" Liz asked.

"We all do!" Sophie stood. "I'll help you."

Jenn got up as well. "I'll be back. I have to go powder my nose."

"We just got drinks," I said, confused. "I don't need another. But I'll come, too," I said, noting the looks my friends gave each other as if they were having a silent conversation.

"I'm going to the bathroom, silly," Jenn said. "I don't think you want to follow me."

"I really want to stretch my legs," Sophie said. "I could stay in here and loom over you or . . ."

I sighed. "No, go on." I grabbed my phone to see if anyone had left a voice message. There was a text message from Aunt Ginny.

Rumor has it Rex and Charles are looking for Richard French. It seems a witness has come forward.

Who's the witness? I texted back.

You're not going to believe it.

I shook my head and texted. *Who?*

His second wife, Julie. She said he was angry because Velma had come into some money and could still draw off his Social Security, leaving hers to use later.

That doesn't seem like enough motive for murder, I texted. *But it makes sense she would say that.* I heard laughter, and the girls all rushed forward. Looking up, I noticed they wore party clothes.

"Bar crawl!" Liz shouted and wiggled a dance.

Jenn put a sash around me that said "Bride" and Sophie attached a small veil to my messy updo.

"Wait, what??" Stunned, I didn't know what to do when they each took an arm and Liz pushed me from behind toward the door. I tried to get my footing to stop the madness, but they kept me moving. "Wait! Are we going out? But you said it was a slumber party. We were all wearing pajamas."

"We *were*," Jenn said. "But now we're going to crawl the bars."

"Crawl?" I felt confused as they crossed the threshold and the colder night air hit me. "What bar?"

"Every bar," Sophie replied.

"I have to go back to my apartment and get dressed," I said, desperately looking left and right.

"Oh, no, you don't," Jenn said, as they tossed me into a carriage and squeezed in beside me.

"I can't go out wearing pajamas. My mom will kill me." I panicked. "And when did this carriage get here?"

Liz looked from me to the other three. "She's right, you know." The other two looked confused. "I believe our bride hasn't had enough to drink if she's going to be killed by matricide."

"Shots, shots, shots," Sophie started chanting. Soon the carriage was so loud that all the people who were still out and about turned and looked. I felt the heat of a blush rush up from my chest to the top of my head. Most folks clapped and yelled, while a few glared and shook their heads.

The carriage stopped, and I was mortified as they pulled me into the first bar. There was a moment of stunned silence from the patrons when we entered, until Jenn, the traitor, shouted "The bride-to-be is in the house! Shots! Shots!"

Before I knew it, everyone stamped their feet in unison and joined in the shouting. Pulled to the bar, my so-called friends sat me down on a green-covered barstool. A shot of tequila was pushed into my hand. I looked from one side to the other, taking in the glee on my friends' faces and shrugged, then tossed it down.

By the second bar, I discovered that striped footie pajamas weren't a bad outfit for a bar crawl. I was much warmer than my girlfriends, who were dressed in club clothes. Also, I didn't have to wear high heels. While Liz, who was on my left, didn't either, she had on combat boots, a short plaid kilt, and a white blouse tied at her belly. She looked adorable, her hair in two small pigtails in front. She had turned to talk to a cute guy wearing a too-tight black T-shirt to show off his arms and his oversized chest, matched with jeans and boat shoes. We usually could spot a ridiculous rich boy two miles away. What was Liz doing?

A tall handsome blond man approached. "Harry?" I tried to say it, but it didn't come out as loud or as sober as I'd hoped. He ignored me and headed straight toward Sophie, who was dressed in a very short, red bodycon dress with four-inch stilettos that made her as tall as he was. I had to remember to give her those shoes my mom kept insisting I wear. They kissed intimately, and, embarrassed, I turned away while someone put another shot in my hand. I swallowed it without even a thought.

"Looks like it's you and me again, kid," Jenn said and tossed down her shot and asked the bartender for more.

"Where's Shane?"

"He's at Rex's bachelor party." Jenn looked around and danced to the music. The bartender brought one more shot. Jenn put it in my hand and lifted her glass. I followed. "The original bachelorette's dreams have come true. To the bride and the matron of honor."

"Hear, hear," I said, grinned, and down the alcohol went. I wiped my mouth and said no to the next round by putting my hand over the shot glass. "You look pretty amazing for a wife, new mom, party planner extraordinaire, and momzilla wrangler."

"Oh, this little thing?" She laughed and pointed to her kelly-green dress, which clung to her hips and her chest. Then she leaned in conspiratorially. "Shane's been working too many long hours, and I got my mom to babysit tonight." She winked. "This is for him, and if I'm a little eye candy in the bars, that's pretty flattering, too. I'll be right back. I'm going to the ladies' room."

"Oh, no, you can't go without me," I stood, a little wobbly in my footie pajamas. She pushed through the crowd, and I walked in her wake, not paying attention. Suddenly I tripped, and two strong, familiar hands caught me and pressed me against his chest as he tried to straighten me. I looked up into a face so handsome it always made my heart beat a little faster. "Trent?" I asked, not sure if he was real or I'd really had too much to drink.

"One and the same," he said and held me against him as he adjusted my veil. "Imagine my surprise when I come home, only to run into my true love in . . ."

"Striped footie pajamas," I said with no shame.

"Wearing a veil and a sash that says 'Bride.'"

My mouth went a little dry from the way he said it. He still hadn't let go of me. I remembered his scent—expensive, subtle, all male. My fingers dug into a fine wool suit. It was either gray or dark blue. It was hard to tell in this light with a bit too much to drink and the handsome man in front of me. The suit fit his broad shoulders and was tailored to reveal a flat stomach and long legs. One of his hands that steadied me held his signature cowboy hat.

"Wait, what?" I was confused.

"My true love."

I could feel the words rumbling in his chest. I looked up into his dark eyes. "You left."

"You knew I had obligations in Chicago after my

dad died," he said so softly I had to lean against him to fully hear in the noisy bar.

"You left," I kept repeating.

"I knew how important the McMurphy was to you." His breath hot in my ear gave me shivers up and down my spine. "I love you so much, I offered to stay here for the season with you, no matter how difficult it would be for me and my work. The only thing I asked for in return was for you to spend the winters with me. Three months." I felt his breath hitch, and the sorrow coming off of him surprised me. "I had planned a place for you to keep working on your Christmas orders, your winter online orders. I wanted to be together always." He shrugged. "It always was Rex, wasn't it? That's why you stayed."

Even a little blurry, I drew my eyebrows together in confusion. "I told you I needed to be here for the winter to show people I wasn't a fudgie, but part of the island community."

"I texted you for months, called every week, but your answers slowed, and then disappeared." He had a wry smile on his face. "If you love someone, let them go. If they come back, they truly love you," he repeated the old saying. His dark eyes glanced from the sash to the veil. "Now I know why."

A lump filled my throat at the sorrow I felt roll off him. My happy little buzz was gone. It was hard to see a dear friend, boyfriend, ex, hurt. I gave him a big hug. He hugged me back and planted a warm kiss on the top of my head.

"I want you to be happy," he said and took a step back. "Rex is not the most reliable in a marriage. If he ever hurts you, call me. I'll be by your side in a heart-beat. I'll move back here and never let you go again."

With a tilt of my head and a tear in my eye, I couldn't help the soft smile on my lips. "Thank you."

Suddenly, Jenn was beside me, putting her arm through mine. "Trent," she said with a nod.

"Jenn," he replied.

"Come on, Allie, time to go. We have three more bars to hit."

As she dragged me back through the crowd, I turned to see him give me one last look and turn to the bar.

The cold outside seeped through my pajamas and my alcoholic haze. Jenn and I walked hand in hand toward the next bar. "The wind cuts right through you," I said. "You must be freezing."

"I've heard it's good for the complexion," she said.

"Let's pop in here and get out of it for a bit." I pulled her into the covered alleyway that led to the ferry dock.

"Oh, man," Jenn said looking around. "Don't you think this would have made a great place to make out when we were in high school?"

"It might still be a great place to make out." I waggled my eyebrows at her, and we both burst out giggling. "We should call our men."

"Your mom would kill you," Jenn said.

"Allie," I imitated my mom, "have some decorum, and for goodness' sake, go change your clothes and brush your hair."

Jenn and I burst out in hysterics until I doubled over. My sides hurt so much from all the laughter.

That's when I saw him. It was Richard French, and even in my inebriated state, I knew he was dead.

Chapter 34

Jenn and I stood off to the side with blankets around our shoulders. I'm sure we looked a bit worse for wear. Rex, Charles, Shane, and George were all on the scene at the same time. They'd been over at Charles's place, playing poker for Rex's bachelor party. As soon as the call came, they left and were on the scene.

I couldn't tell whether my footies pajamas or Jenn's sexy red dress shocked them the most. George had blankets around us within a minute of arriving on the scene. It was scary how quickly they had crime-scene tape up and collected evidence.

"Alright," Rex said in his cop tone. I felt like a child being scolded by her father. "Let's begin with why you two found yourself on the ferry dock."

I looked at Jenn, and she looked at me, and we both started laughing until our eyes watered.

"Murder is no laughing matter," Rex said, in a soft

but deadly tone that for some reason struck me as ridiculous.

I worked hard not to laugh, because I knew if I started, Jenn would start and then there would be no hope for either of us. I looked at Jenn, her mouth twitching as she refused to look at me directly. I cleared my throat. "You are so attractive when you turn on your cop persona. Maybe we should explore that later." I couldn't help it. I really couldn't. It was the alcohol talking. At least that's what I would tell him later. But now was not the time, because Jenn and I both burst out in laughter.

Rex made a face, and I suspect he would have pulled his hair out if he had had any. He waited patiently for us to stop, cleared his throat, and turned to Jenn, as if she were any more sober than me. "Jenn," he said.

"Yes?" she replied, and we both broke out in more laughter.

I elbowed her, and she looked at me, and we both tried to act less drunk.

"Ladies," he finally said.

"Ladies!" we repeated, and another round of laughter erupted.

Rex turned and gave Shane a look, and they both nodded. Before we knew what was going on, Rex tossed me over his shoulder, and Shane tossed Jenn over his, and they pulled us from the scene.

"Did I ever tell you that you have the most interesting backside?" I said, as I hung upside down with nothing to look at but the body part in question. I gave it a nice pat. "Oh, I saw Trent in the bar," I said. "He still loves me. You should have seen how sad he was."

That stopped Rex in his tracks. "Jessop is here?"

"I know," I said. "He still can make my heart go pitty-pat." I patted Rex's butt again. "But not as much as you do. Did you know we're getting married on Saturday? That's only two days from now."

I think he looked straight up and then blew out his breath. "I'm aware," he replied and started walking.

I started humming and then singing "Here Comes the Bride." "We should have them play that at our ceremony. Oh, wait, isn't that song something about ladies heading straight to the bridal bed? We could do that right now, if you want." I patted his butt again and giggled. He opened a door, and the bells jangled. "Oh, are we at the McMurphy? That was close by." I continued humming until we were suddenly in our apartment, and he plopped me on the bed. The bounce of the bed made me giggle some more. He unzipped my jammies, and I gave him my best or, shall I say, worst southern accent. "Why, Police Officer Manning, I thought you had a crime scene to attend to."

He never said a word as he pulled the covers up under my chin as I continued to sing my song.

The next morning, I blinked my eyes when someone loudly pulled the blinds up, letting in too much bright sunlight. "Allie, get up!" It was my mom. I buried my throbbing head under my pillow, but she would have no part of it. "Allie Louise!" She pulled the pillow out from my hands.

"Mom, please," I said, "can you lower your voice?"

The bed rocked, and my stomach sloshed a bit. "Sit up," Aunt Ginny said quietly. I did and tried not to get motion-sick as my mom paced the bedroom. Aunt Ginny handed me a glass. "Drink it. It's Grandma's hangover cure."

I did as she asked and took one swallow of the bitter liquid. I went to put the rest on the end table when Aunt Ginny forced me to drink it all. "You have to drink it all for it to work," she said.

After getting as much of the nasty stuff down as I could, I turned to her. "You're trying to kill me, right?"

"No, dear," Aunt Ginny said and patted my hand. "Not until you tell me all about how you found Richard French dead. He was our prime suspect."

"Allie, take a shower," Mom said. "You smell like death." I stood to find myself in one of Rex's tees that stopped just above my knees. "And for goodness' sake, brush your teeth."

Chapter 35

An hour later, having showered, washed my hair, brushed my teeth, and eaten a nice portion of Aunt Ginny's eggs, I felt nearly one hundred percent normal. Thank you, Aunt Ginny, I thought, as I sat on my couch.

"I cannot believe you've been investigating a murder instead of preparing for your wedding," Mom said, as she paced in front of me like a general scolding his troops.

I sat on my couch, with Mal by my side and Mella on the back of the couch, leaning against my shoulders. Aunt Ginny sat beside me, not saying a word. "Mom."

"Then to get Ginny involved? Ginny?" She turned and gave me a look that combined disappointment and anger. "Allie Louise, I expected better of you. I swear, I taught you better. Have you forgotten everything since you've been on this island?"

"Mom, I'm a grown—"

"Yes, yes, a grown woman who has been running away from her wedding preparations for the last two weeks. I can't believe you would do this. You only have one wedding," Mom said. "And you'd rather be investigating some woman's death? Can't you give this incessant investigating up? What does Rex think about all this? Don't you want to get married?"

"Mom, sit!" I used her own motherly tone back at her. She was so surprised, she sat in my side chair and Mal hopped up on her lap. "I am the one disappointed in you. You're wrong. I'm not trying to sabotage my own wedding," I looked her in the eyes. "You're the one scaring Rex with this 'look how big our family is' tactic. That's also why I've been avoiding all the family and friends you've invited without asking me. Family cocktail party, family picnic, really? I've said it before, and I'll say it again as many times as I have to after that: this is our wedding, not yours."

"But Rex doesn't seem to have a lot of family," she said, making it sound like I was the unreasonable one. It was a talent of hers. "I wanted to show him that we have plenty."

I dropped my head, rubbed my forehead, and cut her off. "What if your mom had done this to you?"

"We eloped before she could," Mom said.

"That's right," Aunt Ginny said. "You eloped to escape Mom's wedding plans."

That quieted Mom for a moment. "You have to understand, Allie. Those were different times. Women's movement or not, parents still ruled."

I leaned toward her. "It wasn't right then, and it's not right now."

She took a deep breath. "I guess I've done nothing but hurt you since I've gotten here."

I stood and walked to my kitchen, where I poured myself a coffee and gave my pets treats. "Guilt is not going to work on me right now." I sipped my coffee and sat back down,

She grew quiet. "But Ginny? Ginny? Really, you got her involved and not me?"

And there it was, the truth behind her anger. "Aunt Ginny is right here," I said. "Stop talking about her as if she's not in the room."

"If you must know," Aunt Ginny said, "I invited myself. I heard about the murder and had been following Allie's investigations in the news and put two and two together. I'll have you know that I happen to do some amateur sleuthing myself, and I find it quite thrilling."

Mom glanced at Ginny in surprise. "No, I didn't know."

"Clearly, Allie got her talent from somewhere."

"I take it this horrible investigation is over, and you can finally pay attention to your wedding plans," Mom said, clearly put out.

"No," Aunt Ginny said. "Allie found our main suspect dead last night. And I'm dying to get her take on it."

Mom stood, and Mal jumped off her lap and into mine. "There's no reasoning with you, after all I've done this week. I don't understand you. All you do is disappoint me time and time again."

"If you don't like it," I said calmly, "there's the door." I pointed to the door, and her face reddened.

"Fine," she said.

"Fine," I replied.

Mom grabbed her purse and stormed off.

"Now that she's gone," Aunt Ginny said, "who do you think killed Richard?"

"I'm not sure," I said, trying to breathe after the conflict with Mom. "Audrey told me Myrtle was wrong, it wasn't Velma who left the computer on the Social Security page, it was Julie French."

"Oh, that's why she made that witness statement against Richard. She'd looked up all the details."

"Yep, Julie seems to be at the heart of all this."

"I agree," Aunt Ginny said. "There's just one problem."

"What?" I asked.

"Julie French was in jail all night."

Chapter 36

For the first time in two weeks, I was able to breathe. I should have had it out with Mom sooner. I did feel a little guilty about kicking her out, but something had to be done, and I was the only one who could do it.

"I'm so sorry I haven't been there for you as much as I promised." Jenn watched me do my hair and makeup. "I've been distracted, and it seemed like you had things under control in terms of handling your family."

"I knew Mom needed constant watching," I said, then put down my makeup brush. "But I'm the one who should have been doing it instead of trying to pawn her off on you. I'm sorry. Benji should come first, and he's had that cold the last few days."

"I hate that colds last ten days." Jenn watched me from where she lay on my bed. "It seems babies get sick at the most inopportune times. Then there was the Franklins' disaster."

"What happened there?" I asked as I put mascara on. This time only one coat, not the seven that Louis was so fond of.

"The couple eloped at the last minute, and the parents were left with all the food, flowers, and one hundred people there already."

I turned from my vanity mirror. "What did you do?"

"I got the couple to video-conference in and turned the whole thing into a celebration of the new family."

"You amaze me," I said.

"Did Rex call you into the police station to interview you?" Jenn asked.

"Yes," I said. "You?"

"Yup," she said. "I don't remember much. Last night is all one big blur."

"I'm the same," I said. "I have to ask."

"What?"

"Did Shane admire the dress?"

"I wouldn't know," she said wryly. "I was asleep before my head hit the pillow. Shame, too. Here I was trying to seduce my husband, and instead I was sound asleep."

"There'll be other days," I said. "And it isn't our fault a man is dead."

"It makes me nervous to know we were in the dark with a murderer on the loose. Think about it. They could have been right there waiting in the shadows. Shane was upset that we didn't take a carriage."

"I know," I said. "Rex ensured someone was by my

side all day. And worse, he wouldn't tell me why Julie French is in jail."

"That's what happens when someone loves you," Jenn said with a sigh. "We worry about them, and they worry about us." She helped me with a stray piece of hair. But I do know why Julie is in jail."

"Why?"

"They discovered her eyewitness account was false, and they let Richard go and arrested Julie instead for obstruction of justice."

"I bet she didn't see that coming." I stood and eyed my reflection. "But it still doesn't tell us who killed Velma and if Richard's death was related."

Jenn put her arm through mine. "Let's let the boys worry about that for now. It's your rehearsal dinner. Let's go and enjoy ourselves."

"Fine," I said. "But I'm not having any alcohol this time."

Jenn laughed. "Me neither."

"You look beautiful," Rex said.

"You're not so bad yourself." He wore a black wool suit that looked like it was tailored for him. His shirt was a crisp white and his tie was lilac. I don't know how he found that color in a silk tie, but I wasn't going to complain.

"Thanks," I said. "I was finally able to do everything myself. I should have kicked Mom out a week ago."

"It's done now," he said and squeezed my hand, then put it through his arm as we approached the tight knot of people near the gazebo. It was lit with white fairy lights, and two lines of chairs faced it.

The officiant, Jaxson Teel, clapped his hands to get everyone's attention. "The bride and groom are here. Let's get started."

Jenn came toward me and squeezed my hand. "Are you ready for this?"

"Very ready," I replied.

"Alright, places," Jaxson said. "The bride, her father, and her maid of honor should be in the bride's tent."

"It'll be right here." Jenn took us to a spot to the right and within four blue flags stuck neatly in the ground. Jenn had marked the chair placement as well with my wedding colors. "Don't worry, it won't block anyone's view. As soon as you and your dad step out, I have a crew who will tear it down before you get five steps from the gazebo."

"The groom will now escort the mother of the bride to her seat," Jaxson intoned. Rex crooked his arm, and Mom gave him a beautiful smile before they walked. "Nice and slow. Good. Mrs. McMurphy, you should take the second chair."

Mom sat and turned toward us.

"And the mother of the groom?" Jaxson asked

Rex shook his head slightly. "No."

"Then you stand beside your best man." Jaxson waved to the spot.

Rex took two steps and glanced back at me. I smiled and blew him a kiss, right before we heard a woman's voice.

"Reggie, darling, are we too late?"

Reggie? I turned to see Aunt Felicity escorting a

woman about ten years older than my mom, along with a woman around my age followed by a man with familiar features.

"Surprise!" My mom said.

It took me less than two seconds to understand the horror of what my mom had done. My gaze went straight to Rex. I watched the expressions flash over his face: shock, disbelief, longing, sadness, then hard flat cop. He turned to me. Our eyes met, and he stared me down.

"No." He shook his head. "No."

Then he walked off, his strides long. I had to race to catch up and still didn't make it before he said, with a tone I'd never heard before, "I trusted you." His words were cold, and I felt like I had been plunged suddenly into the depths of icy, black water and sunk to the bottom.

I must have fallen to my knees.

"Allie, honey," Jenn said softly and gently helped me stand. Then she put her arms around me. "You're cold." She rubbed my arms, but I didn't feel any warmth. Some part of me registered that Shane had gone after Rex. "What's going on?"

I was too numb to speak or even cry. Jenn put her arm around me, and I barely registered that she talked to my father and asked him to become the host tonight and make sure everyone enjoyed the dinner.

Then I was walking, striding, jogging, running until I hit the trail that led to the *Somewhere in Time* gazebo and lost the contents of my stomach. Tears began, as I slid down the nearest tree, pulled my knees to my chest, and rested my head on them, hiding my face and letting the sobs flow. My thoughts floated through the last few years. Rex standing nearby when I fainted the first time I'd seen a dead body. Rex's upset whenever I was on a case. Rex looking at me as if I was a serial killer of some sort. Rex with Mal, coming through the door into the McMurphy and removing his hat. He always removed his hat. The first time I saw longing on his face, then desire. Then a stolen kiss and a bad apology. I hiccupped. Rex was always bad at apologies. My thoughts went on and on and on. Finally, they slowed down. Thankfully, Jenn had her carry-everything-but-the-kitchen-sink new mom's bag with her and had been handing me tissue after tissue after tissue.

"Come on, Allie." Her tone was firm but gentle. She took hold of my left elbow and tugged until there was nothing I could do but stand. "Let's take you home and get you cleaned up."

"I can't," I could barely get the words out. Turning, I looked into her eyes, "I can't go there. Please, Jenn. I can't."

"Okay, okay," Jenn put her arm around me. "I'll take you home with me. Benji is the best thing in the world to hold when you feel you can't go on."

Sniffing and swallowing, I could feel my body shaking. "I can't, Jenn . . ." I hiccupped. "I can't stay. I need to go." I looked up at her. "It's all over. Everything."

Chapter 37

I woke up the next morning in Frances and Douglas's spare room, Mal curled up under my chin, licking my tear-stained face. Mella rested on the top of my head, her tail caressing my neck. "Hi, babies," I said, my voice scratchy and my eyes swollen. "How'd you get here? As a matter of fact, how did I get here?" Then a jolt of embarrassment and horror shot down my spine, and I dropped my head back on the pillow and threw the covers over my face. Rex's family showing up, his certainty that I'd betrayed him. How could I face him? Why would he even think I did it? The look on his face still broke my heart.

"Oh, good, you're up," Jenn said cheerily. She opened the curtain, and to the delight of my pets, she grabbed the covers out of my hands. They pounced on me with joy. "It's your wedding day, and you have a lot to do." She took hold of my wrist and pulled me up and out of the bed.

"You know I'm probably not getting married, right? Even if I'm there, Rex won't be there. Didn't you see him last night after my mom invited his family? He only told me about his parents this week strictly in confidence. Now he thinks I told my mom, and she invited them. He'll never forgive me."

"Something that ridiculous wouldn't keep Shane from marrying me," Jenn said and put her hands on her hips. "If it keeps Rex from marrying you, the first thing that's going to happen is that I will hunt him down and make him regret the day he was born."

Frances popped her head into the room, then stepped in. "Trust me, he'll have an entire mob after him with pitchforks and rakes."

"Pitchforks?" I was as confused as I was glad Jenn would do that for me. Because I know she would.

"Exactly like the mob of townsfolk after Frankenstein's monster," Frances said.

"But the island loves Rex. He's an important figure here." Now I was really confused. "Or are you talking about the million family members Mom invited without telling me."

I let Frances take my right hand and put it through the crook of her arm, and Jenn took my left and did the same. Frances patted my hand, and, together, they walked me to the kitchen table, with my pets close on our heels. There they had hot coffee and an array of breakfast food, from scrambled eggs to bacon and sausage, toast, coffee, cream, and bread waiting to be placed in the toaster.

"Sit," Frances said and pointed to the chair with a full place setting in front of it. Then she filled the plate to nearly overflowing. "Eat. You are not thinking clearly. It's probably because you didn't get dinner last night, combined with the stress of your wedding day."

"But—"

"Coffee?" Jenn asked.

"Yes," I replied, and she poured the fragrant drink from a carafe into my cup and then passed me the creamer before she sat down next to Frances and poured her own coffee. "Where's Douglas?"

"He's gone into work," Frances said.

"Is there something going on at the McMurphy?"

"Eat," Jenn said.

"There's nothing going on at the McMurphy," Frances assured me as soon as I took a bite of eggs.

The warm, buttery taste of egg and toast filled my mouth; I hadn't realized how hungry I was. They sat quietly while I ate, nodding to each other and then looking back at me. I put my fork down and picked up my coffee cup to take a sip. "I feel better. Thank you."

"Good," Frances said. "There's nothing like good food to fortify you for your big day. Now don't you let Rex's tantrum bother you. We all knew his secret. We didn't need you to tell any of us." She patted my hand again.

"What do you mean? Rex said he'd never told anyone but me." I could feel my forehead wrinkle in confusion.

"He didn't have to," Frances said and got up from

the table to start wrapping up the leftovers. "When he applied for the job of police officer, he had to put down any other name he had ever had. A complete background check was done, and all of us had a good solid picture of what happened."

"And you never told him?" I slipped both of my pets a little bit of egg.

Frances shrugged. "What was the point? We were all horrified when we discovered the contract his parents made him sign. It was public record, you know."

"That's why we know everyone who lives here will go after him if he doesn't show up at the wedding," Jenn said. "You do still want to marry him after his tantrum, don't you? Trust me, Shane gave him a good talking to about ruining your rehearsal."

"I do," I said. "I really do."

"Good," Jenn said. "Then let's go do this. I have a list that we need to get started on."

"A list?" I asked as she stood and waved me up to do the same.

"A moment-by-moment list," Jenn repeated. "The first thing we need to do is get you home straightaway to take a nice hot shower. While you do that, I've hired a groomer to come to the island to make sure Mal and Mella have final touchups and are in the appropriate clothes to be your flower girl and ring bearer."

"Do you think that's a stupid idea? I love them, and they are as much a part of me as my parents, even more so. But do you think they'll be happy? Or scared?"

"It's a great idea, and we all know Mal and Mella will love the attention. Besides, Mr. Beecher will walk them down the aisle on halters. The rings will be in a box on Mella's back, and a small basket filled with lilac and white rose petals will be fixed on Mal's back, and every time she wags her tail and wiggles in happiness the flowers will fall onto the carpet."

"Oh, that's wonderful," Frances said, taking my plate off the table.

"Are you sure you don't need some help?" I asked her.

"Not today," Jenn said firmly. "Now, get out of Douglas's T-shirt and back into your clothes. We have a schedule to keep."

Chapter 38

"What's next?" I asked as we left the salon with new nail polish on our fingers and toes.

"Lunch," Jenn replied and put her arm through mine.

"It's only noon," I protested. "Are you trying to fill me up? I had a good breakfast—"

"At eight a.m.," she interjected. "And with the wedding at six and the potluck at seven, you'll need lunch."

"Alright, but I'm going to get something small. I'm not that hungry." We stopped at Mary's Bistro and Draught House.

Jenn looked me up and down. "You need to eat. Trust me, you'll be so busy that you may not get to eat at the reception. Everyone will be pulling you this way and that." With my arm through hers, we entered the restaurant. It was filled with activity. Wait staff moved quickly from table to table. A bar with a chalkboard behind it listed the day's variety of beers. Behind that was the kitchen, chef and sous-chefs moving quickly, putting orders of food up as fast as the staff could pick them up. Underneath the bustle, rock music played.

The restaurant had a tall ceiling with pipes showing, all painted black. The walls were smooth pine. Tables held four, but they could be put together for larger groups.

Jenn passed the first four seats at the bar and looked around, as if we were to meet someone. She must have spotted them and drew me through the crowd, my canvas shoes sticking to the dark wood flooring with each step I took, making a funny squeaking sound.

I spotted my mom and Aunt Ginny, even with their backs to the door, and stopped in my tracks. "Nope."

"Yes," Jenn said and, holding firm to my arm, pulled me toward them. "We're going to get this ironed out before your wedding. I won't have any emotion other than joy when you walk down the aisle."

I sent her my "I want to kill you" look, and she laughed as we kept walking. "Hi," she said to the table, pulled me around to the side facing the door, and put me between the wall and her. I imagine it was so that I couldn't run. I gave Jenn the side eye. She ignored me. Frustrated, I refused to acknowledge my mom.

"Hi, Aunt Ginny," I said, as nice as I could be, considering the circumstances.

"Allie, I'm glad you could make time on your wedding day. Isn't the weather perfect for it?" she replied.

"Yes, it certainly is."

The waiter came over, and Jenn ordered us both iced tea and a sampler plate to share.

Mom was silent until the waiter left. "Allie, I'm sorry," she said and tried to reach for my hand, but I put both hands on my lap. She went quiet until Aunt Ginny elbowed her, then she cleared her throat. "I simply couldn't understand why on earth his family wasn't here. What kind of mother doesn't attend her own son's wedding? I don't care how many times he gets married."

I closed my eyes and took a deep breath and tried to stand, but before I could get up, Jenn pushed me back down.

Aunt Ginny nearly slapped my mom. "Ann, you're making it worse. Why must you always make it worse?"

"I don't understand how," Mom said and then saw my expression. "Oh, *oh*!" At least she looked embarrassed. "I didn't mean to imply anything," she tried again. "I've made a mess of things, haven't I? Why can't I learn?"

Aunt Ginny coughed loudly.

"But this isn't about me," Mom said quickly.

The waiter came over with our iced tea, and right behind him, another waiter brought Mom and Aunt Ginny their lunches.

Aunt Ginny glanced at him. "That looks positively delicious," she said. "Do you mind if I get a photo of the tray before you put the food down?"

The waiter stopped and thought about it. I stared at Aunt Ginny as she got out her phone and started clicking before he could answer.

"Thank you," she said. "I hope you don't mind an

old lady needing something to put on her social media page. Plus, it will make this place look wonderful."

I watched him as he put Mom's lunch in front of her. He wore a polo shirt with the company logo and short sleeves, and his biceps seemed to bulge out of them. There was something about him that I recognized. But with everything that'd been going on, I couldn't place him. I gave Aunt Ginny a confused glance. She simply smiled and thanked him as he put her plate down in front of her. As he straightened, I noticed long shallow scrapes on his left bicep, and I looked at Aunt Ginny. She sent me an innocent glance.

Mom continued. "I made a mess with Rex's family, who, by the way, were extremely difficult to find."

"How did you find them?" I asked, and as hard as I tried, I wasn't able to keep the frustration out of my tone.

"I was determined to find them and give them an earful about their behavior," she replied. "I hired a private detective. He told me everything." Mom got more and more upset. "I simply had to call them and tell them what I thought of them."

I closed my eyes for a moment. "Then how did they show up last night, during the rehearsal?"

"When I called," Mom went on. "I gave them what for, but then Crystal, Rex's mom, said that she certainly deserved it. She burst into tears, and I discovered that she regretted making Rex sign that contract. She actually called it a contract, as if their son were a business partner." Mom shook her head in disgust. "She told me that the day she was forced to go with the lawyer to present it, she didn't have a choice."

"Everyone has a choice," I spat out. It had double meaning. My mom had had the choice to leave well enough alone, and Rex's mom had had the choice not to make him sign that contract.

The waiter was back with our appetizer and set it on the table. This time, I paid attention to how big he was. This man was surely XL in size, like Richard. "Anything else, ladies?" he asked. When we shook our heads, he left. I frowned. How many men on the island were the same size as Richard? "Who's our waiter?" I asked Jenn. "He looks familiar."

"Brian Bautita," Jenn said as she grabbed a plate and served herself from our platter. "He's Myrtle's son."

"I feel like I've seen him before."

"Maybe because he spends a lot of time with Myrtle," Jenn took a bite of smoked sausage and closed her eyes in delight.

"Was he there when I discovered the body?" I asked.

Jenn shrugged. "I don't know, I wasn't there, but if Myrtle was there, then he wasn't far."

"Allie," Mom said, drawing my attention back. "Rex's mother really had no choice. Her husband had insisted she go as a show of support. You see, he had control of all the money. Even the credit cards were all issued in his name. The house was his, her clothes, her car, all of that could be gone in an instant if he decided. There was nowhere she could go. She didn't have any family and grew up in foster care. It's not as if his family had any money. They weren't trust-fund people, but he was a surgeon and made a good living, and she had never known anyone with money. The long and short of it is, she truly believed she could never go against his wishes unless she wanted to be homeless and on the streets."

"She had friends," I spat out. "Everyone has friends."

"They were all his friends." Mom leaned closer. "Think about it. It's a classic case of abuse, and the poor thing had no idea or even an example to tell her differently."

I felt my heart soften a bit. Rex had grown up in an abusive household. He was a good man. A man with integrity and loyalty. The proof was in the way he treated his ex-wives, especially Melonie. It made me love Rex even more.

"Eat," Jenn nudged me. I tried, but the food turned to sawdust in my mouth.

Mom went on. "Rex's dad died last year, and as soon as everything was through probate, Crystal planned to get a private detective and find her son."

"You invited her to the wedding without asking me," I said, as a frustrated Jenn handed me a roll filled with cheese and meat. I took it, and before she could kick me, I took a bite. It caught in my throat, and I had to swallow some water to get it down. "You should have asked first. Rex is so upset that I'm not certain he'll even be there for the ceremony since he left the rehearsal before we even got started." I tried to keep the tears out of my eyes, but the tremor in my voice gave my emotions away.

"I realize that now," Mom said and had the good grace to look guilty. "I don't want to lose you." She reached for my hand, and I pulled it away. "Please, Allie."

"What other 'surprises' do you have for us, Mom?" I asked. "Tell me now."

"Nothing, honey, I swear."

"Hmm," I stood. "Excuse me a moment, I need to head to the restroom."

"So do I," Aunt Ginny said.

Great, now I needed an escort to go to the restroom.

Aunt Ginny walked beside me, chattering away about nothing. I was lost in my thoughts until we hit the restroom. "Wait!" she said. When I went to ask why, when she put her finger to her lips, telling me to be quiet. Then she checked all the stalls. "All's clear."

"What are you doing?" I asked.

"I figured it out," she said. "The killer is right in front of us."

Chapter 39

"The waiter," I said.

"Yes," she agreed, her eyes twinkling with delight.

I shook my head. "Rex will never go for that. Just because a man has a similar build, we can't prove he had anything to do with it."

"He has scratches in the right place," she interrupted me and got out her phone to show me the photos she had taken of his face and his forearm.

"It's not enough, Aunt Ginny," I said. "Besides, he's Myrtle's son. What was his motive for killing two people?"

"Think about it," she said. "There's one person connected to both victims."

"Julie," I said. "But what does she have to do with Brian? Besides, Julie was in jail when Richard was killed."

"And why was that?" Aunt Ginny asked. "Think about it. Why was Richard out of jail, but Julie in jail?"

"Jenn told me it was because she lied about Richard," I said. "They got her on obstruction, because her claim that Richard made her bury the T-shirt sounded suspicious. Spouses are immune from testifying against each other. So why would she do it? All that I can think is that Rex put her on a twenty-four-hour hold until he could figure out why she did that."

"And Richard?"

"My guess would be that they really had no basis for holding him," Ginny said.

"Why arrest him then?" I asked.

"Maybe they hoped to get a confession out of him. Or by arresting him, they could have access to his DNA. Either way, it's your wedding day." Aunt Ginny patted my hand. "Don't you worry, I'll find concrete proof. Now, are you going to let your mom off the hook?"

"She ruined last night, and I'm not sure Rex can ever forget that or forgive me," I said. "Plus, she's been awful the last two weeks. If anyone is ruining my wedding, it's her."

"Of course it is," Aunt Ginny said and opened the door for me. "But we both know Ann, and she's always been obsessive. How can she change now?"

"I should have told her we'd already eloped," I muttered, and Aunt Ginny laughed. "I'm not sure that would have made a difference." On our way back to the table, we passed Brian taking orders for another table. That's when I noticed his work boots and nodded to Aunt Ginny to look as well. They had what looked like blood on them. We both had our phones out in a flash and took pictures, me from the left and Aunt Ginny from the right.

Brian finished taking orders and turned to leave. “Oh,” he said, seeing us standing there. “Is there anything I can do for you ladies?” He seemed confused that we stood on either side of him.

“Yes, please,” Aunt Ginny said. “When you get a minute, can you bring our table a dessert menu?”

“You got it,” he said and headed toward the kitchen.

Aunt Ginny and I quickly compared pictures. “We need to contact Rex.”

Chapter 40

"Allie?" Mom asked as we sat down.

I knew what she wanted. "It's not me you need to apologize to," I said. "This time, you need to talk to Rex."

"I tried, but he's busy with a killer," she said.

"He has to stop sometime, to get married." I didn't sit down. "*If* we're getting married today."

"What does that mean?" Mom asked.

"If you'd been paying attention to what Allie said earlier, it means Allie isn't sure Rex will go through with it after the stunt you pulled." Jenn grabbed her purse and mine and stood with me.

"Well," Aunt Ginny said. "Looks like you need to go down to the police station, Ann."

Mom paid the bill in cash. "I guess I should."

"Good," Aunt Ginny said. "I'll go with you." She followed Mom out and turned and winked at me.

"What did that mean?" Jenn asked.

"We think we found the real killer this time." I linked arms with Jenn. "Or at least an accomplice."

"Anyone I know?" Jenn asked.

"Yes," was all I said.

By three thirty, Jenn and I and Frances got into a closed carriage and made our way to the bridal tent. Jenn had already stocked it with our dresses, shoes, extra hair spray and makeup, anything we might need at the last minute.

She beamed approvingly at me. "You have been doing amazingly today. I'm very proud of you."

"Thanks, Mom," I teased, then frowned. "My eyes still look swollen, even after the cool cucumber eye mask."

"Speaking of moms," Frances said. "Where's yours?"

"Dad will bring her along soon," I answered. "I called and told him it was his job to keep an eye on her after she apologized to Rex. And he promised he would."

Frances already wore her wedding ensemble, which was a beautiful lilac-colored, floor-length, A-line gown with a V-neck and flutter sleeves. Her shoes were matching flats. Even her cocktail purse matched. She looked positively regal.

I watched the beautiful landscape go by. It smelled like lilacs and spring flowers as the horses clip-clopped our way up the hill past the governor's mansion to the trail with the gazebo on it.

When we got to the gazebo, I saw that the bride's

tent was quite large and fully set into the ground until it barely fluttered in the wind.

The coachman, Ken Marley, stepped off his perch as soon as he put the brake on. He wore full regalia—a dark topcoat with matching slacks and a white shirt tucked into a gray-striped vest and morning coat. He wore a top hat. I had no idea how he kept the thing on in the wind, and yet somehow, he did.

He came around and opened the door, then helped Jenn down and handed her the hatboxes she'd brought.

When he helped Frances down, she smiled at him. "Thanks, Kenneth."

He turned to me and helped me down so that my feet landed on the rice-paper aisle runner and not the grass, even though I wore white tennis shoes. "You're going to be a very beautiful bride," he said.

"You're going to be there, right?" I asked.

"Yes," he said. "We're all taking time off. Our riders can walk just as easily as taking a carriage. Don't worry, we'll bring up anyone who will be attending first."

"Thank you," I said. Then Jenn grabbed my hand and pulled me into the bridal tent.

"People are already coming up to put their chairs in the spot they want," Jenn said. "You need to get inside now."

By 5:15, I was ready. My wild, crazy hair had been magically slicked down and put into a twisted bun at the base of my neck. A simple veil comb was placed at the top of it, holding Carol's veil. My makeup was subtle and more like me than what Louis would have done. The dress fit me perfectly, neither too tight nor too loose, and my silver sequined flats were very comfortable.

I had my grandmother's handkerchief as something old, my veil counted as something borrowed, the dress was something new, and my garter had a touch of blue. A few weeks ago, Jenn had taken me to a jewelry shop, where I'd bought simple pearl drop earrings, although I had no idea when I'd ever wear them again.

In short, I was ready. The bridal tent buzzed with laughter and nerves as Mom and Jenn fluttered about. Amazingly, Rex's mom was there, but it would be a long time before I forgave her.

My mom and his mom got along quite well. I smiled and introduced myself, as that was proper, and then turned my back and spent most of my time talking to Jenn. I looked calm and happy, but my stomach had butterflies. I couldn't decide if it was because all eyes would be on me or because this was such a big step in my life.

"Allie." I turned, as Betty Olway stepped into the tent.

"Betty," I said and gave her a quick hug. "What brings you in here?"

"You look gorgeous." Betty took me in from head to toe. "It's the perfect dress for you."

"Thank you." Betty being here was confusing, and I realized I'd cocked my head, concerned. Sometimes Betty could be obtuse. "What can I do for you?"

"Oh," she said, with an embarrassed giggle. "I forgot I was supposed to give this to you." She handed me an envelope. "It's from your Aunt Ginny."

"Thank you," I took the envelope, with my name written on the hotel stationery.

"Gotta go," Betty said. "Toodles."

I opened the envelope and took out the note. I realized the entire tent had grown silent with curiosity. The note said, "Brian only helped move Velma. I know who the real killer is, and I'm to meet them at the Skull Cave to find out their motive and bring them to justice. Don't worry, I'll be back in time for the wedding. Love, Aunt Ginny."

Chapter 41

"Aunt Ginny!" I cried out, my thoughts whirling. Meet the killer? What was she thinking? I pulled Carol's veil out of my hair and handed it to Rex's mom, then lifted my skirt and rushed out of the tent. I had to see that Aunt Ginny was safe. Running past the townspeople in chairs, I hit the trail to Skull Cave and realized my dress slowed me down. I lifted my skirt, tucked it into my waistband, leaving my petticoats showing, and continued my race to Skull Cave. Would I find her near death? Or worse, dead?

I ran faster, glad for the ballet flats I wore. The trails twisted and turned. I heard barking getting closer that I would recognize anywhere. It was Mal. She must have gotten loose from Mr. Beecher. Before I knew it, she raced beside me, and I wished I was as fast as she was.

Finally, I got to the cave and stopped, careful to take in my surroundings. I searched the area for Aunt Ginny or the killer. I knew I was an easy target because I stuck out like a sore thumb in all white. Mal sniffed around with her nose to the ground and headed straight to the cave. I followed quickly, trusting Mal to help me find Aunt Ginny.

The cave had a very small entrance, and I had to get on my hands and knees to crawl inside. Once a tribal burial ground and a place to hide from invading soldiers, the cave was no taller than my shoulders and shallow. It was so dim inside that I wished I had a flashlight. Mal barked and ran back and forth between me and the back of the cave. "Aunt Ginny! Aunt Ginny!" I called and heard a low moan. I crawled deeper until the moan was right in front of me. Mal licked my hand as I reached to find my aunt lying on the ground. "Aunt Ginny," I said, as I felt for injuries. "Aunt Ginny, can I move you? We need to get you out of the cave."

She moaned again. Her forehead was slick, as if she'd been hit by something, and I found a break in her right arm, and then something warm and wet on her abdomen. I couldn't decide if I should move her with a head wound, but I couldn't leave her there. I had to do it. I tore my now-ruined skirt and secured it under her arms, then pulled.

She groaned louder as I dragged her, broken arm and all. The ceiling was so close that I couldn't stand, but thankfully the cave was shallow. I finally got her top half out and was able to stand and leverage the rest of her as best I could. Suddenly, Mal went shooting out of the cave from behind me.

I turned my head to see my mom. She ran toward

me, her face red and her breathing loud. “Allie,” she said and stopped next to me to catch her breath. “Oh, Ginny!”

“Mom, call 911 and stay with her. I’m going after whoever did this.”

“Are you sure that’s a good thing to do?” she asked and helped me pull Aunt Ginny all the way out. There was a gash in her head that bled profusely. Her arm was broken and her foot was turned in an unnatural position.

“I’m going whether it is or not,” I said and knelt down close to my aunt’s mouth. “Aunt Ginny, who did this?”

She tried to form words, but they came out garbled.

“Okay,” I said. “Don’t try to speak. Can you point me in the direction they went?”

She shook her head slightly and moaned from the pain. Then she licked her dry lips and croaked out, “Run.”

“What direction?” I asked, but she closed her eyes. “Aunt Ginny? Aunt Ginny?”

Mom was on the phone with Charlene when I got up. I was going to run alright. “Mal, get ’em!”

My pup sniffed the ground and ran toward the trail. I followed, keeping up with her pace. Shortly, Mal turned off the wide trail and followed a much thinner, hidden one. It twisted and turned. The brush and trees caught on my dress, pulling bits off, and I realized that was a great idea. I would leave a breadcrumb trail. I tore small pieces of the eyelet and dropped them every few yards as I kept running as fast as I could.

We crossed turtle park and kept going through the trees. The bushes here were few and far between, but as on the other small trail, the tree branches were thick and hung low.

As we ran wildly through the brush, I realized the killer lead us on a wild goose chase, hoping they wouldn't get caught. Where were they going? Frankly, it was hard to think when I was running fast and trying to breathe.

The sound of someone crashing through the bush, following me, was of little comfort. I knew I could outrun most of the people here. Ignoring whoever followed me, I saw someone in the distance. They, too, ran, but much slower than I expected. It was a short woman, wearing a gray running outfit. Clearly, Mal had the wrong person, but at the very least, she was on the same trail, and I could ask her if anyone had come by.

It was odd, though. All of the islanders were gathered at my wedding. Why would anyone be out here running off trail? If it was a fudgie, maybe they were lost? Mal caught up to her first, barking and circling her, as if it were a game. The woman sped up, but still wasn't as quick as me. Why would she run faster? People who are afraid of dogs always seem to stop, because they know dogs love to chase anyone running.

I caught up with her quickly and slowed down. "Behind you," I said. It was always a courtesy to let runners know when they were being passed. But instead of passing her, Mal stopped in front of her and barked. "Mal!" I scolded.

She stopped, and I swerved to keep from running into her. "I'm sorry about my dog." When I turned, I was completely shocked.

It was Myrtle in the running suit, and she was covered with blood.

Chapter 42

"Myrtle?" I asked and took two steps back. "Are you hurt?" Part of my mind told me she wouldn't be running if she was hurt. The other part couldn't believe that Myrtle would hurt Aunt Ginny, who'd been trying to keep her out of jail for the last two weeks.

"You know darn right that I'm not hurt." She took two steps toward me and pulled a hunting knife out of her pocket.

"But why?" I asked, as I took another step back and to the side.

"Why Ginny? Or why Velma? Or maybe Richard?" She followed me step for step.

"Wait, Velma?" I was incredulous. "But I thought you loved to bicker with her."

"That nosey old biddy was going to tell and ruin everything," she said as she circled me.

"Ruin what?" I asked, doing my best to stall.

"My Brian's life," she sounded crazed. "All my baby wanted was to rescue Julie from Richard's abuse, but he controlled the money. The only thing to do was to steal it, bit by bit, until they had enough to disappear. But for some reason, Velma decided to go down to the lake after checking out her books and caught them in an embrace."

Myrtle jabbed at me, but I dodged her just in time. Mal grabbed her leg and tore at her clothes, but Myrtle shook her off and then kicked her hard.

I hated the yelp Mal made before her eyes shut. Anger raced through me, and I rushed Myrtle and punched her, sending her backward two steps. "No one hurts my baby," I said.

But she recovered quickly and swung at me with her knife. "That darn dog wouldn't leave things alone. First finding evidence, then pointing you onto the trail I took."

"Mal," I called, but my pup didn't get up. My anger grew, and I rushed her again, but this time she was ready and cut my fisted hand.

"How did you know?" I asked through gritted teeth. "How did you know she saw the embrace?"

"When I left the library, she ran toward me, shocked. Brian chased her, and I instantly knew what she'd seen and stopped her. Brian grabbed her and dragged her behind the library." Myrtle jabbed again, but this time, I wasn't fast enough, and she nicked my upper arm. "She kept saying she was going to tell Richard. There was no reasoning with that crazy old biddy."

"So you killed her," I deduced.

"It was easier than I thought," Myrtle said. "I grabbed a nearby rock and bashed her in the head until I saw brain matter. All I had to do was wipe the rock clean of prints. The kids arranged her body. I waited for them to leave and made my way around the bushes, cried out, and fell to my knees, letting the rock roll next to me."

"Why stage the scene?" I asked, deftly twisting out of the way of her next lunge.

"I knew you'd be coming any minute, and you were the perfect person to find her. I even left you a trail of books to be sure you did," Myrtle said and advanced on me again. This time I dodged clear of the deadly knife. "Sweet, naïve Irma would vouch for me, and you'd investigate, clearing me and pinning it on someone else."

"After you killed her, there was very little blood on you. Hitting her with a rock had to have covered you in blood splatter."

She gave me a bone-chilling smile. "I took off my top and switched with Julie. She put it on inside out and quickly ran home to change. The rest didn't matter. I knew any blood on my hands would be attributed to my touching Velma."

"And Richard?" I jumped back in time to miss a swipe to my gut.

"He was so easy to frame. Especially when he kicked the rock into the lake, but the stupid cops wouldn't hold him. It's too bad he discovered that Brian and Julie had robbed him. He had to go." She jabbed again, this time barely missing my throat. "But then you and Ginny had to go and tell the police about Brian's boots."

She shook her head. "I told him to get rid of those things. I'd buy him new ones. Or at the very least clean them up. Children rarely listen to their mothers."

She lifted her arm and swung downward to put the knife through my heart. I blocked it with my arm and pivoted.

Suddenly, someone crashed through the trees, and before I could think, Rex tackled Myrtle. She struggled and dropped the knife. I kicked it away before she hurt anyone else. In an impressive move, Rex pulled off his necktie and tied her hands behind her back.

Myrtle kicked and screamed, swearing we were hurting a senior citizen and she'd done nothing wrong.

Rex lifted her up by her arm and pulled her to a standing position, her clothes now covered with blood and dirt. I rushed over to Mal as she got up and shook her head. As I picked my baby up, Mal woke up fully and growled at Myrtle. "I hate dogs," she sneered, "even worse than I hate cats."

Charles, then Shane and Jenn, and then half the townspeople arrived in time to hear her. There was a loud, combined gasp.

Myrtle immediately turned on her "little old lady" act. Tears welled in her eyes, and her voice wobbled. "I don't know why you're doing this," she said feebly. "I can't remember anything before you tackled and handcuffed me."

She wasn't talking to us. She was acting for the crowd.

"Myrtle Bautita," Rex said. "You're under arrest for two counts of premeditated murder, as well as two counts of assault and battery. Charles, can you take her?"

"I can," he said with a nod and stepped up, grabbing

her by her forearm and walking away. She looked over her shoulder, tears running down her face. "I couldn't have done those things," she warbled. "I don't even remember why I'm here. My doctor did diagnose me with dementia."

Rex pulled me to him and hugged me tight, with Mal between us. I hugged him back, leaning into the comfort of his arms, tears of relief flowing down my face. He kissed the top of my head. "You simply can't keep out of trouble, can you?"

I laughed through my tears and looked up at him. "Not where my family and friends are concerned. How's Aunt Ginny? Do you know?"

"She's in good hands," Rex said. "George arrived as your mom told me which direction you went."

"What a relief," I said.

"It was very smart of you to create a breadcrumb trail using bits of fabric from your dress." He looked at me with pride.

"I knew you would be here, but how?"

"My mom came running out of the bridal tent, calling my name and waving a note. When I hurried to her, she said that the note had sent you running out of the tent, then your mom and Jenn followed. It alarmed her, and she wanted to know if I had a runaway bride."

"Oh, my goodness," I put my hand over my mouth in horror. "I bet it looked like that to everyone." The heat of a blush competed with the red on my face from running at breakneck speed.

"I knew better." He kissed me, then noticed the cuts on my hand and arms. "Jenn, text for a carriage. We need to get Allie to the clinic."

Suddenly, I felt the pain of the wounds pounding with my heartbeat as they oozed blood all over what was left of my white dress. I felt dizzy and stumbled a bit, and Rex picked me up. "Mal," I said. "She attacked Mal, and someone needs to check my baby out."

"Don't worry," he said. "Shane, can you take Mal to the vet?"

"I'm here," said Nathan Danovitch, and he stepped forward. "Come here, little girl." He took her from my arms as the carriage pulled up.

Ken jumped down and opened the door, and Rex gently placed me on the seat and then climbed in next to me. Jenn jumped in as well, and the driver closed the door and took us swiftly to the clinic.

It turned out that Myrtle had led us a few feet away from Lakeshore Drive, not too far from the library, where this whole thing started. It was a warm and welcoming place, and I would be back, regardless of the murder. We stopped at the clinic, and Rex insisted on carrying me inside. At the sight of me, the nurses put me on a bed and cut my bodice off to check for other wounds. Jenn looked deeply concerned as they found another wound on my chest and a tear in my corset where the knife had been unable to penetrate.

She held my free hand as Rex stood beside me, his anger growing with each wound they discovered. Luckily, the ones I had were quickly cleaned and stitched up. I was given pain pills, hugged, and sent on my way, wearing a scrub shirt over my torn bodice.

Rex and Jenn walked me out, one on either side, in case I needed support. "Are you feeling well enough to marry me?" Rex asked, his expression one of concern. "We can put it off until you heal."

"Oh no, we won't," I said. "You're not getting rid of me that easily."

Suddenly, it dawned on me that, while Rex was covered in easily brushed-off dirt from tackling Myrtle, my gown not only had ground-in dirt from crawling in the cave but was covered in blood and in complete tatters. Any sense of control I had over my hair was lost. Even my lovely ballet shoes were covered with dirt and scuff marks from the trails. I was sure it would be a funny tale in the future, but for now, I wanted to cry. What was I going to do without the dress of my dreams?

I let go of Rex and turned to Jenn, with tears in my eyes. A quick swipe of my hand from my hair to my shoes told her enough. She glanced at Rex as Shane came running up. "You guys go on." She put her arm through mine. "We'll meet you there, but first we have a few things to take care of."

Someone must have called Sean O'Malley, because the clip-clop of horses rounded the corner, and he pulled up in front of us.

"Need a lift?" he asked.

"Yes, thank you," Jenn said, as he climbed down.

"That was a brave and noble thing you did, Allie," Sean said. "I don't know anyone else who would leave their own wedding at the drop of a hat to run off and save their aunt."

I winced. "I didn't mean to give everyone such a scare."

He looked at all the people who had run after me, knowing I was going to catch a killer. "Not everyone," he said, "especially not the people who know you." Then he closed the door of the carriage. Rex and Shane took Ken's carriage back to the wedding site.

"How are we going to fix this?" I asked, trying not to cry. Even my petticoats were in tatters.

"Don't worry," Jenn said. "I'm a wedding planner, remember? I've got it all under control."

Chapter 43

"How did you do this?" I asked. Once again, I was transformed into a bride. This time, I wore the gown my mom had bought for me, and for once, I was grateful. When we'd arrived back at the tent, the dress was there, along with all the undergarment pieces and a pair of lovely silver flats. Thankfully, I had taken off Carol's veil before my sudden flight, and I was able to still make it my something borrowed. In fact, most of my traditional borrowed, new, old, and blue were still intact. Louis had come running with his kit the moment he saw my hair. Jenn did my makeup, and by seven o'clock, the harpist we hired began to play. Rex walked his mom down the aisle and Shane walked my mom. Both men ended up next to the officiant. Next down the aisle were Mal, who had the vet's seal of approval, and Mella, accompanied by Mr. Beecher. Then, after giving me a happy hug, her eyes filled with tears of joy, Jenn followed them down the aisle.

"Thank you, Daddy," I said. "For the dress, the McMurphy, and all the love you've shown me."

Now he had tears in his eyes and patted my hand. At the music crescendo, we stepped out. Rex looked handsome. He'd gotten a new tux somewhere. His blue eyes welled up, and I widened my smile, trying not to cry myself. The walk was both too slow and too fast. The flower petals on the rice paper were perfect, which meant Mal had done a good job. Mal sat in Frances's lap, and Mella wrapped herself around Douglas's neck like a fur stole. I was happy to see Rex's family in the seats across the aisle from mine.

Then, suddenly, Daddy gave me away with a kiss, and I faced the man I loved, both of us grinning. Traditional vows were said, except "obey," of course. Rex knew that would never happen.

"I now pronounce you man and wife," Jaxson said. "You may kiss the bride."

Rex took me gently in his arms, careful not to touch my wounds, and gave me a smoldering kiss, filling my heart with joy. Catcalls and whistles filled the air, and we took each other's hands and walked back down the aisle.

The reception line was long, too long, and I tried to smile, even though I was suddenly exhausted. Our relatives and friends chatted, laughed, and headed straight for the potluck.

The caterers were busy at work on the charcoal grills, cooking up hamburgers, hot dogs, and brats, which were all ready and warm when the line began. The bride's tent was gone, as promised, and people took their plates full of food and cups filled with beverages from the four bars we'd set up and sat in chairs or on blankets, like at a picnic. Even my uptight aunts and uncles were in the spirit of things and sat on a red-and-white picnic blanket, designer regalia and all.

During the dancing, Rex and I watched from the sidelines. I leaned into Rex as we watched everyone from the seniors to my family, and even Rex's family, having fun. He held me tight.

"Your family's still here," I said.

"My brother and sister and I talked. Dad told them I was dead," Rex said. "They were young enough to believe him. We're going to take it slow and get reacquainted."

"And your mom?"

"I'm not ready to talk to her yet," he said, his voice gruff. "I'm not sure I'll ever be ready."

I squeezed him as tight as I could without hurting myself. "I totally understand. It was very kind of you to let her stay for the wedding." I blew out my breath. "I never expected today to be so crazy."

He smiled. "Just another day on Mackinac Island, with you risking your life for a friend. A killer caught. Crazy family coming out of the woodwork, and now"—he turned me toward the lake—"fireworks."

The sky was suddenly filled with explosions and colors popping.

I kissed him while everyone else oohed and aahed over the fireworks.

"And tomorrow?" I whispered.

"It's back to fudge and marriage."

Acknowledgments

Thank you to the wonderful librarians who work at the Mackinac Island library for letting me wander around, looking for the perfect place to murder someone. And to the amazing team at the Island Bookstore, for their support for me and suggesting my books whenever someone comes in wanting to read a book set on the island.

Special thanks to my editor, Michaela Hamilton, and the team at Kensington Books who take my manuscript and turn it into a delightful book. Thanks to Paige Wheeler, who has supported this wonderful, long-running series. And to my readers, who support my books by preordering, telling their friends and family about them, and reminding me that I'm not alone in my love of Allie and her friends and wonderful Mackinac Island.

Don't miss the next delightful Candy-Coated mystery
by Nancy Coco!
Keep reading to enjoy the first chapter of
Some Like it Fudgy . . .
Available from Kensington Publishing Corp.

Chapter 1

"Bearding the lion in her den, I see," said Frances Devaney, my hotel manager. Frances had her brown hair cut short. Her wide-set brown eyes seemed to peer into the hearts of others. Today she wore a turquoise blue T-shirt, a flowy white skirt with a turquoise pattern and her usual tennis shoes.

"That's a very weird saying," I answered. "I'm only going to try to be nice to a neighbor." As a newlywed, I found things so rosy that I thought it might be a good thing to make nice with Melonie, my husband's ex-wife. After all, she'd become the new manager of the Old Tyme Photo Shoppe right next door to the McMurphy Hotel and Fudge Shop. The McMurphy had been owned and run by my family since it was built in the 1870s. People loved to stay because the lobby always smelled of delicious fudge and hot coffee.

Now it was my turn to own and care for it. I loved all

the quirkiness and creaky parts, the history of people who have come and gone over the years, and the link to my family. Then there was the tradition of making fudge and performing fudge demonstrations while telling my Papa Liam's stories to the crowds who stopped to watch.

After my ten o'clock demonstration I gathered up a five-slice box full of fudge. I chose dark chocolate Traverse City cherry, white chocolate apple cinnamon, classic chocolate, peanut butter with chocolate chip, and Melonie's favorite fudge, rocky road. At least that's what the seniors I hung out with told me.

I didn't expect a warm welcome and even braced myself for her knocking the box out of my hands. It's why I planned on going at ten thirty when her shop would be full, and she couldn't really make a scene.

"As long as she lives next to us, we should at least be civil," I explained.

"Good luck with that," Frances said without looking up.

I sighed. She was probably right. But I had to try. I hung up my chef's coat and ran a hand over my hair, which I'd pulled up into a high bun, hoping the natural waves stayed in place this time. I tugged down on my shop's signature pink-and-white striped polo and brushed off my black work jeans. After working all morning, I knew I was covered in sugar and smelled of fudge, but why change before the afternoon demonstration.

I gave Mal, my Bichonpoo pup, a pat on the head. She snuggled back into her dog bed next to Frances's reception desk. She seemed to instinctively know when she could go and when she needed to stay. As I left, I waved to my assistant, Roxanne Jones. The older woman proved to be invaluable in the fudge shop. She was quick to learn and able to work on her own when I needed a day off. She took care of everything the week I got married, and for that I'll be forever grateful.

Taking a deep breath, I pasted on a smile and walked out the door of the McMurphy. It was a busy day on Main Street. The sun was bright, and the street smelled of popcorn and fudge. The sound of low murmurs, laughing families, and children playing was muted by the clip clop of horses that carried either fudgies—the endearing name we gave tourists—or the various goods it took to run the hotels and restaurants around the island.

The Old Tyme Photo Shoppe specialized in portraits of people dressed in Victorian costumes. I had become friends with the last manager and had been through the building many times. If I remembered right, costumes were provided in the back of the shop near two dressing rooms. The pictures were taken in the well-lit middle of the building. The front looked like an old apothecary—a nod to the fact that film and cameras were once generally sold in pharmacies. As you entered, the middle of the building was divided by a wall with a waiting room on one side and the studio on the other. A modern camera was set up in the studio with various scenic backgrounds rolled up or down depending on the costumes the customers picked.

I walked in, noting the scent of rosewater, the sound of tinny old-time music, the click of the camera, and the pop of the lights. The waiting area was wallpapered with pink cabbage roses on a background of mint green. The chairs and tables looked like they belonged in an ice cream shop—extending the pharmacy theme as many pharmacies once had ice cream counters. Swallowing my trepidation, I sat in a bistro chair in the tiny studio waiting room. I could hear a small group of people laughing and chatting in the costume/dressing room area. The longer I sat there the more I noticed the camera clicking and clicking and the pop and flashing of the studio lights.

The back door opened and closed. But from the chatting I could tell not everyone had left. Then it got strangely quiet, and I heard a man say, "We should go out the back and find someone who can help."

Help? Was one of them hurt? If so, why not interrupt Melonie and ask her? Meanwhile, the nonstop picture-taking with no instructions to the customers continued. I got worried. No photographer I knew had ever taken so many photos in a row. So I got up and stepped around the corner to see what was going on. No one was having their picture taken. Confused, I looked from the empty seating area to the camera.

There, on the floor, was Melonie. I put the fudge on the cash register counter and hurried to her side. Carefully, I shook her, but she didn't respond. Checking for a pulse with my fingers on the side of her neck, I felt nothing. Next, I put my cheek near her mouth to check if she was breathing.

No pulse. No breath.

"Is she okay? Because she looks dead," a woman said over my shoulder.

I nearly jumped out of my skin. I was so concentrated on Melonie that all I heard was the click and the flash. The killer could have come out of nowhere and killed me, too. "She is dead," I replied and took in the surprising woman and the beautiful Great Dane with no leash sitting beside her.

The woman was at least five foot nine based on how close the top of her head was to the top of the photographic lights. Her long legs were covered by gray cargo pants, the pockets bulging with mysterious things. Thin but shapely, she wore a pale blue camp shirt with the sleeves rolled and held in place by tabs sewn on the sleeves. Her arms were slightly tanned. Braided leather, twisted colored string, and beaded bracelets encircled both wrists. A smart watch sat in the middle of the bracelets on her right wrist.

We stared at each other until the woman said, "Oh! Oh, no, I wasn't here when it happened. The door was open, and Finn came in. That was unusual for him."

"Who's Finn?" I asked, wondering if I needed to watch for another person to pop in.

"Oh, um, Finn's my dog. He's really well-trained and, you know, loves kids and pets and wildlife. He basically loves anybody. And when I heard the constant pop of the lights and clicking of the shutter button, I thought someone might need help." She paused and stared at the body. "Not, you know, first aid kind of help." She fumbled for appropriate words. "I'm a photographer." She lifted the expensive-looking camera around her neck. "But not a people kind of photographer, I stick to pets and wildlife mainly." She took a deep breath before continuing. "Newbies often have equipment problems, but she's beyond help. Isn't she?

Wait, is that Melonie Strausberg? I guess she has a different last name now. I heard she's been married at least twice. Anyway, I didn't realize this was her shop. Last I heard she was in Texas or some other warm place. Oh my goodness, I'm rambling. To be fair, I've never seen a dead body before, except, you know, when my great-great grandma, Harriet, died. Oh, and my Great Aunt Helen, my Great Uncle Harry—and yes, their mom loved the letter H. Anyway, that's just my mom's side. Then there's my great-great grandpa on my dad's side, my Aunt Mary, and my mom, of course. But they were embalmed and wearing makeup and nice clothes with their hair done, not just, you know, dead. It's weird, I can almost see the little Xs on Melonie's eyes like in the cartoons. Only her eyes are open." She took a deep breath and gave me a half-smile. "See, ramble."

It took longer than I hoped to sort out the important information from her babbling. "It's okay," I said. "I passed out when I found my first body. We all react differently." I stood, watching her every move. "Did you know Melonie?"

She moved her head from side to side as if to say sort of. "We went to school together for a while. But she and her parents moved. Aunt Fanny keeps me up to date on what's going on with my classmates. She told me that Melonie's first husband was a horrible man. So Melonie changed her name and came back here to be safe after her divorce. Then, within a year, Aunt Fanny said that Melonie had married again, this time to a guy with a movie character name." Rowan looked up at the ceiling, tapping her chin in thought. "Some movie, some movie, some—Oh! I have it. She said Melonie had married a Rex Manning and there was this old movie with this character named that and now the movie's this kind of cult thing, you know? Some people even have a Rex Manning Day. Have you ever heard of that?"

"No," I said, half curious about the movie, half horrified that people actually celebrated Rex Manning Day. "I'm going to call 911 now."

"Okay." She nodded and glanced around while her dog sat quietly beside her. Then it was as if she'd just remembered something. "Oh, I have a camera. Is it okay if I take some, you know, crime scene photos for Shane?"

I looked at her, surprised and concerned. First, she knew Melonie, now she knows Shane? Was this going to be one of those situations where everyone knows her except me? "You know Shane?"

She seemed to calm down when she snapped photos in a careful, thoughtful way from one side of the room clockwise to the other, including the floor and the ceiling. The beautiful dog remained at her side. "We went to elementary school together," she said between snapping pictures. "And then we went to junior high and high school until graduation." She paused, looking around to see if she missed anything. "After graduation, I went to Yale and graduated from their photography program, while Shane went to Michigan State. We haven't really kept in touch, but Aunt Fanny tells me he got married to a lovely transplant from Chicago, I think, and has a new baby boy."

"Okay," I said wondering if she was nervous babbling because she had something to do with the murder and was now inserting herself into the investigation. None of this was helping Melonie, so I dialed 911.

"Nine-one-one what is your emergency?"

"Hi, Charlene," I said.

"Oh, for goodness' sake, Allie, who is it this time?" Charlene asked. "I'm keeping a tally."

"Charlene!" I chided her. "What if I just wanted to see if you want to get a coffee sometime? It would be nice to meet in person."

"Allie, you know better than to call 911 for that," Charlene said.

"Right . . . oh, and Melonie Manning is dead on the photography floor in the Old Tyme Photo Shoppe."

"I would love to get a coffee with you soon but seriously, you found Rex's ex-wife number two dead?"

"Yes, that Melonie Manning," I said calmly. "Charlene, please send Rex and the usual crew to the Old Tyme Photo Shoppe and let them know to hurry. People have begun to gather at the door. Also, get Shane here ASAP. There's a woman here—"

"Rowan, Rowan Giles," the woman said.

"Rowan Giles," I repeated. "She's taking photos of the crime scene."

"Rowan? Really? Goodness, I haven't seen her for close to fifteen years," Charlene said. "What's she doing at Melonie's? Everyone knows they're mortal enemies, have been all their lives."

I gave Rowan a curious look.

"Can you put her on?" Charlene asked.

"Charlene wants to talk to you," I handed her my cell phone. It seemed odd that she had just appeared when I found Melonie dead, and then started taking pictures. Were the pictures meant to distract Shane from other evidence?

"Charlene, hi," Rowan said, letting her camera fall against her, held safely by the thick strap around her shoulder. "I'm good. How have you been? Really? Yup, I did work in New York, but I met someone and now I'm back. No, I didn't know Melonie worked at the Old Tyme Photo Shoppe. Who am I dating?" I watched as a blush spread across her flawless, creamy skin with a touch of freckles across her cheekbones. "Locklan Forester, yes, I know." Her blush grew deeper, and her eyes avoided me. "Oh, yes, of course, we should catch up, but right now probably isn't the best time. Okay, I will."

Rowan handed me the phone, but Charlene had already hung up.

"Charlene told me you went to school with Melonie, too. I didn't know she lived up here. I thought she moved here later," I said.

"I did go to school with her, but she moved her junior year. I don't know where her family went." She shrugged. "We weren't the best of friends."

Someone peered around the wall to see what was going on. Rowan snapped her fingers and pointed to the door. Her beautiful, blue-eyed, lavender merle Great Dane gently pushed them back out the door. Since the dog didn't come back and no one else came in, I assumed the dog went straight to the door and blocked anyone from coming in. I loved my sweet little Bichonpoo, but Mal wasn't quite so obedient. She was, however, very friendly and treated everyone like part of the family. Everyone except for killers. Somehow, she always knew who not to trust.

"I'm so sorry," Rowan said. "I didn't catch your name."

"Allie McMurphy . . . er Manning," I said, and she stuck out her hand, so I shook it.

"Manning and McMurphy? What a coincidence," Rowan said. "You and Melonie having the same last name. You must have married someone in the same family as Melonie's second husband. From what I know, small islands are like that. I mean there are only so many people to marry and all that. And McMurphy? Like the hotel? Finn and I are staying at the McMurphy Hotel and Fudge Shop next door for the next week. Is that like your family place? It would be nice to have a family business. I mean ever since my mom died when I was ten, my dad sort of disappeared into himself. So we lived with my grandma in the tiny two-bedroom place my grandpa built in the fifties. Dad did odd jobs, and I worked part time when I wasn't in school. I guess that was our family business, you know? Part-time gigs. Anyway, it would be so nice to work in a place that your family has owned for generations."

"Yes, it's been in my family since it was built and I'm the current owner."

"That's so amazing," She couldn't seem to stop herself from babbling. "Wow, I mean, I was so happy to find your hotel. Most hotels won't take Finn even though he's well trained.". She brushed her curly red hair off her face. I was strangely envious of her hair. It wasn't an orange red, but instead a deep red brown with highlights of lighter red that showed in the light.

Then there were those curls, real curls. While mine was simply wavy, not straight or curly, and mostly frizzy. That's why I tended to keep it in either a bun or ponytail.

"I have a little Bichonpoo who has free rein of the hotel. I don't believe the size of the dog matters as much as the dog's behavior," I said. "Just out of curiosity, did you see anyone when you entered? Besides Melonie and me, of course."

"I thought I saw five people all going out the back door," Rowan answered. "The first one to leave had dark hair and a blue T-shirt. The other four seemed to have come together. You know, two couples. Most of them wore souvenir shirts or sweatshirts. Mackinac Island stuff. The ladies carried gift shop bags. Probably things they found in the shops. The plastic bags had boxes of fudge inside. It struck me as odd that they all went out the back way. I mean, I assume they paid because she didn't have the back door locked or alarmed, which she should anyway. You never know who could slip in while you're working. It's not safe." Rowan glanced at Melonie. "I guess she found out the hard way, didn't she?"

I cleared my throat. "Would you know the people if you saw them again?"

"The two couples? Maybe. I saw mostly their backs but some silhouettes of their faces. Finn will help, of course. He's got keener sight and scent."

The sound of activity came from outside the shop. "Brown, get these people back. Davis, set up a perimeter," I heard my new husband, Rex, say. "Hello, dog. I'm going in. Good boy." Rex walked around the corner and looked at Rowan with his policeman's eye for detail. "That your dog?"

"Yes, that's Finn. Isn't he so smart?" she said with love for her dog visible on her face. "I told him to guard the door so that no one would get in."

"He let me in," Rex said and glanced over his shoulder.

"Oh, of course. He knows the difference between a civilian and a police officer. He was rescued from a horrible situation as a pup by two police officers," she explained. "He's loved them ever since. Finn can even recognize a law enforcement person in civilian clothes. There's just something about them that he can sense."

"Smart dog," Rex said then turned back to us, his expression fierce until he saw his ex-wife on the floor in an unnatural position, her eyes staring into nothing. His expression went neutral. He did that when he didn't want to show his emotion. Especially on duty. "Melonie?" he asked as he looked at her with sadness in his eyes. The camera still clicked, and the lights still popped.

"Yes," I said. "Are you okay?" When he didn't answer I pushed a little further. "Maybe you should sit until the shock wears off." I grabbed a stool and brought it to him, then gently pressed him down until he sat. "Um, maybe you should let someone else be in charge of the case. She was an important part of your life."

He didn't stop staring at her. "Brown!"

"Yes?" Charles stepped into the scene. "Is that . . ."

"Melonie," Rex said. "Have Davis keep the crowd back and for goodness' sake, turn the darn camera off."

"She's probably on top of the remote switch and will

have to be turned over before you can turn it off," Rowan said, with Finn now at her side. "You should wait. Oh, your name tag says Manning. Are you Melonie's ex-husband, Rex Manning? I heard you divorced over her hatred of cold and snow. Aunt Fanny says you loved it here and refused to be a snowbird. Which makes sense if you're a police officer and work here year-round. I bet it's hard for police officers to be snowbirds. I totally understand. No wonder you divorced."

Rex turned toward her. His jaw was tight and a muscle at the back twitched. His beautiful dark blue eyes narrowed, and his mouth formed a firm line. I took a step and put my hand on his shoulder.

"This is her first murder scene, and she tends to babble," I explained.

"Oh, yes, sorry, I do tend to ramble when I'm faced with surprises. And let me tell you, this was a surprise. I mean, I love true crime stories, but this is next level. Since I've never seen a dead body in real life before. Except for, you know, relatives who've died like my—"

"Let's not get into that right now," I said gently, squeezing Rex's shoulder to remind him that although he was torn up and angry, I wasn't going to let him take it out on Rowan. His shoulders relaxed a bit at my touch, his jaw faintly loosened. A movement so small that only I would know.

Interestingly, Rowan wasn't the least little bit intimidated by him. And trust me, my husband could be intimidating. He looked like an action hero from his bald head to his wide shoulders and well-muscled arms and chest. Put that together with his well-pressed, perfectly tailored police uniform and add the gun on his belt. It rarely got more intimidating than that. He turned to Officer Brown while keeping his gaze on Melonie. "Where's Marron?"

"On his way," Charles answered. Charles was around six feet tall with broad shoulders. He was big boned, with light brown hair and dark brown, hooded eyes. Popular with the young women on the island, he tended to date away from here. And he was very private about his life off shift. I always wondered if he simply hadn't found the love of his life. Maybe he didn't want to hurt anyone on the island. Anyone he'd have to see every day he did his rounds.

Most of the time the police stuck to the crowded tourist areas to ensure people didn't walk in front of a horse-drawn vehicle and the pedestrians gave the carriages and wagons plenty of room to get their work done.

"You need to take the case," Rex said.

I knew it was hard for him to give a case over to a junior police officer, but Charles was very capable, and Rex knew he was too biased to do a good job.

George Marron walked in pulling a stretcher with his new EMT, Henny Pilgrim, pushing the back end. Together they made a head-turning couple. George's high cheekbones, hawk-like nose, and sculpted mouth were as striking as Henny's round face, brown eyes and full lips. While his skin was copper colored, hers was a deeper, richer brown. They both had straight black hair, his worn in twin braids and hers worn in a single braid down her back.